D0021336

PRINTER'S
D·E·V·I·L

PRINTER'S
D·E·V·I·L

Christian D. Stevens

ST. MARTIN'S PRESS
NEW YORK

This is a work of fiction, and any similarity between the incidents or characters in this novel and actual events or persons, living or dead, is coincidental.

Design by Amy Bernstein

Library of Congress Cataloging in Publication Data

Stevens, Christian D.
  Printer's devil.

  I. Title.
PS3569.T45114P7   1987   813'.54   86-27952
ISBN 0-312-00176-2

First Edition

10 9 8 7 6 5 4 3 2 1

In memory
of
my mother and father,

Temple Smith Stevens
and
Charles L. Stevens,

. . . who taught us all the Good News

It is an honest town once more, and the man will
have to rise early that catches it napping again.

—Mark Twain,
   "The Man That Corrupted Hadleyburg"

Contents

Acknowledgments

I wish to thank St. Martin's Press for kind permission to use excerpts from "The Fall of the House of Usher," by Edgar Allan Poe, and from "The Man That Corrupted Hadleyburg," by Mark Twain, taken from *American Literature: The Makers and the Making*, Vols. I and II, edited by Cleanth Brooks, R. W. B. Lewis, and Robert Penn Warren, St. Martin's Press, New York, 1973.

C. D. S.

PART ONE
Breadline

I

About three months after the Great Falls *Independent,* Montana's Fastest-Growing Weekly, and I had collapsed, I received a desperate telephone call from Birdie Johnson. I was used to desperate telephone calls by then—mostly from creditors—but Birdie's was different. He was having trouble with his five-day daily in Marksburg and wanted me to come down immediately to edit the paper.

At the time, I had a hollow feeling in what was left of my stomach after an ulcer operation. Birdie and I had never really seen visor to visor about newspapering. When we both worked for the *Tribune* in Great Falls years ago, he was described in the newsroom as Advertising Enemy Number One. And if he was Ad Lad, I guess you'd have called me low man on the factotum pole of journalism, not to mention the Guild's pay scale.

I covered routine news—the city run, police court once a week, that sort of thing. I enjoyed it all. In fact, I loved it just as long as it was newswork. But, as the business editor once put it, Birdie was usually playing golf at the country club and enjoying crème-de-menthe-flavored sherbet with the head of the Chamber of Commerce while the rest of us were eating hamburgers at Hank's Stand on the corner.

I wondered why Birdie would call me. Perhaps, I thought, it was because he knew that I never could resist the sound of a newspaper going to press. I mean, when I was first hired as a copyboy on the *Tribune* at fifteen, I was amazed that the *paper* was going to pay *me*. Or maybe, I mused, it was because I have one of those faces sources feel naturally superior to, which was why the occasional feature came my way. I didn't have as much talent as I thought I did. The city editor usually sent think pieces to other desks.

However, one time I wrote a three-part series on the soaring cost of malpractice fees, and it was referred to in a fiery *Tribune* editorial. Condemning all such inflationary practices (particularly in relation to newspapers), the editorial called for further investigative reporting. Between that and the fact that I always put the correct change in the newsroom's stamp box, I had become known as "Even Steven."

Frankly, I always wanted to be known as the crusading, foreign-correspondent type, with trench-coat collar up and wide-angle-lens camera at the ready in perilous places. You know, "Ace Reporter Steve Hadleyman." But "Even Steven" stuck.

Birdie was a different type. "Dirty Birdie" was the label pasted on his reputation at the Pennant Bar, where we used to conduct autopsies on the final edition or simply end a shift liquidating the frustrations of a deadline. We called our sessions Nights of the Round Table, and I can remember that Birdie was often a lively topic of conversation with the boys.

"He's the kind of brittle, up-and-running hustler that puts a newsman's instincts on alert immediately," one of the wire-desk men complained one night. "Man, that guy has a real talent for antagonizing anyone on the desk who won't condone some plot or other to give a used-car dealer or a realtor ten inches of extra space in a feature section."

"Yeah, but he's a good advertising salesman," someone else said.

"You can say that again," the police reporter added. "Birdie could sell a half-page spread demanding funds for the Male Chauvinist Society of America to the National Organization for Women and get the whole thing published, rip-off included, in the *Gay Universe Gazette*."

"Well," the deskman retorted, "let me tell you that doesn't endear him to the city room. We can grouse over here all night about the way he's become the white-headed boy of the business office. But we're powerless when he gets enough clout to bludgeon his way onto the wire desk during vacations. That's when he performs all those commercial stunts on the news side."

"Can't the Guild do something?" someone asked.

"We've all screamed about him at meetings," the police reporter answered, "but there isn't much we can do. Have you noticed the way he's cajoled his way through the chairs? And now that he's secretary-treasurer of the local—watch out!"

"And meanwhile," the deskman said, laughing over a foamy head of beer, "our beloved city editor goes stomping around the newsroom, roaring like an old flatbed press, a page proof in one hand and a straightedge in the other, gasping at an unusually erotic brassiere ad on the religion page and making derogatory references to the effluent chamber of Dirty Birdie's alimentary canal."

We all laughed at the thought of the city editor in a rage, but personally I never had any real reason for taking offense at Birdie's activities. He generally operated on a higher echelon, smiling benignly at me as our paths crossed in the hall leading to the men's room, where Birdie had usually pasted up the byline of the most recent reporting star against the back of a urinal. He would pass me jauntily, all welkin-eyed and gleeful, bearing a certain air of mansuetude that covered a devilish sense of mischief. Such a bearing kept us all on the *qui vive*. He was, in a word, slick.

Furthermore, Birdie had an apparently unlimited credit rating at the Pennant. After some entrepreneurial coup, he would pacify us all with as many free steins of Great Falls Beer as could be downed after deadline. Actually, I shouldn't say "us all." Whereas the mild protests of many reporters (who had spent the working day cussing him out) were no more substantial than a foamy head on what we lovingly called "a Great Falls scoop," I privately referred to such soporifics as "Birdie's bribes" and always paid for my own. Birdie never seemed to mind. He would just give me one of those strange smiles of his and lift his scoop to me, as if to say, "That's okay, Steve— every man has his price."

The *Tribune* was an honest sheet, so it was inevitable that, for all his smoothness, Birdie would one day get the sack. It happened when the sports editor caught him taking kickbacks on a ski-resort ad.

Birdie drifted to the West Coast then and we all lost track of him, although sometime later, after I had started my weekly, I received a check for four dollars from him with a request that I send him a subscription to a post-office address in California.

A few months later, rumor at the Pennant had it that Birdie was back in Montana and had his hands full of worries as acting publisher of the Marksburg *Dispatch*.

Now here he was on the phone. I was impressed. The call wasn't collect.

❧ II

"Can you come down for even a few months, Steve?" Birdie asked.

"Where's your regular editor?"

"He's been drunk for three days, owes everybody in town, and I think he's run off with one of the printers' wives. Besides, he couldn't write."

"Well, there *is* a minimum-wage law, you know."

Birdie had a tendency to forget about things he had to give instead of receive—like wages. As a Guild organizer in less halcyon days, he would proffer suggestions at union meetings that would have scared the overalls off a Wobbly in the IWW's heyday. But the boys at the Pennant noted that no sooner had he become an acting publisher than he was so grasping he would sit up nights reading *David Copperfield* under the impression Uriah Heep was the hero.

"Hell, Steve," he said against the echo of a clattering linotype over the phone, "come on down. You need the work and I need a fill-in editor for a while. Got a guy coming in from Michigan—I hope."

"Who y' kiddin', Birdie? I can hear that old K linotype fallin' apart way up here."

"Aw, come on down."

I thought it over. I had seven dollars and forty cents in my pocket. There was a pile of bills on the telephone stand. My bank had a list of accounts receivable for the *Independent* that were about as collectible as a World War I Balkans reparations claim. And there were worse fates than the Marksburg *Dispatch*, even though Birdie and I had never enjoyed common views about publishing.

"Okay, Birdie, but who writes the editorials?"

Silence.

"Birdie, I said who—"

"All right, all right," he whined. "But take it easy, Steve. I've got advertisers, you know." There was a strained, almost childish tone in his voice.

"I'm in the slot?"

"Okay." But he sounded reluctant. I knew he was lying; that was Birdie.

"Hundred and seventy five?"

"One forty."

"Uh—I don't think I can, Birdie. Maura's expecting again,

and besides we couldn't bring the kids. That means double rent. It wouldn't work out."

"Look," he said desperately, sounding like the old Birdie, "come on down for one forty a week and I'll get you a place to stay for nothing if you're baching it, okay?"

One forty was below Guild scale, but even the sound of it evoked a sort of cash-register ringing in my ears, so I didn't quibble.

"And, Steve . . ."

"Yeah?"

"See if you can dream up some hot stuff. The staff here has run dry and Terrill's giving me a bad time."

Terrill was the owner of the paper from the East. It was a legend in the state that Terrill, a wealthy businessman with plenty of interests in New York, had never set foot west of the Mississippi. Some people said he kept an independent daily going in Montana merely as a tax write-off. However true that was, it was common knowledge that Terrill had had a stomachful of trouble with the publisher before Birdie, a man named Caxton.

That was a story in itself. Caxton had simply disappeared. It was the first top wire story out of Marksburg since the Ku Klux Klan had burned crosses on the wheatfield of a Hutterite colony. After three years of Caxton's publishing, the town was so mad at him the odds were high at the Pennant that no one would be able to take over the job. That's probably why Birdie got it. I wondered why he wasn't still playing up the story. The case of the vanishing publisher was hot copy, I thought, and I said so.

"That's *too* hot," Birdie said.

"Haven't seen anything on the wire for some time."

"We're playing it down," he answered vaguely. "Business reasons."

Whose business? I wondered.

That was Birdie's way of saying that the story was a sacred

cow: closed. Of course, Caxton's disappearance meant that Birdie could be publisher, a position of power that he had no doubt dreamed of all his life. He would cling to it like a badger. And everyone knew that Marksburg couldn't have cared less what happened to Caxton.

I've known some truly hated publishers in my time, but I never saw a case like Caxton's. His name—"King Irwin," they called him in the state capital—was like a firebrand before Marksburg's public eye.

One time, he led a campaign to bring in a branch of the Society for the Prevention of Cruelty to Animals. A week later, he found his two Persian cats and his toy terrier all tied to the front porch and painted blue, orange, and chartreuse, respectively.

Caxton called the police, another time, after delivering a speech upstate on the importance of Montana wildlife. He had stepped through the front door of his house and discovered a cluster of various-sized porcupines backing a skunk into a corner of the hallway, where it was playing havoc with the carpet.

But, of course, the police couldn't—or wouldn't—do anything. The chief even suggested that Caxton was lucky someone didn't charge *him* with disturbing the peace.

You could say it was just a guess that the town wasn't fond of a man like Birdie Johnson. But it was an absolute certainty that King Irwin would have been lynched with his mouth stuffed full of his own editorials if he ever showed his face again in Marksburg.

About three years before Caxton had hired Birdie Johnson as his advertising manager, which was only a few months before he disappeared, Caxton reportedly bought the *Dispatch* from Terrill. I say "reportedly" because the actual cash transaction was never clear.

The rumor was that Caxton had met Terrill in the East and they had come to some sort of agreement. After Caxton disappeared, I learned that Terrill had got the paper back for one dollar at a sheriff's auction. But nobody much cared how Terrill retrieved it, just as long as Caxton was gone. It was then that Birdie was hired as acting publisher.

I was busy with my own one-man operation in Great Falls, which was becoming known as a tri-weekly—I'd get it out one week and then try the next—so I didn't follow the *Dispatch's* progress very well. It's pretty tough to hold on to the job of publishing a five-day daily in a town of five thousand people with a collection of defunct churches, an empty library, twenty-three flourishing bars, and fourteen hog ranches. But I can remember the Pennant bunch saying if Birdie could make a go of it, he might eventually have a good thing.

I heard that Caxton had originally promised to pay Terrill a fantastic price for the ancient machinery and then conveniently neglected to pay anything down—that is, beyond a few thousand in earnest money. They say you had to know Caxton to appreciate his ability to talk high prices whenever he wanted anything.

Handsome in a John Wilkes Booth sort of way, Caxton was as suave as a mint julep. Irwin Royal Caxton III was a Virginia dude with the softest tongue since Wilson Mizner: he had managed to sweet-talk the town out of its tree roots, draining the paper, apparently, without making a single improvement on the plant along the way, or so it seemed at the time.

At first, Caxton had created a sensation in the state with editorials against provincialism. I recall a series of articles he had published in his paper on the need to create a Wheat Research Agency in Marksburg. The articles were filled with highfalutin theories concerning agronomy and land-development schemes. He had circulated offprints of the series all around the state, and I remember the *Trib's* aggie editor in Great Falls chuckling over them as just so much hot air. Still, Caxton's Southern rhetoric had saturated the wire copy like molasses. It made him an enemy of practically every citizen in Marksburg overnight.

The state enjoyed it thoroughly. Caxton was a popular attraction up and down the knife-and-fork circuit in the cities where his speeches were making him politically prominent.

In Montana—about the size of both Germanies, with the population of Stuttgart—almost any human noise has a way of ricocheting throughout the territory. Caxton's aristocratic tones, filled with barbs and high-sounding phrases, had echoed through the canyons from Rattlesnake Creek to Canada and back. The word in Helena was that Caxton was well on his way to the governorship. His prospects had been considered quite good in the capital. And he might have made it, too, except for one thing. He wasn't around anymore.

Birdie wanted to forget all about it. Every time someone mentioned King Irwin, he complained to me on the phone, the *Dispatch* lost a subscriber. He had given the story of Caxton's disappearance a good play when he took over, but now he was fence-mending. In the future—and he stressed the point at the end of our conversation—it was hands off. It was obvious that Terrill, perhaps unhappy at the idea that all of Marksburg knew he'd been had, didn't want to look back either.

I had to hand it to Birdie. Anybody who could keep that paper going after Caxton's three-year spree was a real adman.

ɜ III

When I hung up and turned to Maura to discuss the telephone call, she already had my briefcase open and was filling it with a toothbrush, a clean shirt, some shorts and socks, and the last two apples in the house.

"It's a mighty low salary," I explained, "but at least it's news-work, and we've been broke so long, Maura . . ."

She looked up at me then as only Maura can do. Her head was slightly tilted in that Irish way of hers, the wine-dark of her hair casting a shadow across her soft cheek. She leveled a gray-eyed, intelligent expression at me that spoke more than volumes. It was, in a sense, an *explication de texte* of her entire being. Every time Maura looked at me like that, I fell in love all over again.

"You'll take care of yourself, won't you?" she said.

The past year unfolded for me at that moment. Starting a weekly against pretty heavy odds and no financing had been a headstrong venture that I figured from the start would be tough on me, and when I collapsed at home with a miniature Krakatoa in my duodenum it was no more than I should have expected. But what I was only lately beginning to appreciate was how tough the year had been on Maura and the children. Yet I don't remember Maura ever rebuking me for it. I *do* remember her staying up all night to help fold the first edition of the *Independent*, and keeping the kids and me cheered up during some tough Thursdays, or crying and giving out as she stared bleakly at the stove after trying to stretch a ten-dollar bill all the way across a supermarket.

It suddenly dawned on me that if I went to Marksburg, Maura and I would be apart for the first time since our marriage. It didn't seem fair. Some wives have to combat mistresses, but Maura was doing battle with an entire concept. In a going romance with the newspaper profession, I had embraced a weekly all on my own. Now I was beginning to realize that my priorities had been out of kilter, that Maura and the kids came first.

"Maybe I'd better take a rain check on this one, Maura," I muttered guiltily. "Birdie said the job would be for at least a month, and that's a long time for you to be on your own, especially in your condition. I saw an ad this morning for a shoe salesman at Hoffman's store. I could . . ."

"Ah, don't be silly, Steve," she said, coming over to me then and putting her hand on my arm. "I'll be fine and so will the children. Look—I didn't fall in love with a shoe salesman. You're a newspaperman, and a good one, and if it's an honest job—well, we'll be grand. Maybe you can come home on the weekends, or we could come down on the bus. Don't worry. Just get back when you can."

That word "honest" sank way in. I've never known anyone straighter than Maura. She's a beauty by any standards, but an *honest* one, with the kind of manner that tells you—by means of a quick stride or straightening of the shoulders—that the way to stay honest is to work hard.

And as far as the low pay went—well, Maura had never been deluded about a newspaperman's salary. The fact that she had to pay the hotel bill on our honeymoon gave her an early introduction to the kind of financial circles reporters revolve in. My being a Big Publisher in the West and all that didn't faze her in the slightest.

"Birdie Johnson wants me down there right away," I said. Maura handed me the briefcase and suddenly gave me one of those kisses that sting the soles of your feet.

"I'll miss you," she whispered.

"Me, too."

"Will you be editing?"

I nodded as the kids waved happily at me. After splitting the seven-fifty with her, I had just enough money for gas and a hamburger.

I still felt guilty as I climbed into our battered, seven-year-old Volkswagen with its wonky doors and vibrating steering wheel. Giving myself two and a half hours for the trip, I figured I would just make it to Marksburg by ten-thirty that night, when Birdie was expecting me. In the rearview mirror I saw Maura waving from the porch as I pulled away, and I was glad I had managed to sneak the two apples out of the briefcase, leaving them—with a twenty-dollar bill I had kept hidden for emergencies—on the telephone stand.

ᔰ IV

Marksburg, I recalled from a fishing junket or two in the past, was a good place to pass through en route to high lakes and excellent trout streams. Set in some of the most breathtaking country in America where the Great Plains and the Rockies meet, Marksburg, like many Montana towns, is a haven for sportsmen trying to escape pollution and suburbia, or for rural people who know where to go to find enough hunting and fishing to feed the family for winter.

There's rich land there, too. Wheat, cattle, and tourism are big industries, with plenty of hogs thrown in for change.

But the similarity between Marksburg and her sister communities ends there. I can promise you now that there never was a town—*anywhere*—like Marksburg. To say that the citizens are long on complaints and short on taxes is more than a platitude; it's economic miosis.

There's a story that one time an Internal Revenue Service agent had the audacity to identify himself in a notorious Marksburg saloon—Kelly's Southside Bar & Laundromat—and the last anyone saw of him he was stuffed naked and upside down into the mouth of the American Legion cannon on the headquarters lawn. The weapon, some claim fortunately, was as inoperable as a White House press release. Mock obsequies were held, nonetheless, in every bar in town.

I knew these people hated taxes just by the condition of the highway leading to Marksburg. Besides big potholes in the road,

there were immense bullet holes reminiscent of Smith &
Wesson's large-caliber stock that appeared with increasing frequency in road signs as I drove closer to my destination.

Don't get me wrong. Montana's towns are something any
state would be proud of—usually. Places like Bozeman,
Lewistown, Butte, Great Falls—well, they have their problems,
but the people are warm, human, unusually friendly. But not
Marksburg. They say the death rate triples on a certain week
every summer when the townspeople hold their annual orgy: a
sort of drinking man's rodeo as contrived by the Marquis de
Sade.

I once covered a rodeo in Augusta, Montana, and felt fortu-
nate to walk away from it with all limbs intact. But even to go
to the Marksburg Buckaroo requires the commitment of a ka-
mikaze pilot.

Whereas most Montana towns and cities have their Republi-
can and Democratic—or, at least, liberal and conservative—
strongholds, with large groups of voters in between, the people
of Marksburg didn't vote at all. It wasn't that they didn't trust
politicians. They didn't believe in politics. I think I can accu-
rately state that no candidate for any Montana office ever went
near Marksburg during a campaign.

How can you garner votes in a place where the concept of
voting has not been sown? Oh, the town had a mayor and
council, but how such dignitaries were selected could probably
be better described in a nineteenth-century Vigilantes Manual
than a constitution.

They were prosperous and vocal enough, I reminded myself
as I churned the VW over a long gravel-and-dirt stretch. The
rich really had it in Marksburg. There weren't any poor people,
because anyone who was broke was more or less encouraged
simply to pass through town; it has never had a Salvation Army
station, a food-stamp service, or a civil-rights group.

Although they wouldn't go so far as to vote, the citizens
of Marksburg enthusiastically supported Senator Burton K.

Wheeler's opposition to America's entry into World War II, not because they favored the Montana senator's isolationist policies but because they were unanimously convinced Adolf Hitler was in the right.

That was Marksburg—the kind of town that obviously would not take to the Caxtons of this life any more than he took to it. And I was pretty sure the town wouldn't be overjoyed to welcome an ex-publisher like me: Steve Hadleyman, former pilot of a high-flying weekly with dreams of rattling the Eastern newspaper chains; the Great Falls boy who was suspect enough just coming from that sloth-ridden pit of urbanity, not to mention being a newspaperman.

No, the band would not be playing.

But I was going anyway. It was a news job, after all. And when the night shadows of the mountains appeared on the horizon, and storm clouds began to give out tow-rows of thunder, grumbling in the distance where the town lay stretched out like some gigantic Moloch of the netherworld, I heard my voice saying scratchily, "Okay, Hadleyman. Here we go."

 V

I reached Marksburg a little earlier than I had calculated. The rain began to slant its way over the surrounding hills with gusto, as though forming a fast-dropping, ominous curtain that would shield a worldly audience from an as yet incompletely rehearsed metaphysical drama.

The deserted, darkened streets resembled slippery laneways in a sort of Cretan labyrinth. Those streets were more like fragments of an argument than avenues. I entertained a fanciful notion, as I drove slowly down Main Street, that if I pursued it to its logical conclusion I might arrive at a fallacy, at the heart of some ludicrous and nefarious idea: a place that was more a state of chaotic thinking than a town square.

The *Dispatch* building, which was on Main, was dark. It was just after ten and I could not see anyone about, so I decided to get a cup of coffee and a doughnut while waiting for Birdie. It seemed senseless to book a hotel room for the night, since Birdie had lined up a place for me and I couldn't have paid for it anyway. So I went to the bus depot, the only establishment that was open, to sip coffee and fret about the job.

I knew Birdie would want me to make an early start in the morning. There would be a lot to do. I'd been around a deadline long enough to know why Birdie was in trouble. Publishing is a tough racket, but if you are stuck with an editor who is not a self-starter, it's almost an impossible job.

I went over the items in my mind.

1.   Terrill: New York businessman and kingpin. Probably a tightwad. Unhappy with the paper ever since he had hired . . .

2.   Irwin Royal Caxton III: Round peg in one of the squarest holes in the world. Three years of rapscallious humbuggery . . . hated by the town, had obviously conned Terrill. Then he mysteriously disappeared. That was a few months after he had hired . . .

3.   Birdie Johnson: The man with the zipper mouth. My old pal would try anything to make a profit. No newspaperman, he was nonetheless a hard-sell adman who could make money. Since he was on the job when Caxton disappeared, he was a natural selection for the publisher's

spot. . . . But Terrill would demand that he produce. No doubt the pressure was on. That meant . . .

4. Minimum payment to the staff: Witness the low offer to me. Probably no other newsman would even bother to locate Marksburg on a map. Who could have any interest in such an antisocial town, anyway? Birdie must have been picking up what he could at the door. In any case, he was the kind of employer who would probably have to hire goons to break up a strike called by scabs. He no doubt was employing a journalism-school dropout or a few alkies who bounced from paycheck to paycheck. . . .

The girl behind the bus-depot counter came over to pour me a second cup of coffee. She was a pale blonde, in a pale, food-stained uniform, with pale lipstick and pale, opaque, life-dulled eyes. I asked her if she had a copy of the Marksburg *Dispatch* I could look at, and she produced a crumpled, coffee-stained twelve-pager from the midst of a pile of dirty dishes.

The coffee stains were the most interesting thing on page 1. The wire editor must have been eight sheets to the wind when he had come to work. I don't know if you have ever heard of helter-skelter makeup or not—a sort of hodgepodge design that is still popular with certain country weeklies—but the *Dispatch* was a classic in that style. It looked as though someone had grabbed a handful of type lice and spattered the front page with the reckless abandon of a Dada-era fanatic.

It was my guess that the staff was made up of a high-school reporter and some 93-year-old former editor of the Concabula *Harvester* out of one of Dan Cushman's novels, working afternoons at forty bucks a week. He probably read proof, too, judging from the typos. There were even grammatical errors in the masthead. Stringers from every hamlet in the area—and they were numerous—seemingly had got all their gray copy on page 1, ranging from bridge-game results to visitors from the Dakotas.

And the type! It was so hairy I had a feeling the machines predated the Paige typesetter. It was awful.

The biggest headline on page 1 was not over 24-point. The lead story was a hailstorm over Two-Dot. The big newsbreak on the wire services that week had been a nuclear-test-ban yarn that had the world holding its breath over banners in dailies from *Pravda* to the San Francisco *Chronicle*. I found the story in the *Dispatch* buried on page 5—one paragraph hidden beneath six inches of agate type recording the results of the Nugget Club Bowling Tournament.

That was the *Dispatch.*

Birdie's trouble was zip—the sheet had none. He needed color. Something big. He was understaffed, I was sure, and though I'm no Lincoln Steffens, even I could see he needed someone who could chew out the wire editor, set up a time schedule on local and wire news, and get people moving.

Advertising was different. The paper was bulging with huge display ads. It was well over the legal percentage. I wondered if the post-office regulations were being observed. In fact, I was beginning to wonder if Marksburg even had a post office.

We would have to talk, Birdie and I. I hoped he was waiting. I needed a briefing on the town. I also wanted to know if I could get an advance. Finally, I was curious to see what Birdie had had in mind when he had reluctantly agreed that I could be the editor and not just a flak.

But I never found out.

I left the bus depot at ten-thirty. I drove back to the *Dispatch*, where I now saw a light shining in the back office. That must be the editorial office, I thought, so I parked on Main and went over to the front swinging doors.

They were unlocked. I went straight in, peering through the darkness of the front part of the main floor, which was cluttered with office supplies, boxes of cut paper, and poorly arranged desks. I could just barely make out the editorial section where a single desk lamp was on and where Birdie sat in a chair at the editor's desk near the teletype machine.

The editorial section only amounted to a half-dozen desks in the rear of the building, behind the advertising and printing and supply sections. The UPI ticker was still chattering away. It shouldn't have been on at that time, since the *Dispatch* was an afternoon sheet that would only require the morning roundups. Birdie looked asleep.

I walked toward his desk, started to say hello, stopped. Something like a little train of spiders wearing feathers on their feet skittered down my stomach.

Birdie was not asleep. His head was resting on his arms. An editor's spindle was sticking into the top of his head. A line of scarlet flowed down his forehead and coagulated on some papers on the desk. A pair of editor's shears entered his throat at the left and came out the right side of his neck.

"Birdie . . ."

My voice sounded as though it were coming from behind me. I felt frozen. There was a rip down the back of Birdie's shirt and a large, dark shadow across his back, which I could not look away from. I remember trying to decide whether it was a shadow, in fact, or blood.

Even though I couldn't see his face, I would have known it was Birdie Johnson. I recognized the green visor, the old-fashioned kind, that Birdie habitually wore in the old days while reading ad proofs. The visor had been perched with apparently maniacal whimsy over the spindle and on his head backward.

I stepped away. I stumbled against another desk. My mouth was extremely dry. The UPI ticker kept rattling on. My ears seemed to be ringing.

There was a phone behind me. I reached for it. Stopped. I reached again. The police would have to know.

It's strange what you think of at times like that. Even as I dialed 0, I wondered where my fingerprints could be found.

I looked around nervously. I could see shadows that loomed

up like phantoms throughout the entire downstairs of the plant. There was a suffocating silence while I waited for the police to answer.

Just after I had hung up the phone, I thought I saw a movement up front in the advertising section. I told myself it was my imagination. But it wasn't. I had to go back to the front doors to pick up my briefcase where I had set it down on my way in. Now I hoped the police would get there in a hurry, because one of the doors was still swinging.

ཙ VI

When I reflect on my brilliant performance during that first crisis in Marksburg, I am reminded of a book my mother checked out of the library for me on my eighth birthday when I announced that I was going to be a newspaperman. The book was entitled *Fundamentals of Apprentice Plumbing.* I should have taken the hint. But I never was much good at getting messages, especially concerning the best way to keep out of trouble.

My dad, noting frequently that I was born in the year of the Crash, called me a fiscal disaster, something he, being a veteran newsman, knew a great deal about. For years, in fact, I thought I was the direct cause of the Depression. Often my mom seemed depressed just looking at me. I had what she called "that gormless look of the Hadleymans" on my face, combined with a certain bucolic innocence, which was no doubt enhanced by the outsize WPA overalls I had to wear all the way through the thirties.

You'd think any product of the Depression would have had at least enough moxie to know the *Dispatch* spelled catastrophe: (1) I should never have taken that job in the first place, and (2) after phoning the police, I should have sat tight. Instead, I was intrigued by those swinging doors. I stepped out on the pavement, now darkened by a greasy rain, and looked up and down a deserted Main Street that would have made Sinclair Lewis heave just another sigh. The entire town seemed a study in gray.

I counted two or three places where a person might hide before reaching an intersection. I don't know what I expected to find, but I decided carelessly to have a look. The dull orange reflection of the streetlamps on the slippery pavement cast accusing fingers of shadow-black up and down the sleepy avenue.

There wasn't anyone in sight. A dog barked somewhere. I remember thinking that whoever had just pushed through those swinging doors could not have made it to the corner by the time I came out. That's the kind of thought my mom would have labeled "Hadleymania."

Of course no one could make it to the corner, which meant that whoever had been sadistic and violent enough to drive a spindle through Birdie's cranium was still in the *Dispatch* building. But did I think of that?

There I was, the Pride of Newspaperdom, peering in and out of doorways as the shopwindows reflected the blue sheets of lightning that glowed beyond the mountains and as the raindrops began to pummel the street like huge insects hurling themselves to earth in a suicidal frenzy.

There I was, getting progressively wetter as I tried to light my pipe with a shaking hand that seemed to be detached from my body.

There I was, on a brooding Montana night, fidgeting through the pockets of the shabby vestments of a forgotten Western town, in search of a reason—any reason—to avoid thinking of my last view of Birdie Johnson.

Yet mid-panic it occurred to me that, for some reason that

now escapes me, perhaps it would look better to the police if I were standing exactly where I had been when I telephoned them. So I went back through the doors.

Just through. Something caught me behind the right ear. I was angrily surprised to hear thunder inside the building. A flower of crimson brightness splashed in front of my eyes. I could smell blood and, in that brief, panoplied moment, what seemed like strong whiskey.

I can recall thinking that my head was growing on one side of my face only, and probably looked like a distorted portion of a football bladder. I also recall having one more thought before I went to sleep. It was of an 11-year-old boy named Cookie Molesworth. He was a new kid in the neighborhood at the time I had reached the sixth grade in the Emerson School, the Greatest School in the World. I was delighted to see him, since he was smaller than I, and for some time I had been in last position in the school's pecking order.

Every Friday for what seemed a lifetime, the cigar-smoking Polson twins, Alvie and Ollie (accompanied by their Missouri River colleagues, who, like themselves, were repeating the sixth grade for at least the fourth time), would take out all their cantankerousness, stored up during the week's series of frustrations in Miss Carson's militarized homeroom, on me. You know the kind of thing—Donna Mae Ingebritzen's panties tied over my head, or maybe my lunch nickel seized as insurance money, or just plain contusions.

Then Cookie showed up. His real name was Bertram, but we called him Cookie in tribute to his insatiable yearning for and apparently cornucopian supply of anything sweet. He was as frail as a sick whippet that had been reared on nothing but cookies. He spoke with a funny lisp. His folks lived on the north side and had chocolate-covered almonds in a blue glass bowl on a mahogany sideboard on any random afternoon. Most of us on the south side never saw anything but Ex-Lax on the kitchen sink, and that was usually gone by ten in the morning.

Anyway, Cookie seemed like the perfect scapegoat for me and I tried my best to get Alvie and Ollie Polson interested in persecuting the newcomer. But it wasn't on. The others were the same. They seemed happy enough pantsing me on weekends, and in spite of the fact I thought Cookie was the model sissy, they gave him a wide berth, the way a wolf pack will circumvent a bobcat.

There was only one thing for it, and that was for me to get things started by beating up Cookie on my own. But that wasn't on either. Cookie turned out to be tougher than hell. He just took off his store-bought glasses and whomped the daylights out of me—and I was back where I started, at the end of the order with just one more enemy to peck away at my weekends.

It was years before I learned (I think it was Ollie Polson who told me, one time, when he returned from the state prison in Deer Lodge to reminisce over the Emerson joys) how Cookie had had enough know-how to insure a newcomer's security by keeping the entire sixth grade—myself excepted—supplied with cookies that he filched every recess from Old Man Moss's corner store.

Now, while I was just passing out on the whirling floor of the *Dispatch*, that was my final thought: Cookie Molesworth. I mean, I was beginning to get the message.

❧ VII

Flybuzz. Cotton taste and bzz-bzz and a slap, like the sharp sound of a breaking stick.

Someone was slapping someone. Me. That was it. Someone

was slapping me. Awake. Swinging brownish walls up and down and flybuzz. Strange taste of cotton. Don't tell me, I asked myself with a whimper, they're operating on another ulcer?

I was sitting, sort of, in a chair. A bright desk lamp was shining in my face. It made me angry. My ear hurt.

I could see some hazy figures in uniform. Then an immense, shaggy-haired, purplish-faced head came into focus immediately in front of my eyes. It blocked out everything in view. The shaggy hair seemed to fade away and come back again on top of a mordant face. Red forehead. Mean, porcine eyes that were set close together, bloodshot and diamond hard. A large mouth twisted here and there beneath a once-broken nose.

The face went away and became part of the shaggy head that rested atop a huge body. The body had a sort of grizzly-bear way of moving and kept lumbering menacingly in my direction.

All that was the chief of police. For a moment, I thought he was going to put his thumb on my head and squash me. I could smell whiskey on his breath.

As you've probably gathered, whiskey's a popular drink in the Northwest. Whiskey and water, with about a dram of water to a barrel of whiskey, is called a "ditch" in Montana. Montanans are known as "ditchdiggers."

"You the guy that called us?" the police chief graveled.

It was more order than question. You would think an ordinary question like that should sound peaceable enough. But the chief had a way of making the slightest sound seem like a rusty bayonet sliding out of a sheath. He looked as if he wanted to cuff me across the mouth.

"Yes."

"Well, you said someone had been killed. So?"

I went through the motions of trying to sit up. I wanted to fit things into place—physically as well as mentally. I realized that I was in the editorial section of the *Dispatch*, sitting at Birdie's desk. Birdie's desk! It was like trying to drink a cupful of half-live moths! I shuddered and leaped up from the seat.

Not only was Birdie missing now, however, but so were any signs of violence, except for the bruise behind my ear. The papers were still cluttered about. The ticker still rattled away. The light was on as before. But there were no indications of a crime such as I had seen. The editorial shears, instead of sticking through Birdie's throat, were lying harmlessly on the desk as a paperweight for some copy. The spindle—that unforgettable spindle—rested there, upright and as innocuous as the straight-edge beside it. The blood I had seen coagulating on the papers on the desk was completely gone.

The chief breathed a little liquid fire in my face and looked at the uniformed men around us. They reminded me of X. Biedler's Vigilantes of a century ago, with myself in the star role of Henry Plummer ten minutes before lynching time. Clearly, they did not like newspapermen.

"Birdie—Birdie's dead," I said, clearing my throat. "Where is he? I tell you, he was here when I came in. He—he was stabbed to death or something. Dead . . ."

The chief glowered. "You'd better come down to the station, buddy. We'll talk there. Hey, Will," he snapped at one of his men, "call the doc and tell him to come downtown and fix this guy's head." Then he said to me: "Looks like someone clobbered you with a baseball bat. We found you lying up front in your own blood . . . and so far that's the only blood we've seen around here. Maybe you'll be able to get your story straightened up a bit once we're in the right surroundings."

He paused for a moment, his men smiling at him like the subordinate actors in an old Lon Chaney film, then added: "We'll look around the joint and check you out, buddy. But so far we haven't found Birdie Johnson or anyone else—except you. And that don't seem like much."

The trip to the station was a car ride of three blocks, sirens and all, and I counted so much artillery in the front office when we got there I thought we had arrived at the National Guard Armory. The chief saw me staring at the rifle rack.

"We like a nice, peaceful town," he said menacingly, "which is how we aim to keep it. An', pal, we've got good aim."

My head was still ringing when the doctor finally showed up. I was sure I could smell whiskey on his breath, too. He was a frumpy, ashen-faced little man with a squint, who said he specialized in veterinary cases. Maybe the whiskey smell came from the stuff he put on my head. He applied a small bandage, commenting in disgust that I didn't need stitches. His tone implied that I had picked up a hammer and hit myself with it several times.

"Don't you think you'd better find Birdie?" I asked the chief. He ignored me.

A policeman came between us and nudged me with his arm and I fell backward into a chair. A young rookie who had been coming in and out every few minutes handed the chief a note. Its contents seemed to make the red brow redder.

"You're a newspaper fella, aintcha?" he asked, taking out a fat, stubby cigar—the kind that the late General Curtis LeMay used to smoke while handing out press releases at the Pentagon.

"That's right."

"Where from?"

"Great Falls."

"Lousy town."

You guys should talk, I thought—but that's all I did, just think it. You guys with apparently more cops than there are citizens in Marksburg and a whole fort of cannons—you ought to be searching every dive in this burg for whoever slugged me.

"You know, you look sorta like a dood to me," the chief added thoughtfully. Some of the men laughed.

"I like to wear a tie," I quipped.

The man nearest me, a big Swedish guy who bulged out of his faded blue uniform in several directions, slapped me across the mouth—and I mean slapped. I bit my cheek. The slap turned my head sideways and I caught a glimpse of a policeman at the booking desk. He had one foot up on a bench, shoe off. He was scratching his toes.

"Easy," the chief said. "We ain't got nuthin' on him—yet."

"What does that mean?" I asked, feeling the steam rise a little. The area behind my ear hurt again and my stomach wasn't all that sound either.

"It means that part of your story checks out—whatchername?"

"Hadleyman . . . Steve Hadleyman."

"Yeah. Hadleyman. Well, the waitress at the bus depot corroborated that you were there just before you called us. And we've checked Birdie Johnson's house, the bars, and his usual hangouts. He ain't around. Seems to have disappeared."

I thought of Caxton.

The chief put the fat cigar between his bloated lips and worried it for a moment. I went over my story for him again—and again. I could see no one believed me, but no one could believe anyone else, either. So far, there was no Birdie—no body— and, as far as they were concerned, no crime, except that someone had slugged me, which the chief seemed to consider some sort of public service.

"Well," he said reluctantly, "d'ya wanna register a complaint or somethin'?" It sounded like a threat.

"I'll think it over, Chief."

He jerked the cigar out of his mouth, a spiderweb of saliva clinging to the business end of it. "Now listen, Hadleyman," he growled, "you can leave here, but if I was you I wouldn't wander any further than Great Falls. When we do come across Birdie Johnson, we may want you again."

"Don't worry," I said, rising stiffly and feeling my head. "I'm not even going as far as the highway. I'm staying right here."

The chief did a second take. "Staying here?"

"Yup. I was hired to put out the *Dispatch* for a month. So I'm going to put out the *Dispatch* for a month. I don't care what you guys think or what happened to Birdie or anything else. I need the job, I was hired, and that's that. Sue me."

The big Swede who had slapped me said something about my watching my mouth and shoved me toward the chair again. It made me mad. I caught my balance this time as he came forward and hit him in the throat with my elbow. He made a funny, breathless face and went backward. I was mad enough to keep it up. The chief caught my arm. Everybody came alive. Even the cop behind the booking desk stopped scratching, came around the desk, and just stood there, one shoe off and one shoe on.

"Now take it easy," the chief said, with the first hint of a smile. He was talking to the guy who had shoved me. It was a good thing for me the chief held him back, actually. He looked like a tiger catching a whiff of a wounded gazelle downwind. "Hadleyman's right. He can stay if he wants to. No need for rough stuff." Then, turning to me, he glowered again. "Just keep out of trouble, okay?"

"Well," I said, trying to steady myself, "that doesn't look like it'll be easy. But for the next month, at least, I'm going to be an editor, so you guys had better brush up on your public relations."

To get to the front door of the police station, I faced the Herculean task of pushing past the chief with his belligerent mouth and whiskey-shot eyes, three hulking cops who looked as if they had grown out of the floor, and, finally, the policeman from behind the desk with one shoe off and one shoe on. I timed my staggering so that the edge of my shoe sole came down on three of his toes. Then I hurried out.

My head began to clear as I walked in the dark from the police station onto the unpaved road that ran in front of it. The rain had stopped and starlight was showing. I could see well enough to thread my way back to the *Dispatch*—well enough to note that the good citizens of Marksburg, if there were any, apparently never voted for enough taxes even to build a sidewalk around City Hall.

I could imagine the kind of salary structure that existed for law officers, and I was beginning to appreciate the kind of problems a police chief might face in this town. The chief may have looked mean, but he did not strike me as a fool—perhaps mainly because he did not strike me, period. For one thing, he obviously knew his law. And there was a glint behind those bloodshot eyes that said he had his hands full with what must be one hell of a police force.

₰ VIII

It wasn't hard to decide my next move when I reached the *Dispatch*. First of all, I would make a nice comfortable bed somewhere in the office. Whatever had happened that night, I had to get some sleep, and I preferred the *Dispatch* to the looks of the city jail.

Second, I would call a staff meeting—whatever that consisted of—the first thing in the morning. I wanted to make sure the sheet kept going whether the story of the night before was believed or not. Finally—and this would be a big step, apparently—I would try to find out what had happened to Birdie.

Some newspaper office. It hadn't been swept out in weeks. I didn't want to go poking around at that time of night, but just a glance at the cluttered desks and outdated mats and cuts lying around told me that the sheet was in serious trouble. It was as though nobody cared what was happening.

That wasn't like Birdie. If anybody ever cared about a tidy, moneymaking circumstance, it was that guy. Birdie was a high-stepping climber with ideas of being on his own and eventually getting a sheet where he could put his theories to work—a sheet like this one. He could sell an idea for a two-page spread before nine in the morning, have it laid out by lunchtime, and be well into a plan for the magazine section, on a clean desk with a full waste-paper basket, by three in the afternoon.

Sure, he was a hard driver, but who would want to kill Birdie Johnson? He was a big, good-looking son of a Norwegian farmer from the northern part of the state who generally kept his mind on his work. A bachelor, he appreciated the voluptuous attractions of, say, the well-endowed switchboard operator back at the *Tribune*. But he always seemed to be in too much of a hurry ever to settle down to a steady girlfriend. He was also known to be a hard worker. With an opportunity to publish a daily at hand, he was the last person I could imagine letting his big chance slip away from him by carousing in bars and making enemies.

Birdie did have the ability to nudge people on occasion. But what publisher doesn't make an enemy now and then? Compared with the leonine "King Irwin" Royal Caxton III before him, Birdie was a tame, if greedy, little pussycat. Yet someone hated him enough to . . . well, to kill him.

I looked back at the now darkened area where I had seen Birdie's body. No matter what the chief of police thought, I saw what I saw. That was one stabbed Birdie, all right—a bleeding Birdie, with what I would describe as a genuine enemy.

I grabbed some dusty cushions from the unsold office chairs in the supply section and made a mattress out of them on top of the advertising counter up front. As I settled down, I thought about Birdie's early days in Great Falls.

He had always impressed me with a certain force, a dynamism that spurred his ambition. It was tragic that his career should end in this way. Was that—that body I'd seen the same man who had swaggered into the Pennant one day to seek me out?

I could still remember his wide grin and quick, alert expression when we shook hands. The word had got out that I was starting a weekly on the west side of town, and he was telling me over a scoop that he would probably be in California before I got rolling. In spite of the fact he had been sacked, it was the self-confidence with which he spoke that stuck in my mind. He seemed to know something I didn't.

"You look skeptical," I had said.

"Well, Steve—you'll never make it, you know."

I was piqued. I mean, I had lined up enough advertising for the first four issues. I had plenty of merchants on contract and the promise of a good circulation on a side of town that had no area paper or throwaway. I also was launching one of the first offset weeklies in the state. Oh, there had been some unhealthy signs here and there, but could Birdie know about those, I wondered. In fact, how did he know I wasn't a cousin of the Hearsts or William Allen White's soul mate or taking payola from the Anaconda Company or something? Rich, I clearly wasn't, but he hadn't seen inside of me. Or had he?

"What makes you so sure?" I couldn't help asking.

"You won't make it," he repeated, giving me that iceberg-colored stare you occasionally see in a veteran politician's eyes on the first Monday of a crucial November, "because you don't have the jugular instinct."

I can remember asking Birdie to elucidate.

"Well," he had drawled, quaffing his beer, "I'll tell you. And I know, because I work the streets instead of sitting up in that word tower of yours. While you reporters count ideas, I count dollar inches. That's what it takes. The jugular instinct means you have to grab a newspaper with your bare hands and hold on to it. You have to force out any competition. Get as many readers and advertisers as you can. Play any trick in the game that's necessary. Keep those readers and advertisers in your own pocket.

"The trouble with you, Steve, is that you have made an ideal of newspapering itself. It's a business full of whoring and back-alley deals. You gotta compromise . . . bend, or break. Cut out the social do-gooding or any sentimental journalese. Put reporters in their place and tell 'em what to write. It's not the other way around.

"You gotta worry about the ad rates, Steve. The facts will take care of themselves. And to the highest bidder—be he politician, merchant monopolist, union thug, or strip-joint operator—so goes your pen.

"You know newspapering from the shuffling pit on up, but you don't know life. That's why you'll wind up on the breadline."

When Birdie talked about his jugular instinct in those days, most of the newsmen in the Pennant would just nod knowingly at the old nemesis of the profession and insist that no newspaper would sell to a fish market without news. I agreed with them, of course, but I thought about what Birdie said more than once when my own weekly began its downward slide.

Birdie could push things pretty far, I thought, pulling a copy of the *Dispatch* over my head and trying to get comfortable on my advertising-counter cot. But apparently someone with a jugular instinct of his own had followed Birdie's advice seriously, judging from the position of the shears I had seen sticking through that vital vein in his throat.

I wondered fleetingly if it might have been a newspaperman who had taken him literally, for once, or maybe one of those pragmatic bidders on Main Street he was always talking about, or even another publisher.

I decided to sleep on it. No matter what had happened in that building, I somehow felt assured that the action was over. And, in any case, I needed the sleep. It would be tough enough meeting the staff in the morning and trying to keep them together to put out the sheet after I had described what I had seen this night.

❧ IX

The bell—as shrill and insistent as a fire-drill warning—announced the commencement of the first runoff as the steel rake on my dad's old flatbed press swept up high as the ceiling, like

thin silvery fingers clawing to get out of hell, and then flashed
back down again, clutching newsprint that billowed in full sail,
and flipped out the sheet over a row of blue drying flames with a
roaring cough, and my eyes followed the progress of the first
sheet, but the frustrated rake lifted once again and I could not
help following its quixotic sweep as the press belt increased in
speed and a bubbling sort of rumble seemed to swell up from the
bowels of the earth, or even deeper, by way of the nickel-plated
flooring of the plant, into my legs, through my stomach and
somehow blend with the pulsating beat of my own heart, while
beyond the rake, atop the monstrous machine, seated on high
like some demented, old-time coachman from a Hawthornian
tale, the press operator swayed in reckless abandon and laughed
and shrieked, lashing at the rake with a rolled-up newspaper
that would suddenly elongate itself, snakelike, as he brought
down his long arms in wild, menacing ecstasy; nor would he
look at me, this ink-shrouded phantom pressman, and now the
bell rang again, which it was not supposed to do, while I tried
to tell myself that the pressman was really Jake Rimple, who,
drunk or sober, put out my dad's weekly every Thursday in the
Depression; but anyway I shouted at the roaring press to bring
back my dad, and then I looked at the dark demon pressman
again, and this time he aimed his newspaper whip at me and
screamed, and hot slugs of lead rolled out of his bannerlike
mouth as I hurried to catch them and as the pupils of those
eyes, the color of the tiny glinting tips of purple drying flames,
gleamed at me unseeing, and the thunder of the press crescen-
doed and red-hot slugs of metal rained down upon me, and
through the purple flames and dancing blueblack shadows I saw
the steely-colored rake coming down with hellish certainty,
nearer and nearer, until I was quickly caught on its glistening
tines, snatched by the stiff, unrelenting fingers, now raised on
high, a helpless, Dantesque victim on the fork that dangled me
over the press's mouth that was aligned with the jagged, fang-
glike purple drying flames, and when I was lowered over the

first-run page I could see the headline: BYE, BYE, BIRDIE! in 72-point gothic type, and now I was dropping closer and closer to the flames and a huge molten-lead soup bubbling in a linotype pot and behind me the screaming had turned into the ringing press bell and I screamed back for help and called out: "Dad! Dad! Dad! Dad! . . ."

❧ X

When I awoke, I was shivering. My clothes, still damp from the rain and my feverish sweat, clung clammily to my flesh.

The advertising counter was hard against my back. I had knocked all the cushions off and was lying on the flat glass top of the counter. It was my own screaming that woke me. Then I realized there was something else. The ringing wasn't just in my dream. The telephone was practically jumping on a desk back in the editorial area. Anything was better than the infernal nightmare I had just gone through, spread out as I was on a cold slab of glass between Classified and Display.

I rose stiffly, peered through the gray light of early morning at the large editorial clock registering ten minutes to six (that meant little over four hours' sleep), and staggered to the phone. A bedraggled gray cat was sitting on a chair nearby blinking at me.

It was long-distance from New York: Lawrence Terrill, owner with the loot, whose person or purse had never once made it past the Mississippi.

"Who *is* this?" he barked before I could even say hello.

"Benjamin Franklin," I replied, and hung up.

I didn't like his tone. At six in the morning who wants to hear the sound of a gravel truck shifting gears?

The phone started dancing again. I tried again.

"Is that the new editor?"

"Yeah. Is that you, Terrill?"

"Now look. I don't have any time for games on the phone. I don't know much about you or exactly what you're doing in the *Dispatch* office, but Chief Laken called me in the middle of the night saying Birdie Johnson has disappeared. He says you claim he was murdered. What's it all about?"

"That's about it right there, Terrill. I'm Steve Hadleyman. I used to put out the *Independent* up in Great Falls. Birdie phoned me yesterday and asked me to come down to edit the *Dispatch* until he could get a full-time editor to replace the guy who walked out on him. When I got here, I found Birdie dead, and I wound up slugged myself. When the cops showed up, Birdie was missing. The chief interrogated me last night and then told me I could go back to Great Falls. The way I figure it, I've come here to put out a paper and that's what I plan to do."

Terrill swore. "Why didn't you call me?" he demanded. "I've tried every hotel, motel, and bar within fifty miles of Marksburg. What are you doing in the office now? It must be six in the morning back there."

"I was born in an editorial office, Terrill."

"*Independent . . . Inde*— Did you say the Great Falls *Independent*? The weekly?"

Did I detect a hint of derision? "Yeah. It went down a while back."

"I remember," Terrill said dryly. "I also remember some editorials that you shouldn't have been writing against your advertising percentage. That was Caxton's trouble before Birdie Johnson."

"I heard Caxton had plenty of other kinds of trouble, too," I said.

"Anyway," Terrill went on, ignoring me, "Chief Laken tells me he found a Guild card in your wallet and an old Montana Press Club membership card. I also just finished talking to your old boss on the *Tribune* in Great Falls, who told me you weren't worth waking him up in the middle of the night about. . . . But apparently you've never been fired or the direct cause of a major libel suit. Tell me, can you handle a daily until I get out there?"

"Sure, Terrill. I can handle it even after you get out here. But that doesn't mean I'm going to."

Terrill swore again. "Now you listen to me," he said gruffly. "I don't know what this is all about, but when a man loses two publishers from under his nose—one of them trying to walk out with the wastebaskets . . . or even if both of them were—well . . . Even if something *has* happened to them . . . Now, I don't want to have to come out there right away, but if . . ."

Terrill went on like that for several moments. I just kept breathing heavily into the receiver and waited.

"Emm . . ." he said finally. "How much was Birdie going to pay you?"

"Not enough."

"Okay. I get the idea. So you're acting publisher at Birdie's scale. But get this straight. As long as you're there, I want you to keep that paper publishing, understand? Just between you and me, Birdie was beginning to get that paper on its feet. Now, you know what missing a deadline can mean. I don't exactly know what the staff situation is out there, but if you're no better than the last two jokers . . . Hell, Hadleyman, for all I know you could have taken care of both Caxton and Birdie Johnson . . ."

"Now hold on," I started.

". . . or know who did. All I know is that if the *Dispatch* closes its doors for one day it will close them for good. That was my policy before and that's my policy now. The town lost faith in the paper when Caxton got his hooks into the editorial page. Can you handle it?"

"The question is, Terrill, can *you?*"

"What do you mean?"

"I mean," I started, getting a little hot in the forehead as I looked past the desk at the cluttered junk and gathering dust. I paused, then said, "Ah, forget it. Don't worry about the *Dispatch.* It'll come out."

"Good. Listen, I can't get away from here, but I don't want any more trouble before I do get there. I've already had to buy that rag back from myself at a sheriff's auction once. I don't want to look foolish like that again. It can make money, but it *has* to be a newspaper, understand?"

"That'll be a switch."

"What?"

"I said I'm itching to go. And, by the way, it would help if you'd start putting some hard cash into this plant. It's falling apart. For one thing, the ticker paper is arriving in boxes marked C.O.D., and my guess is that the machinery is running on hope and hairpins. For another, I'd appreciate it, Mr. Terrill, if you would ring up whatever bank the *Dispatch* is chained to in this town and give me a credit clearing for all expenses— today."

"No dice."

There was a long pause. "Right," I said. "I'm leaving for Great Falls after breakfast."

Another pause. "Okay, okay!" he said, at last. "Take it easy. Don't you disappear on me, too. I'll call the Central Bank this morning. But don't go spending like a wild man. Keep the staff hungry. Play it by ear. And lay off the editorials, do you hear me? Write about the United Way and the courtship of predatory animals or something. No politics. I can't figure what's with you people out there, but whatever Caxton and Birdie put into that sheet, someone didn't like it. I'll clear you with the bank. But I accept no apologies if you wind up murdered."

I hung up and went back to the advertising counter, but the sleep had worn off. So I shaved in the sink back by the makeshift darkroom the *Dispatch* apparently relied on for pictures. Then I went out to charge breakfast at the bus depot.

I was back by seven-thirty, and set about cleaning up the desks, spindling the wire stuff that had rolled all over the floor, continually pushing that dumb cat out of the way as I spiked dead copy, and trying to put Birdie's desk in order before the staff arrived. I found Birdie's confidential file on the staff after forcing open the one locked drawer in his desk. It seemed intact but mighty sketchy on some of the people.

There were great gaps of missing information. Across the cover of the folder Birdie or somebody had apparently written: "Ref: X-2." Since the lip of the folder was marked "X-1," I figured that Birdie had, somewhere—either at home or in the office—another file. That would be even more confidential, I presumed, or at least it would fill in the gaps in X-1. I looked around for a while, but I didn't spot anything else.

XI

I spent the time until 9 A.M. going over the file I did have. It told me little. Certainly there was nothing in it to indicate that when the employees began to show up, some demonic monster would surge through the swinging doors and give himself or herself away with a drooling leer.

In fact, at nine sharp, Shirley Weaver, the receptionist who also handled a lot of the circulation details, stuck her head through the doors and stared at me curiously, then demurely entered. She was in her late twenties, I estimated (since her age was not on file). She had a soft complexion that would have been more attractive if her hair wasn't still in large pink curlers. She was chewing gum and staring at me through huge, round, pink-rimmed glasses. When she took off her raincoat, she seemed quite skinny.

"Hi, there, Porno," she chirped.

I sat up straight in Birdie's swivel chair. "I beg your pardon?"

"Er—I mean—" she stammered. Then I realized her glasses were slightly off center. She was looking at the swivel chair next to the one I sat in. The scraggly cat possessed it, staring at me as though I were some Egyptian pharaoh.

"I—I meant the cat," she said, with an inscrutable smile. "Our cat, Porno. He's sort of the paper's mascot. Are you Steve Hadleyman?"

"Right."

"Birdie told me you were coming down from Great Falls. I thought you might be with him now. Otherwise . . ." She put a hand to her curlers. "Usually," she added, picking up her purse and looking hesitantly toward the back of the shop where the sink and mirror were to be found by the makeshift darkroom.

"Go ahead," I said.

She gave me an appraising look that said, quite rightly, "Oh, oh, here's another male-chauvinist boar," and hurried off to do her hair. The cat followed her, giving me a similarly appraising glance.

When she returned, looking quite pretty, I briefed her on the situation, leaving out any reference to Birdie's death. I simply said he wouldn't be in. I wanted to announce the little item of murder to all the staff at once. I think it was Hercule Poirot or Maigret, or possibly Sherlock Holmes, who wanted to study the mass reaction of a group in order to discern the singular nature of the villain, in some case or other I had read. But in my mind

I felt it would be interesting, if not downright dramatic, to announce the murder of Birdie Johnson in front of everyone directly connected with the *Dispatch*. I had to admit that such a moment would make me the center of attention, something I had not been for some time.

Ego and self-pity aside, if you can lay such things aside, I knew that a show of authority would have to be made at the outset. Once Birdie's death was announced, the news would no doubt have the effect of a firecracker in an anthill. I didn't want people to scatter—just the opposite. The more central and authoritative I appeared to be, therefore, the better our chance of survival. That's how I had it figured, anyway.

I asked Shirley to inform each person on the staff as soon as he or she came in that an important conference with the new editor and publisher would be held at 10 A.M.

The word "publisher" caught her by surprise and her lips parted. But she brightened considerably when I also asked her to draw checks for one week's wages for everybody in the place—including me—on the office checkbook, which, it turned out, was a Marksburg Central Bank office checkbook that Shirley kept in her desk.

She had the checks ready in a few minutes, commenting as I signed them, "Good idea. You know, several of the staff have back wages coming."

"I'm sure," I replied. "I'll get to that as soon as I can. This is just to get things started. Who does the books?"

"Birdie and I."

"We'll go over them later. But tell me, Shirley. The advertising looks sky high. How about accounts receivable?"

"They're getting better. But a lot of firms are pretty hard up right now. We've quite a few on the books, and . . ." She paused nervously.

"Yes?"

"Well . . . the cash flow has increased recently, but the *Dispatch* is still far in the red."

"How so? I mean, the advertising . . ."

"I suppose," she went on, lowering her voice and gathering the checks, which her pink-polished nails neatly separated for insertion into envelopes for each member of the paper, "you should talk to Birdie about that, really, but between us girls, Mr. Caxton—when he was here—lived pretty well, if you know what I mean. Besides, a lot of money goes to New York every quarter. At least, it goes out of this town. But where, exactly, I'm not sure."

"Right," I said, stretching. "Okay—we'll start getting some of that back. You'll find out soon enough that Birdie's out of the picture now. And I've been cleared at the bank by Terrill. 'Bout time he started putting cash back into this sheet."

Shirley really came to life then and said with a new tone of excitement that she would make coffee for the conference.

I studied her. Bright girl. She had a good accounting degree from the university and, as far as I could see, wore at least three hats. She not only was receptionist and a sort of unofficial circulation manager, but also appeared to be the firm's accountant. And I didn't doubt she was underpaid, too.

I may be—as she so quickly observed, and as my wife would have cheerfully confirmed—a male chauvinist, and I admit it. But when it comes to women's pay for work done, I am strictly on the side of the angels.

Knowing Birdie's reputation, I was certain that he would exploit anyone of either sex, but he had the kind of bluff attitude to be found in certain men in authority who would exploit females first and foremost. It was my bet that Shirley had been one of the first to suffer. When I saw the size of her weekly salary as I signed her check, I knew I was right.

Somewhere in the back of my mind, however, I heard another thought creaking about. This was a sensitive and bright girl. Pink was her color on the outside. But was there a deeper shade of red—blood red—in her temperament? Just how vindictive could she be? Vindictive enough to use a pair of shears on Birdie?

ᕲ XII

Between nine-thirty and ten the staff trickled in, going from the swinging doors to the coat hangers in the back by the darkroom where Shirley had coffee started. They gave me puzzled looks after she tipped them off about me. They all looked like human beings to me—not a Dracula in the crowd. Yet *someone* had murdered Birdie, after all, and if that someone happened to be a staff member, it seemed at least possible that he or she would also be unhappy to find a new publisher already at work.

If Birdie's enemy had wielded that spindle and those shears for personal reasons—well, I guessed I was safe enough. But what if someone was trying to kill more than a man—say, a newspaper? In that case, I knew my life wouldn't be worth a thirty slug in the hellbox until the mystery was solved.

The staff meeting turned out to be a pretty cozy affair. The department heads plus the editorial side made up practically the whole sheet. Everyone had a title, and that was about all. As they gathered in the editorial area, I studied them carefully and mentally went over their dossiers that I had seen in Birdie's X-1 file.

The first person to sit down opposite me after looking at and pocketing his check was a beefy, dull-eyed printer from Missouri named Leon Ermann. He had an air of having sprawled before a television set in an overheated room for a week solid without changing clothes. He announced that he was the shop foreman, recently appointed. He seemed to have reacted to

Shirley's tip that there was a new publisher in the *Dispatch* with all the ebullience of a hippopotamus being hit by a mud ball. It just didn't make any difference to Ermann. He simply hung up his baggy jacket, lumbered over to a chair and sat down heavily, rolls of fat doubling up everywhere, and stared at me through almost closed lids. Then he belched.

I had checked Ermann's dossier. He was supposed to be a troubleshooter in the manner of the itinerant printer. I had met many itinerant printers in my time, including the great lino-composition master, the Wandering Jew, who worked most of the Montana dailies; but Ermann was a troubleshooter of another kind, really, with the emphasis on trouble.

I could see he was a heavy drinker, first of all. That meant he probably migrated whenever he ran up debts or missed too many shifts. He had worked every pressroom, apparently, from Laredo to Banff. After a few minutes of talk, I could tell that he was not exactly tops in his trade. I also gathered from his remarks that he had little love for Birdie Johnson or anyone else.

"To tell you the truth, Mr. Hadleyman," he said in a confidential tone, sleepily scratching himself, "I didn't think Johnson would last very long."

"Why not?"

"Well, in the first place he didn't pay us enough—or on time. I know he had his problems, but you can't keep union printers around if you're gonna keep cutting wages. Even though he made me foreman, he didn't increase my paycheck none."

"Didn't you get scale?"

His thick-lidded eyes rolled languidly as he studied the grimy wall. "Well—yeah. But the guys who—"

"How long have you been here, Ermann?"

"Uh . . ." Ermann paused, figuring on his fingers and avoiding my glance by feigning calculation with his eyes, now aimed at the ceiling. "Uh . . . eight months."

"I see."

There was a pregnant pause, a pause with little promise of a child of inspiration. "Tell me something," I continued, cutting my fingernails with the shears. "When did you last see Birdie Johnson?"

Ermann gave me a funny, nervous look—a look, I thought, that didn't quite go with his face.

"Oh, 'bout four-thirty yesterday, I guess. Right after we printed, I told the boys to clean up and then take off, same as always. Why? Birdie skip town or something?"

"Something like that," I replied.

We were interrupted by Jim Strong, a blond-haired, blue-eyed pressman in his late forties who was in excellent shape for his age. Strong had chatted with Shirley, gone to the pressroom for a routine check, then returned. He sat down quietly next to Ermann, the flicker of a smile in his eyes as he fingered the unopened envelope containing his surprise check. He rose again as we shook hands.

I liked Strong's looks. Certain printers have a way about them, a quiet knowledge and easy confidence that is more assuring to an editorial man than almost anything else in a plant. Strong looked like the kind of man who could print a paper with a roll of gelatin and a pulley.

I thought of Strong's file. He was just the opposite of Ermann. Steady, non-drinking, methodical, he was the oldest employee from the point of view of seniority on the *Dispatch*.

He had been reared in Marksburg, had learned the trade from the age of thirteen on. With the exception of a stint in the navy during World War II, he had been tinkering with linotypes and presses, cutters and routers—the works—most of his life. Furthermore, he was in a position to know everybody on the staff better than anyone else was, having seen the *Dispatch* move from a rural weekly to the current, grocery-store throwaway daily that it now resembled. He would be a useful man.

But there had been a hitch in his file. Apparently he and

Birdie Johnson hadn't hit it off too well. Ermann, a newcomer, had been made foreman over him. I noticed that Strong had been demoted once before, too—under Caxton.

As Strong and Ermann chatted, I mentally compared them. Strong didn't look like the kind of man you would demote—certainly not one who would be demoted for financial reasons. There was something else.

"You two should be informed that I'm not exactly the best pressman in the world," I said, fidgeting with the spindle on the desk. "I'll be counting on you pretty heavily."

Their glances didn't commit them one way or another. I was anxious to discern their interest in the paper as a paper, or even their interest in a spindle as a weapon. Nothing.

"What happened to Birdie Johnson?" Strong asked. It was a plain question, even in tone. It implied nothing.

"That's what I want to talk to the staff about," I replied.

About that time there was a high-pitched shriek up front, followed by an angry slap. I looked up and saw Shirley, her face aflame, staring angrily at a good-looking, brisk-striding, suburbanized male already stepping, bright as a political ad, in our direction.

"That'll be Willy Dunkle," Ermann said, with a wet grin and without looking around. "The girls always react like that when Willy comes in."

Willy Dunkle looked every inch an adman. Judging from the linage in the sheet, he wasn't doing badly, either. He looked like the kind of man Birdie would pick to work the streets. Of medium height, he appeared very athletic nonetheless, with that kind of outdoors look you find on men in these parts who know the best fishing spots and who go after game in jeeps. I pegged him for about thirty-two or so.

There was a curious omission from his file. His background wasn't listed. Instead, there was a reference to X-2, the file I couldn't find. The reference was marked in where Dunkle's birthplace should have been listed.

"That Shirley," Willy chuckled, pointing his thumb at the receptionist, who had apparently been caught with her guard down. "That's the fourth time she's proposed to me this week." Willy sat down hard, still chuckling and smiling at all of us and scratching Porno behind the ears as the cat came over to him.

"Someday," Ermann said rather solemnly, "Shirley's boyfriend is going to be paying a call when you make your usual morning pass at her."

"Aw—I'm just kiddin' around, Ermann. Don't take it so seriously. Shirley doesn't mind."

Willy shifted in his seat, suddenly looking directly at me. "Hi," he continued, giving me a short wave. "I'm William Lloyd Dunkle—Madison Avenue's answer to the Marksburg crisis. My friends call me Willy. And you're our new trail boss, right? Steve Hadleyman?"

"That's right," I replied. "Glad to meet you, Willy. We'll wait for the others."

Willy sat back restlessly, looking around and tucking his check into his sports jacket. He smiled at nothing but still managed to look as though he'd just been shot out of a cannon. In spite of the early hour, I smelled whiskey. I couldn't help thinking that the glad hand was a front. He had something of an "I've been through it" look underneath. Maybe it was in the way he walked when he slowed down—on the balls of his feet, like a boxer—or the cut of his chin. He had a mean look, sort of, but it wasn't located on any particular feature of his face. It was, in fact, rather a composite of various good-looking and pleasant features that added up to a certain cloudiness.

He saw me staring at him, smiled at me through level brown eyes, and rubbed his ear. I couldn't help wondering what was missing on him in the file that the mysterious X-2 folder might reveal.

Van Jellinek, a gangling young journalism-school product whom the file had described as "bright but could have attained a higher scholastic average with greater effort," came up next.

The *Dispatch* was his first job out of the university, a job he'd held for about three months. After hearing from the receptionist that I was replacing Birdie, he looked around the room nervously. He paced about the plant for a few moments, going to the back to hang up his windbreaker, to the swinging doors to study his check in apparent disbelief by the morning light, then to his desk to put the slim envelope carefully away. Finally he brought a couple of swivel chairs over to the group.

He sat down near me. I realized that most of his height was in his legs. Clean-cut and as Dutch-looking as a yellow tulip, he wore his hair cropped short. He was constantly in motion. I caught a glimpse of him looking at the bandage behind my ear.

"Do I smell coffee?" he asked cheerfully, glancing over my shoulder toward the sink near the darkroom. He was up again. He went to the coffee urn to investigate.

"Does that kid ever stay still?" I asked.

Jim Strong smiled.

"It's a good thing he does move, Mr. Hadleyman," Willy Dunkle said. Shirley, I noticed, hadn't wasted any time in spreading my name around, emphasizing the new signature on the checks. "Jellinek has to do most of the legwork on editorial—sports, courthouse, cops, and federal building, council every other Monday night. You name it. A real workout for a kid. Birdie Johnson stayed close to the office, covering some local by phone."

"Birdie was the type to keep his hand in advertising," I commented.

"That's right," Willy replied, with a slight frown. "Best damned adman I ever saw."

"What do you mean, *was* the type?" Ermann asked me.

"We'll get to that in a moment," I replied.

"Hey, Van!" Dunkle shouted. "Come over here and light, will you? This is no way to greet a new publisher."

Van Jellinek came back to the group, holding a cup of steaming coffee. He sat down carefully and smiled, as though waiting for permission to drink.

"Glad to meet you," I said, extending a hand. Jellinek stretched forward awkwardly, hitting his elbow on the corner of the desk. About half of his cup of coffee spilled on my pants.

"Good start, kid," Ermann gibed.

Jellinek grabbed at some paper on the desk to wipe off my pants. "Gee, I'm sorry, Mr.—"

"Not that!" I exclaimed. He held a part of the confidential file in his hand. "Don't worry," I added hastily. "It doesn't stain."

Fortunately for Jellinek, Harvey Kressnach made his entrance at about that time. I was beginning to get something of an idea of the staff and why the Dispatch looked the way it did. Kressnach's appearance sort of put a head on it.

If you can imagine a suet pudding walking on two loaves of bread with a curve-stemmed pipe attached somewhere near the top, you more or less have the right picture of Kressnach. With a sort of professional trepidation, I pegged him for the wire editor. He had proofreader's hump, glasses with bottle-thick lenses, and absolutely no neck at all.

"Mr. Hadleyman. I'm Harvey Kressnach."

His high, curiously squeaky voice was a surprise, coming from that waddling package of some sixty years of humanity. He wore a tie that had gone out of fashion in the Harding era. About two inches down from his collar button—that's right, a gold collar button—there was a loose knot. Still farther down the tie was a collection of once-edible specimens that had gathered for who knew how long.

Oddly enough, the tie seemed to go with him. He wore it absentmindedly, with a sense of malaise, as though it were an appendage he was cursed with.

As we shook hands, I caught the sewerlike whiff of his pipe, which gurgled stuffily above the definitely adenoidal wheeze of his breathing. It wasn't a very long walk from the receptionist's desk to mine, but Kressnach looked as though he'd just made the Bataan Death March. I considered giving up my pipe.

He collapsed in a swivel chair and looked around, nodding in what might be described as a friendly way to everyone there. There were specks of ink on his glasses. Everybody was so impressed with his entrance that no one spoke. He took his pipe out of his mouth with a sort of popping sound and began to unscrew the stem in his pudgy fingers. Then he did a strange thing. He giggled like an old lady.

"Well," I said, trying to get my bearings, "is everyone here?"

Strong spoke up. "All except Mabel."

"Who?"

"Mabel Reitz. She's the society editor."

Jellinek chuckled and Kressnach fanned himself with his check and giggled again.

"Just for the record," I said, taking a long look at the collection in front of me, "who reads proof on this sheet?"

They all gave me a knowing look.

"Mabel and I," Kressnach muttered, giggling a third time. He was running a secondhand pipe cleaner through the pipestem. "That is, when there's time."

"Well, you'd better make time from now on," I said icily.

Kressnach slowly lowered the stem of the pipe and stared at me through those thick glasses that made his eyes look like BBs. His face was suddenly so still, his stare so steady—as though he were seeing me for the first time—that I had the impression he was trying to see through me.

I could not make out the emotion in his expression. His thick lips, which were always slightly parted, twitched, and he ran the tip of his tongue over the upper one. Then he went back to cleaning his pipe. I don't know why, but the way he fingered the pipe bowl and kept scratching away at the stem irritated me.

ଈ XIII

It was a good five minutes before Mabel Reitz finally wandered in. We had lapsed into a strained silence, with occasional idle comments and some business back and forth about the coffee. I was determined to wait until I had them all together before I told them about what I had seen—rather than what Chief Laken would no doubt later report.

I must confess that Mabel was not what I had expected from her dossier. I had guessed the society editor to be a part-time old-age pensioner—I mean, the name Mabel, sweet as it may be in its trochaic nostalgia for the nineties, isn't exactly *au courant*. But this Mabel was.

She was about twenty-six, but you could add a good round dozen to that number for some of her other statistics. In motion there seemed to be more curves around than on U.S. Highway 89.

She had a way of coming through the swinging doors that titillated one's tactile responses. She seemed to float through and then stand there for a breathless moment, waiting for the doors to swing back with impudent virulence and give her a gentle paddle forward.

Shirley glared at her and she glared back. She accepted her check envelope like a Spanish lady receiving a bull's ear from a matador.

She was dressed in what some B-movie makeup man might consider newspaper style: alligator-leather jacket with a belt, no less, and a high collar up, the way Maggie Higgins probably wore her field jacket in Korea. A bright green scarf blazed beneath a Rita Hayworth chin. The emerald flash against her short-cropped, genuinely auburn hair seemed to turn her chic little hat and tan matching purse—very much the style in those days—into something meaningful. On someone else, those clothes would have been as corny as a revived *Big Town* series. On Mabel Reitz they looked as well designed as Sally Rand's fans.

Yet in a big town, small town, or no town at all, appearances—like the makeup of any newspaper's page 1—mean little without solid content. After all, I had read the society page of the *Dispatch*. Whatever this fiery-haired girl reporter could do, she couldn't write. In fact, she couldn't spell.

Once a week, the *Dispatch* ran a woman's page with an eight-column logo across the top: "Women's Reitz." You might expect that such a pun would evoke at least one up-to-date story: a women's liberation report, perhaps, even for those pre-ERA days, or news items related to women's social problems, or a feature on careers, the future of the modern working girl—that sort of thing. I could hardly be called a grass root in support of the modern feminists, but even I could see the importance to the press of such a news-dominating movement.

But no. Most of the stuff on Mabel's page was boilerplate material from some syndicate that must have been started by Louisa May Alcott. The syndicated stuff was material that had been dug up from the files before World War II. One controversial piece I saw, for example, was a rehashed feature defending Eleanor Roosevelt's right to go on the radio. A big item in another issue was a ten-inch, double-column story on how to economize by using a new technique for darning socks.

It is true that Mabel ran a column, signed "M.R.," and I expected that here, at least, a reader might find some originality. At first I was encouraged to see that Mabel's interest was in the occult, a popular enough subject even in those days. But the copy was agonizing. I don't mean she had an agony column; I mean that her astrology chart would have boggled the mind of a medieval physician. The spelling was the only thing truly mythological. Worst of all, the suspiciously anonymous letters were inevitably from male admirers of M.R. Their styles, furthermore, were injudiciously similar to Mabel's own.

One example should suffice:

Abel Mabel: Thanks macho for youre vues re the true libberated male today. I drive truck and the guys who kid me for washing the dishes, when Ime hoam dont joke when there loanly in the bars on those nites when me an the ole ladys awoopin it up at hoam. the reel sissys in this wurld is the BeXXX Birt Rennolds XX tipes who like to show off the hares on theyre chest an scairt to put a aprin on. Beleev you me Mabel a free women meens a free man an good luck in the coz. Yrs truely. An admirer.

PS—You were shur rite about me bein a astrological mixter of Tara the Bull and Pissies. How did you now?

That word "astrological" was the giveaway. It was the one word in her various columns that the fictional letter writers spelled correctly. All misspellings were consistent.

I looked at Mabel as she walked toward us and it seemed to me I could hear a clarinet whining its way up the scale. She fluttered what must have been half-inch-long, real eyelashes at all of us. She gave me a quizzical look as she searched for a chair. Jellinek was on his feet, sliding one of the swivel chairs over next to himself for her. She sat down gracefully, crossed two remarkable ankles, and waited for Jellinek to light her cigarette with his shaking hand.

We all looked at her thoughtfully, silently. I cleared my throat. Suddenly she winked at old man Kressnach, who promptly giggled.

There wasn't much in her file, except that she was a local girl whose father was president of the Marksburg Central Bank, which carried about three buckets of gold out of the paper, apparently, every month. The bank also ran a quarter-page advertisement once a week on the women's page.

ઋ XIV

"Now that you're all here," I started, "I'll fill you in on what has happened. As you all know, I'm Steve Hadleyman, the person who told Shirley to inform you of this meeting and of my appointment as new editor. I'm a newsman from Great Falls. What some of you don't know is that I'm more than the new editor as of now. I'm the new publisher."

There was a bit of a buzzing. I continued: "Birdie called me up yesterday afternoon and asked me to come down and fill in for a month or so. When I arrived here last night, though—well, there's some bad news, I'm afraid. I—uh—found Birdie sitting here, in the chair I'm sitting in now. He'd been murdered."

There was a sort of unanimous gasp. Kressnach dropped his pipe. For the first time since his arrival, Jellinek stopped moving and sat stock-still, his eyes glittering with excitement. Mabel brought her fist to her mouth, the knuckles shining white. Willy Dunkle went sort of limp, but Ermann didn't seem to change visibly. Yet I thought I heard him take in a little breath. His piggy eyes didn't leave my face. Jim Strong looked past me at Shirley, who still sat at the reception desk, her eyes wide behind the pink-rimmed glasses as she stroked the cat on her lap thoughtfully.

"I—I think I could use a cup of coffee," Mabel said, rising unsteadily. She walked into the back area and returned with the tray and cups and the coffeepot and fixings all rattling like a typewriter.

I realized that my direct tone had held them spellbound for the moment, just as in the movies, with the exception that they all had a look as if to say I was probably the murderer.

I went on: "Chief Laken was here last night. After I discovered Birdie's body, someone slugged me. But I had time to call the police. When the chief arrived, Birdie's body was gone. . . ." More silence.

"In case any of you are wondering about me," I said a bit nervously, "the cops have more or less cleared me. The place has been cleaned up, in a manner of speaking. Laken believes Birdie Johnson has simply disappeared—like Caxton before him. But I saw the body. It seems to me that somebody is trying to stop the *Dispatch* from publishing . . . and that means that we could all be in danger—especially if the murderer is among us."

They all looked at each other, and then, as one person, at me. It was a strained moment.

I filled the silence by messing with my coffee, which, in spite of heavy quantities of milk and sugar, still looked like mud—an earthy testimonial to the fact that Shirley's fourth hat, the domestic one, didn't fit. I couldn't bring myself to taste the stuff.

"Fer the love of Pete," Mabel said brassily as she started to pour coffee for those who didn't have any. "This is fantastic. Bodies just don't up and take off. I mean—it's spooky."

I said nothing.

"What are you going to do?" Strong asked. "Close the doors?"

"That's up to you people," I replied, looking at each of them in turn. "I talked to Terrill this morning. He has named me publisher. I think I can handle the sheet with your help, but I realize I can't hold any of you here, and it is only fair to tell you what I think."

"And what's that?" Ermann asked flatly.

"I think," I said, "that we should put out a newspaper. We could fold up and skedaddle, but I think we would all be letting our end down. On the other hand, somebody may have had a personal grievance against Birdie, and we won't be bothered. From my point of view, I need the job. I think we can turn out a pretty good paper if we work together. We've sure got the news. What do you say?"

"I knew there was a catch in those paychecks," Willy Dunkle said, with a chuckle.

They all buzzed together again for a moment. Strong eyed me suspiciously. Leon Ermann just looked at me sleepily. Shirley came over to the rest of us silently, still holding Porno. Van Jellinek looked keen enough, but Kressnach was clearly upset and seemed to be frowning at Willy, who had picked up the spindle on my desk and was playing with it.

Mabel studied the contents of her purse, but looked up when Willy Dunkle grinned and said, "What the heck, Hadleyman. If you can take us, we can take you. Let's make a long cast and see if the fish are biting."

I studied the others. They all either nodded or at least made no sign of protest.

"Okay," I said, rising. "It should be interesting. As you know, even without a murder we wouldn't be working under the best of conditions. I'll talk to each of you about duties as we progress."

Their faces didn't change much. If there was a killer among them, Maigret himself couldn't have picked out the culprit. I wondered just how quickly they could sharpen up. The *Dispatch* was, as I've indicated, a mess.

"Any questions?"

Silence.

"We'll concentrate on coming out as usual this afternoon, then. When's the deadline, Jellinek?"

"Three o'clock, Mr. Hadleyman. Page 1 is at three-thirty."

"Right. My name is Steve."

They all nodded.

"Oh, yes, before you leave, I think I should tell you one other thing to remember, even though it may be unnerving while working."

They all looked up expectantly.

"It's only fair to remind you," I said, "that if someone in this group *is* a murderer, then he, or she, is insane."

I said that mainly because that's what the hero always says in books or films, but, to tell you the truth, I wouldn't know if a killer was insane or not anyway. The way I figure it, anybody trying to kill *me* would have to be nuttier than the state of California.

In any case, I didn't get the melodramatic response I was expecting. Willy Dunkle tapped his fingernails on the desk impatiently. Leon Ermann seemed to have fallen asleep. The cat jumped down from Shirley's arms and rubbed up against Willy's ankle as Shirley went back to her desk. Jim Strong simply got up and headed for the pressroom, and Mabel sipped her coffee.

Only old Harvey Kressnach seemed to respond to the dramatic moment, if you could call it a response. He just giggled.

❧ XV

After the group dispersed, I settled down to bashing out an editorial. It was the kind Terrill wouldn't like, since you could say it took a stand on something.

On the other hand, he might have approved of the fact that

it was only one paragraph long, which I consider the required maximum length for editorials, and that I announced hotly (it was for page 1) that the *Dispatch*, in spite of a change in management, would not miss a deadline.

I was just typing up an assignment sheet when I noticed that nobody was in the plant except Shirley. I called her over.

"Everybody's gone over to the bank to cash their checks," she said, blowing a bubble with her gum.

"Well, tell 'em to get back here—now!" I barked. "Especially Ermann. He'll head straight for a bar."

"Right."

Shirley went out, leaving a pile of account sheets with me that showed how Birdie had been struggling to keep the wire services paid. There was evidence of trouble elsewhere, too. The newsprint bills were piling up. The outward flow of cash was too high—way out of proportion, as far as I could tell. Someone was milking the joint, all right. It was clear that even a moneymaker like Birdie couldn't keep the paper out of the red. A real corker on one account sheet revealed that some of the staff had actually borrowed money at the bank in the past and lent it to Birdie to meet the payroll!

Under the circumstances, it was understandable that things could get so fouled up that someone might be hurt enough to want to take it out on Birdie in a violent way. Yet it was hard to believe that any of the group I had just talked to was capable of murder.

When Jellinek came in, I picked up a series of labor stories I'd found in Birdie's top drawer and walked over to him. He was going through notes and getting ready to walk his beat.

"What's this all about?" I asked.

Jellinek frowned. "That was one of Birdie's typical goofs," he said. "There was a clerks' union strike, called by the area council—a big one. Birdie asked me to get on it. I picked up quite a yarn from union heads on a state level. It gave labor's side of the issue pretty strongly. I was working on it when Birdie buzzed me to come up to the front office, and—"

"Front office?"

"Yeah. Up there." Jellinek pointed to the front of the building. I'd never noticed before, but beyond the advertising counter a small office had been built out of what was once the display-window area of the old store. You wouldn't notice it from the outside, since venetian blinds covered the window. I would have to check that out later, I thought.

"Anyway," Jellinek continued, "Birdie called me up there for a private talk. When I went up, a member of the Marksburg Merchants Association was there. Big wheel. The president. Not to mention the fact he's also the paper's attorney and an important politician in town—guy named Brownlee."

"Pressure?" I asked.

"You kiddin'? Brownlee's in everything around here. Anyway, the association was taking out a page ad. He had a letter or statement, sort of, all written out. Birdie took it from him and handed it to me and said, 'Put an eight-column head on this and run it—as is—on page 1. That's our strike story right there.' He said he had some additional material from Brownlee, too, that he was going to put into the page ad."

Jellinek shook his head in disgust. "Boy," he said, "was I sore. I just couldn't believe it. I guess my mouth dropped open a foot, because Birdie told me to get going and not ask any questions."

"What did you do?"

"What *could* I do, Mr . . . uh, Steve? I said maybe he would like to think it over. I told him—Birdie—that I'd been interviewing the union heads from the area council by phone. But Birdie just turned beet-red and told me to get the copy downstairs. Before I left, I asked him again if he didn't want to think it over. The president of the Merchants Association fidgeted in his chair. Know what Birdie said?"

"No. What?"

"Well," Jellinek said with a sigh, pointing at the articles in my hand, "he said he didn't want any *story*. He said that reporters had to learn to run what the publishers said they should run and to forget the stuff I had. The stuff in your hands there—that was the series I had planned to run. But Birdie was, as Willy Dunkle would say, playing Main Street. Boy, was I disgusted."

I felt a twinge of pride when the kid said that.

There are always people who like to run down young idealists, who are jealous of youth, and who want to destroy those verities in newspapering that have always made the press meaningful to tomorrow's editors. Did Heywood Broun ever forget the beginning reporter? Wasn't this desire for objectivity that Jellinek showed—this sense of both sides of a story—the stuff Pulitzer's stars of the nineties were made of? I, for one, have always admired young crusaders, and I wanted to tell Jellinek so.

I tried to form the right words in my mind, pausing to get the lump out of my throat. It seemed to me to be a special sort of moment when a veteran newsman like myself, if he said the wrong thing, could destroy something delicate and truly noble in the future writer. I think I saw a Humphrey Bogart film with that theme once. Now here it was—in front of my own eyes, really. It might be all right for Birdie to "play Main Street" and to try out his hedonistic ploys on a pro like me who would know how to counteract his mercenary style, but what right did he have to exploit a young reporter, to disillusion a beginning newsman whose social conscience . . .

"I understand, kid," I said, putting one of my feet up on the edge of a waste-paper basket, the way I imagined Scotty Reston would do. "No wonder you were disgusted. When I was a cub on—"

"Yeah," Jellinek muttered, taking off his glasses and shaking his head. "How stupid can you get. To think Birdie would sell out for a measly page ad. Why, he could have screwed the Merchants Association out of a whole year's contract of page ads. We also had the state unions by the short hairs. For once,

too, we had Brownlee on the spot, and Birdie let him slip
Talk about cheap."

I stared at Jellinek. I could tell by the way he stared back
that he was studying my tonsils.

"Uh—how's that?"

"Why, I gave Birdie every chance," Jellinek went on. "I
asked him to think it over so that he could get Brownlee out of
the office and work out a deal with me. But no. Birdie was in
too much of a hurry to grab the nearest carrot when the whole
garden was within his reach."

I cleared my throat.

"Birdie thought small," Jellinek added.

"But—but what about your interview with the union heads?
Didn't you care about your story?"

"Care? Of course I cared!" Jellinek replied, flushing a little.
"Why, we had a gold mine in that. We could have used it as
ammo to jack up the price on the Merchants Association. And
if the association wouldn't buy it, I knew already that we could
have pushed the unions for a pretty good price. If we played it
right, we could have made both sides pay off, in fact."

Jellinek stuffed a small yellow notepad in his pocket and
stood up. "Well, I'd better get going."

I went back to my desk, sat down, and thought as I lit my
pipe: There's another one for Heywood Broun.

"I'll tell you one thing," the kid said as he started for the
door. "There were times when I wouldn't have minded putting
a spindle through Birdie's skull myself . . . if there'd been any
profit in it."

I was still rather pensive after Jellinek went out, so I didn't
notice that the others had wandered back from the bank. All
except Ermann. Shirley couldn't find him.

"Did you check any of the bars that might be open this
early?" I asked.

"They're all open this early," she replied.

I moaned. "Well, don't waste time looking for him. This paper has to roll. In this afternoon's issue I want to see some balanced makeup. That means, Kressnach," I added, calling across the aisle to him, "that you dummy up your page loosely enough for the boys downstairs to compose with white space to spare. I want bigger heads, better emphasis on stories that deserve it, and good heavy play on each quarter of the front page. And, Mabel, if you're proofreading, I want a clean paper—I mean *clean*, understand?"

"Sure," she said vaguely, smiling at Kressnach.

"Come on," I said. "How do you spell 'occurrence'?"

She spelled it with one "r" and an "a." I blew up. She tried it again. Kressnach giggled. Then I threw Mabel a dictionary and told her to start living with it. I noticed, as I started downstairs toward the pressroom, that her complexion matched her hair.

Strong met me on the stairs. "We have a machine problem," he said cautiously.

❧ XVI

"What's wrong?" I asked when we reached the pressroom.

Jim Strong gave me a look that said he had watched publishers come and go, generally sticking their noses into the pressroom where they didn't belong and where they couldn't tell a job press from a multilith. But his tone was friendly enough.

"The gears on the main press are all fouled up. Something wrong on the drive side. Also, the folder keeps acting up. Tough to operate. Come on, I'll show you."

"You look as if you could fix it, Jim." We went over to the huge, lumbering press. The rollers were just so many warped tubes to me. "Or do we have a machinist around here?"

"I could get a guy in by tomorrow night, I guess."

"No. We've gotta keep rolling. We can't afford to miss one issue, or we'll miss them all," I answered, skeptically eyeing the folder and baler. The machinery seemed to sneer back at me.

"Well," Strong said, "I'll give it a try. Do you know anything about these babies?"

It was a test. My father once told me when I was his copyboy that you should never try to con a pressman. They can be as temperamental as the machinery they operate. If you've seen a press misregister or throw a plate in the middle of a run, you know what I mean.

"Naw," I said, laughing. "I used to run my dad's flatbed a little bit . . . until I almost lost three fingers and my dad's contract with the Typos."

Strong laughed and relaxed. I had passed the test.

"I'll fix this monster," he said grimly. "We'll roll."

"Good man. How are the linos?"

"Pretty hairy."

"I was afraid of that. Are the fonts in decent shape?"

"Wait'll you see."

We made a tour of the back shop. The building housing the *Dispatch* was a huge old hardware store with three floors, counting the basement. Actually, it had the makings of a great plant—plenty of space that, with proper planning and some important changes, could tolerate enough expansion to put out a paper as large as any metropolitan daily.

I had to give Irwin Royal Caxton III credit. He had big ideas. He had pulled the *Dispatch* out of a dumpy shack on a back street, I'd heard, and, moving the presses roller by roller, had located it in an ideal spot on Main. Even though he'd had to push a few bankers around, knock a hole in the side of the wall as big as a house, and make Marksburg think a little bigger about dailies, he had wound up with a promising, if presently dilapidated, plant.

Of course, there could be no future of any size for such a paper, as far as I could see, unless the town grew like Topsy— which it made no signs of doing. But it was a typical Caxton maneuver, with some typical Caxton idiosyncrasies, I guessed, for him to prepare for a grand delusion.

For example, as I discovered later, he hadn't paid a penny to any of his creditors in town, ranging from the bankers to the movers to the hardware-store owner, who had at first been delighted to find a lessee. So what if the owner never collected his rent? If he couldn't find the mysteriously missing Caxton, what was he going to do? Knock another hole in the wall to get all those tons of metal out in the street? Sue the janitor?

When I saw that the building was plenty solid and the layout well planned, I had to admire Caxton's vision from a professional point of view. He knew what the *Dispatch* could become if it ever did get some decent circulation.

As soon as I had a chance, I was determined to go through the upstairs floor above the main office area, because I knew that someday it could be converted into a perfect editorial section—apart from the other sections and overseeing all, as an editorial office should. Advertising, the commercial section, and the furniture-supply department could then be housed luxuriously on the first floor without jamming the editorial area into a rear corner near a makeshift darkroom. The darkroom itself could comprise a nice unit on the top floor. And in the basement, I noticed, there was plenty of room for a future and enlarged job shop as well as the main pressroom, the shuffling pits, and a mailing room, with a furnace area in the rear. Why, there was enough space in the basement the way it was, I figured, to house two giant gang-run offset presses, if you wanted.

But while the building arrangements were solid, the furnishings, much to my horror, seemed to be collapsing. Jim Strong's face took on the air of an old sea captain watching his ship springing leaks as we moved from room to room.

The men were already hard at it. One was setting straight matter as he chomped angrily on a cigar; another was tinkering with a job press and spitting frustratedly.

I've seen some makeshift pressrooms in my day, but this was right out of the Gay Nineties. I wouldn't have been surprised if Jim Strong told me that the afternoon edition was coming out on butcher's paper against immovable type. And no wonder there weren't any large headlines. All heads were being set on the linotype.

"Isn't there a Ludlow or any handset type around here, Jim?"

"Sure, but Birdie gave an order that we never use it on any copy but advertising."

"That figures. Well, we use it on news matter starting today," I said disgustedly. "I've told Kressnach to send down larger heads. And we're hitting page 1 with an eight-column, two-line banner. Sixty-point. Nice and square. If you don't have any, dig up what you can and meanwhile get someone carving up linoleum letters. Okay?"

"It'll be there," Strong replied. There was a glint in his eyes again. He spoke a printer's language, and though he knew that I knew doggoned little about the back shop and that my rhetoric was probably somewhat off key, he apparently sensed I loved it all and respected anybody who knew the business.

I think he was genuinely pleased—in fact, delighted—to be challenged again. It was there—in his hands and face. Strong was the kind of man who would take it personally if he saw a publisher destroying a paper, just as though he were witnessing a murder. I wondered then if he might even go so far as to seek revenge. Curious thought, that.

Strong was just showing me the difference between the drive side and off side of a press when there was the sound of men shouting in the job shop. Then we heard a crash. By the time we got there, a young apprentice printer was lying on the floor, holding his mouth. Ermann, drunk as a lord, was standing over him.

"Damn you!" Ermann was shouting, his huge fists doubled up. "Tol' you—keep 'way from this machine!"

Ermann staggered toward the kid and kicked him in the rear end. The kid grabbed at the man's feet and twisted. Ermann went down heavily. The other men had gathered around the two of them.

"Let him up!" someone cried.

"Give it back to him, Joe!"

Ermann, with amazing alacrity for a heavy man, was back on his feet in an instant. The kid was just getting up when Ermann shoved him in the chest, knocking him against the cutter. I watched Ermann's face. The heavy-lidded eyes remained half-closed but menacing. He had murder in them. He was enjoying the fight. The kid was game but sixty pounds lighter, and clearly didn't know much about fighting—especially Ermann's way.

Strong was suddenly no longer next to me. He had moved in quickly. He caught Ermann on the side of the neck. It looked to me like a karate punch. Ermann flew against a pillar next to the job press. The punch was strange, lightning quick, astonishingly effective. But Ermann was no lightweight. He turned angrily, smiling at Strong—a smile that could kill.

Ermann grabbed a lead paperweight and let it fly. It was wild. Strong closed in ready to start swinging. So far, everything amounted to only the motions of a fight. No one had actually been hurt—yet.

"Break it up!" I shouted, rushing between the two of them.

Instead of breaking up the fight, I caught a back-right from Strong, who was cocking it to let Ermann have it again. I felt the sting on my right jaw. For a minute the room turned a kind of putrid green color. Men were shouting all around. I could see Strong looking back at me in surprise.

The men grabbed Ermann and Strong. I shook my head.

"What's this all about?" I asked, catching hold of the job press to keep my balance.

"Tol' that idjut keep 'way from this press!" Ermann shouted. "Tol' 'im hunnert times!"

"It wasn't Joe's fault!" Strong shouted back. "I told him to handle it while I was taking Mr. Hadleyman around the pressroom. You're drunk, Leon!"

The two men looked at each other like a couple of savages.

"Who'sh foreman here?" Ermann snarled.

Strong stared at him hotly.

"Okay—okay—cut it out," I said, trying to snarl, too. But somehow it came out sounding a little watery. My jaw was swelling. My head ached behind my ear, and my stomach was ulcerating again. "We've got enough problems around here without tearing the joint apart. Somebody take care of the kid. Ermann, you get upstairs and have another cup of coffee and calm down. Strong, I want to talk to you. Now, the rest of you guys get to work, you hear? And if anybody misses a minute before deadline, I'll dock every one of you a day's pay."

The men exchanged half-amused glances. They knew that the threat of docked pay couldn't make much difference when they hadn't received a paycheck on schedule—except for the surprise check I'd just had issued to them—for the last three months. Yet they seemed to recognize that the threat from me at least meant that I was determined to put out the paper. They grumbled a bit, leading the apprentice kid, Joe, to a downstairs washroom. Ermann shuffled up the stairs, muttering to himself.

"I haven't seen the stereotype section yet," I said to Strong. "Come on."

"Sorry about your jaw," he replied. "I meant that for Ermann, Mr. Hadleyman."

"The name's still Steve."

"Yeah. Steve."

"Tell me something," I said, rubbing my jaw. "Where'd you learn karate?"

Strong laughed. "I picked it up in the navy. But, to tell you the truth, I think it would take more than a lucky chop to handle Ermann. He's one mean—"

"Yeah—but he *is* foreman."

Strong looked away then. We had reached the stereotype section where no one was around.

"Maybe I should have waited for Ermann to give the orders," Strong said, "but the trouble is, he never knows what orders to give. I knew we had trouble and that you should be told, so I asked Joe to watch things while I talked to you. We have a lot of posters and stuff to get out by tomorrow night."

"Okay—I'll straighten it out," I replied. "But pull everybody off posters and all extra printing for the time being. Let's concentrate on the paper."

❧ XVII

I looked around at the collection of antiquated printing junk that was, to put it mildly, a backdrop for a Dana dilemma. A saw and metal router were jammed into a corner behind a boiler. Rags and ink-stained papers were strewn all over the place, perfect ingredients for a first-class fire. Gallon tins, stoneware bottles, and carboys were cluttered about. You could hardly walk around back there. Next to the boiler was a huge, old-fashioned vat like those used by country printers for thinning ink, surrounded by still more stoneware bottles. My dad used to have one when I was a kid, but I couldn't remember anyone using such a contraption since the thirties.

I whistled.

"I wasn't the best foreman in the world," Strong said bitterly, "but I never tolerated this mess when I was giving orders."

I looked into the vat. It was filled with thick, foul-smelling ink, so odoriferous it made me cough.

"Tell me," I said, making a face, "what was it between you and Birdie? I mean, you seem to know your way around. Why aren't you still foreman?"

Strong's lips tightened. "It's a pretty long story."

"Make it short. Caxton demoted you, too, didn't he?"

"Yeah—well, I'll tell you the truth. I couldn't get along with either of them. With Caxton it was money . . . not for me, understand. That is, not for me alone. But for the men, too. Caxton just wouldn't pay enough to meet the union wage, or on time. With Birdie Johnson—well, let's put it this way. When he needed me, I was there. He came to me and appealed for a cooperative effort to get the *Dispatch* in the black again. Would I go to the men and put them on the long finger, so to speak? I did. I not only got the men to agree to a low wage with the promise of ultimately better compensation, but also convinced them to go to the bank. We all took out personal loans and put the cash into a common pool so that Birdie could actually meet expenses—including the payroll. The men went along with it because I asked them to. We went as far as we could with Birdie. My reward was to be demoted."

"How come?"

Strong looked at me. His voice was grim. "Birdie wanted the power. At first he was as happy as Larry. But when he saw the men rallying around me like that, I guess he began to worry. He figured that if he now failed to meet the payroll, the men would actually rebel. Should I lead them, they would take my side, and Birdie knew it. I honestly think, Steve, that he was afraid I had a plot in mind to take over the sheet myself and become a publisher."

I stared at the mess in the stereotype section. The smell of the vat alone, with its sludgy, almost mud-thick ink, symbolized the whole, stultified operation. It made my eyes sting.

"You'd better get someone to clean all this up, Jim. What's that leftover ink doing here anyway?"

"Search me." Jim shrugged. "This area is little more than a junk room now, although I think the router could be fixed. Birdie told the janitor to mix the ink—some economy kick of his. But the janitor quit ages ago. Anyway, Birdie didn't know what he was doing. To prove it, let me show you the ink-distributing rig on the presses. The stuff Birdie mixed back here has it all gummed up."

"Well," I said, with a sigh, "as long as the stuff's here, let's thin it some more and use it up—on posters or whatever. It may smell like hell, but even the newsprint is coming C.O.D. We've gotta economize, too. Throw those cans and bottles out, for gosh sakes, before we have a fire."

I picked up a carboy, which, though empty, reeked with the stench of rotten eggs. "Phew! What did he thin the ink with? Vinegar?"

Strong laughed. "Some sort of homemade thinner," he replied. "Birdie cut every corner he could. Paper, lead, even ink-thinner costs the earth now. Which reminds me, we don't have much linseed oil left, either. I'll have the men clean this up the best they can. Is it okay to charge some tools and stuff downtown?"

"Better yet, get the stuff you need and have the bill sent to me and I'll pay the check."

"Music to my ears."

I could see from all this that it had been touch and go every day for the printers. No wonder morale was so low. I asked Strong to show me the rest of the equipment. It grew progressively worse as we continued our tour.

I was pretty used to primitive conditions on my own weekly—like pasting up messy offset pages, opaquing out mistakes on page negatives, working with cardboard type, and all

that—but that seemed like Publishers' Row next to this gar-
bage-strewn alley. Only one of the two rotaries was working,
and it didn't seem to have much life left in it.

There was an old Babcock flatbed press standing idle in yet
another dark corner. It may sound silly, but I took a cold look
at that press just in case we would need it in emergencies.

Strong laughed. "Believe it or not," he said, "this old Babcock is a pioneer. It was brought to Montana on a train."

"A train?"

"Yeah—a special train. And it was in operation at the time."

"You're kiddin'."

"Nope. Once upon a time, the National Editorial Association decided to go on tour through Montana between the two
parks, and they actually produced a newspaper on the train during the trip. Know what? They generated power off a dynamo
operated by the locomotive. They not only had a linotype in
operation the whole time, but printed the sheet on a Miehle
press as well. It was called the *National Editor's Argus*."

"I remember my dad telling me about that years ago."

"Right. And this old Babcock was in another car just in case
they needed it, which they did, and it was sold when the tour
was over."

"Well, I'll be . . ." I regarded the ancient press with new
respect as Jim tinkered around with it lovingly. He pressed a
button and, sure enough, it started up, although the revolutions
were mighty slow.

"I keep it oiled," Strong said with a note of pride. "You
never know when you might need this baby."

I nodded appreciatively. "Good thing something works."

Strong laughed again. "We've got so many problems," he
said, "that before we can fix one thing something else breaks
down—except these old pioneers. They made great machines
in those days."

"I see what you mean."

"Now, there are the troublemakers," he added, leading me

out of the pressroom into the composition area and pointing at a row of linotypes. He showed me some of the fonts. Even I could tell that they were far too worn, but the machines still operated. I realized Strong had done a great deal to keep them repaired. I made a mental note of that.

Strong's life was clearly the printing profession. He seemed too good a worker to be much of a hater, but you never could tell. *Somebody* had taken care of Birdie, and I learned long ago that you can find a maniac anywhere—even in a pressroom. I might go so far as to say, after considering the *Dispatch's* condition, especially in a pressroom. It's a tough business.

Strong was putting a font back in place when Jellinek appeared behind me. He was out of breath.

He pointed up the stairs. "It's—it's odd. Come and see."

"What's wrong?"

"Upstairs!"

The three of us went up to the editorial area. The whole staff had gathered by my desk. They were huddling around a chair, whispering. Everyone seemed subdued. I saw Mabel Reitz in the middle of the crowd, bending over something on the floor.

"Never saw anything like it," Jellinek said.

"Poor thing."

"What happened?"

"I dunno."

I pushed through the group. Porno, the cat, was stretched out on the floor next to a saucer of milk. Just as I bent down to look, the cat suddenly shot in the air, its fur sticking out like porcupine quills and legs darting out stiffly in four different directions, as though someone had administered shock treatment. With a single, piercing shriek it flipped over in midair, flashed its claws, and landed with a flat thud exactly where it had been lying. That was one jolted cat.

"What . . ."

"I can't understand it," Mabel was saying. "I poured out a little of the milk from the coffee tray for Porno on his saucer and the next thing—"

"Oh!" Shirley Weaver cried with surprising abruptness and a hostile stare, glowering with anger. "That's enough for me!"

She picked up her purse without looking at anyone, went to the coat hangers for her raincoat, and then marched toward swinging doors. I could hear her voice just before she reached the doors, muttering to anyone who cared to listen, "I quit!"

"Jellinek," I said, getting up slowly, mulling things over, "get this animal outside. Mabel, call the cops. The cat's been poisoned."

I had the feeling Mabel was trying to hide a smile when she said, "We know that, Mr. Hadleyman—uh, Steve. But do you really think it's necessary to call the police over a dead cat?"

"You don't understand, do you?" I replied. "That cat was poisoned by milk that was meant for someone's coffee. Probably strychnine or something."

"Oh, but . . ."

"Call the cops!" I snapped. Then, seeing that some of them still thought I was overdramatizing matters, I added, "Don't you see? Whoever put poison in that milk is probably Birdie's killer. I distinctly remember that none of you took milk in your coffee. Now, I don't know how the killer found out—but in fact the only person here who does take milk is me."

PART TWO
Deadline

‌ XVIII

The point was to keep things moving. We were only putting out a twelve-pager, but it was already 11 A.M.—four hours to deadline.

I canceled all lunch hours. Then I phoned Shirley Weaver at her home to talk her into coming back to handle circulation details, at least, later in the afternoon. I said I was sorry about Porno.

"It was so stupid," she said angrily. "I mean, why would anyone . . ."

I explained to her my theory about the milk. She listened attentively, and when she spoke again, her voice still sounded angry, but, strangely enough, not half as frightened as I felt. She finally agreed to come back. I was relieved, since she was the only person who knew the routine on the mailer. She also dealt with the newsboys who would be arriving at the door behind the pressroom to deliver the sheet after three-thirty. I told her to bring a box of sandwiches, charged to the *Dispatch*, from the bus depot on the way.

When I hung up, I found Chief Laken towering over my desk. He was flanked by three cops, one of whom kept staring at Mabel, who was running around the office like a character out of *The Front Page*.

The chief was still pretty horrible-looking from the lack of sleep and what seemed like a hangover. But I suspected that underneath that grisly exterior was a heart of pure barbed wire, not to mention a wolverine cunning that had obviously been doing overtime since my run-in with him the night before.

Much to my surprise, though, the chief accepted my alarm over the poisoning of the cat as reasonable. He also acquiesced when I told him I would still try to get the paper out.

I expected him to give me a hard time about that, but he said, "I talked to Terrill again after your conversation with him this morning. We still haven't seen any sign of Birdie, alive or dead, and frankly, Hadleyman, your story ain't too impressive. But Terrill says he wants the *Dispatch* to keep coming out and you're the only person around to do it. So I guess it's okay."

"You still don't believe me about Birdie, do you?"

"Hell, no. Not until I find a body."

"You don't really think I made all that up, do you?"

"Could be."

I laughed. "Maybe you think I stabbed Birdie with a spindle, a pair of shears, and who knows what else, then called you on the phone, walked up to the front of the office, and hit myself on the head. Then, of course, to throw suspicion on myself, I poisoned the cat with strychnine this morning."

Laken frowned. "The doc's examining that cat now," he said, ignoring my sarcasm. "We'll know soon enough what killed it."

"Maybe somebody better examine the doc, too," one of the cops added, studying my bandaged head.

"If it's all the same to you," the chief continued, as though no one had spoken, "I'm leaving a few boys around the plant here. I don't want any more shenanigans."

Perhaps, I thought, Laken agreed with me privately that there was a connection between what I'd told him about Birdie's murder and the poisoning of the cat, after all.

"Wouldn't have it any other way," I said cheerfully. "But tell 'em to keep a low profile, will you? We don't have time for lunch as it is."

The chief, starting to leave, peered at my face with a practiced eye. "I don't remember you gettin' clipped on the jaw last night," he said, studying my new bruise.

"Naw," I said. "I got that downstairs. There was a little mix-up between Ermann and one of the apprentice printers. Strong came to the kid's defense and I tried to break it all up and—well, I got this." It was still sore, but the swelling had gone down.

"Strong, huh?" The chief chuckled, but he had a strange, resolute expression.

"Wait a minute," I said. "Please don't go booking anybody. Take Strong out of here and I don't think I could even get the presses started."

The chief didn't say anything. He turned to go. One of his men was sitting on the edge of Mabel's desk, leaning over her from a vantage point that afforded a maximum scenic view.

The chief grabbed him roughly by the upper arm and directed him out. He positioned him at the door and dispersed the other cops to remote corners of the plant. Maybe it was my imagination, but I seemed to sense a certain rapport between Mabel and the chief.

I checked on Kressnach. It was clear that he didn't really know how to edit wire roundups or make up a page. Still, he at least had the inside pages dummied in a magazine sort of way, giving state and national news a look-in, even if the emphasis was peculiar.

"Ah, well, it's a start." I sighed. "How are you getting on, Jellinek?"

"Routine stuff," he replied without looking up. "I'll do the rest of my beat by phone. I think I'll make it."

Mabel Reitz had the weddings going, and, shocking as the grammar was, I was grateful this wasn't the day for her women's page. It was not the time to berate anyone, in any case. They were all working with a certain gusto that made me feel good. Instead of going into shock, they seemed almost inspired. Even Kressnach was humming to himself as he merrily tore up wire copy and neatly piled it at one side, presumably ready for downstairs.

"Anyone seen Willy Dunkle?" I asked.

"He usually checks in just before lunch."

"Right."

The clock seemed to leap ten minutes at a time. The pressure mounted.

I grabbed some of Kressnach's copy and carried it downstairs, re-editing as much of it as I could en route. Then I returned and helped Mabel correct the spelling in her copy. It made her nervous, but she kept going. Jellinek was busy on the phone. I picked up the handouts on his desk and rewrote them hurriedly.

The cops stared at us in disbelief. Paper was flying everywhere. Bells would ring in the basement and there would be shouting back and forth—then more hectic writing.

I loved it. But more than the clock told me that deadline was near. My stomach was right on schedule.

ᘒ XIX

Shirley arrived with the sandwiches as though nothing had happened and got back into the routine of things. A few people came and went, but generally we all kept the rhythm. I munched on a sandwich happily and studied the staff as they worked away.

Jellinek was a steady worker, much more of a worker than I had suspected. It was clear that he didn't like Birdie, but I could not imagine his killing anybody.

He had been at the university when Caxton disappeared, but had he been around long enough to work up a violent hatred for Birdie Johnson? The killer was a bad case, I assured myself—a psychopath, a box of crackers. Could this young, clean-cut, journalism-school product, a 22-year-old tenderfoot whose B.A. diploma was still fresh from the printer, really commit murder?

Well, maybe he could, I thought. After all, Billy the Kid and Dillinger had to start sometime, and you read of more impossible types in the daily paper. Maniacs come in all forms, too. The rare paranoid—that four percent of the population in our asylums listed as violent and aberrant—isn't confined to one class or income bracket. Any police reporter knows that a man who wears a dirty T-shirt and breaks beer bottles at the neck before drinking doesn't have a corner on the market of psychopaths.

It may be true, I told myself, that paranoia is more easily recognizable in the man who lets himself go to pot, but the lab boys would agree that the person who brushes his hair and wears a clean shirt every day could also slug his brother with an axe, even if he is a bit harder to spot.

Well, Jellinek didn't look like the protagonist of *The Phantom of the Opera*, but then who does these days? My grandfather—on the Hadleyman side—looked like a cross between Caliban and the bellringer of *The Hunchback of Notre Dame*, to put it kindly, but he couldn't bear to step on a beetle.

Then, there was Mabel. I studied her. She was nibbling the end of a No. 2 pencil while pondering some copy. Clearly, writing was not her strong point. That didn't make Mabel a killer, although I vaguely recalled Mabel going to the back room to fetch the tray with sugar and the lethal milk for coffee. Good thing, I mused, that I had decided I couldn't face the coffee.

Then again, it was Mabel who poured the milk for the cat, too. Would she have done that if she had known it was poisoned? And most of the staff had been back at that coffee urn during the morning as well.

I began to argue with myself. Don't forget, part of me warned, poison is a woman's weapon. But, argued another part, shears and spindles aren't. Or are they? Was it possible that Mabel . . .

Yep, I answered. Even if that pleasant, deep-eyed expression of hers, currently contorted around a transitive verb, didn't look menacing at the moment, it could cloud over a variety of passions, surely. Take away her cigar and even Ma Barker must have had her feminine charms.

I picked up Mabel's file. There was a lot between the lines. She had a sort of buckaroo background that you sometimes find in women of the West—an unsophisticated meetcha-at-the-swimmin'-hole quality that makes them cling to Cokes and pea-nut-butter sandwiches during high-school lunch hours and vodka and lettermen after the Saturday-night game. But Mabel had a little more physical class than most of the girls in Marks-burg—a certain nubile vitality and a subtle body language that defy description. She was different, all right. Five six, fiery, and flirtatious, she had a smooth exterior that seemed to cover a previous toughness.

A graduate of Marksburg High School, she was in trouble a lot in her teens. After some family disgrace that involved her and the local football hero, she had left for the Coast, no doubt financed by her father, to attend the Pasadena Playhouse. She didn't finish her first year there, however, and after what ap-peared to be a lame attempt to break into films, she wound up on the California weeklies trying to learn the news game. Ob-viously she was looking for the kind of glamour you don't find very often in small towns, and when she didn't find it, she returned to Marksburg about the time Caxton bought the pa-per. No doubt Mabel Reitz had come home reluctantly and probably with the intention of not remaining.

That made me wonder about the possibility of anything going

on between Mabel and Caxton, or, for that matter, Birdie, since both men were bachelors. Caxton, I decided, was more her style. He liked cocktails and new cars; Birdie undoubtedly preferred his beer in the can and stomped around the office in his cowboy boots.

Of course, the personal stuff about Mabel—like her being in trouble in high school—wasn't in the file. I picked up some of the local gossip around town very quickly in the days that followed. But even if I had known nothing about her, there was an air about her that said she was holding in a heavy secret. Could that secret, I mused, involve a motive? Or could she herself have *been* a motive?

I realized as I was staring at her that she was smiling back at me. She wasn't flirting with her smile. Just smiling. The flirting would come later. I cleared my throat.

 XX

I could hear Harvey Kressnach's pipe gurgling and watched him idly as he went through the motions of being a wire editor. He seemed to be making up page 1 by doodling.

"You writing the lead story?" he asked me without looking up. His question was quiet, yet so direct that I felt a queer sensation. How did he know I was looking at him? Further, the tone of his question implied that he could read my thoughts without ever taking his eyes off his own work. Odd duck.

"Yeah," I replied. "We'll have a sixty-point banner, two lines, as I said. The boys know about it downstairs. We're breaking the murder, Harvey, so we'll keep page 1 simple. Get me an exterior shot of the *Dispatch* if you can. And no more helter-skelter makeup!"

He looked up then. His BB eyes were practically invisible behind the thick lenses that bounced the light upward, giving him an almost grotesque, empty-socket vacancy that was offset by that ridiculous pipe. His complexion was the color of unbaked pastry. A cerulean cloud of smoke seemed to linger about his head. I suppose that if one word could describe Harvey Kressnach it was "ambiguity." His manner, his appearance, his voice were enough to put you into a coma. And then, behind that vagueness, something sparked alive and I had a sensation much like the one I'd had when I first met him. As I looked into his distorted beady eyes, I could see a strange pinpoint of light in them, as though he not only could see mine, but also could see *through* mine—while all I could really see were two large, glittering crystals like something from outer space.

When he spoke, however, he was far from vague. "You think I'm a murderer, don't you, Mr. Hadleyman?"

I felt that proverbial chill in the stomach that writers are always describing tritely as icy blood or some such banality. Whatever it was, I felt the shock of his statement, realizing that I was about to come to the conclusion that had passed his turgid lips.

"To tell the honest truth, Harvey," I said quietly, "I'm beginning to think any of you could be. But then why should I suspect you? What reason would you have for killing Birdie Johnson?"

"The best," he replied, grinning oddly. "The very best. Uh—did you say sixty-point?"

"That's right," I said sharply. "You've been playing country weekly with this sheet long enough. We may be rolling only twelve pages, and we're lucky to have the inside pages down with canned stuff, but I want the makeup all through this sheet to *look* like a daily, beginning with page 1, see? We have the news. Let's justify it. Give it a heavy play."

Kressnach's expression didn't change, I guess. . . . I couldn't really tell. Only his mouth moved a little. He seemed, judging from the angle of his glasses, to be more interested in my nose than anything else.

"I didn't kill him," he said, in his squeaky voice. "But perhaps I should have. Do you know why?"

"Why?"

"Because in a way he was killing me." He paused for a moment, and I realized that there could well be genuine tears behind those glasses now.

"Oh yes, he was, Mr. Hadleyman. You wouldn't believe it to look at me now. Young Jellinek wouldn't believe it. That starstruck Mabel would never believe it. But I was a great reporter once, and ten times the editor you'll ever be."

He was right—I didn't believe it.

I said nothing. Kressnach fiddled with the stem of his pipe and breathed heavily, staring at me. With headlines and makeup of the kind he composed, I thought, he had to be completely round the bend to convince himself he had ever been an ace reporter, not to mention any kind of editor.

"I once broke a contract with INS and released the biggest gambling story in Chicago. Would you believe it? I wasn't always like this, you know. I didn't always work from ten to six, pulling roundups off the machine and taking two coffee breaks. I didn't always go home to a one-room apartment where a crabby landlady feeds me garbage and nags me every night. I was a columnist once, you know. I had a family, wrote theater reviews once in a while. I was even famous, in a way. It was so long ago that . . ."

"What happened?"

He shrugged and started to make up page 1 again. "What happened?" he asked himself. "What happened?"

He didn't seem to want to go on, so I didn't press it, but something was way off kilter. When I checked his file, it jibed, all right.

Somewhere there was apparently a turning point, a very intimate and decisive turning point. If he had ever been the news-man he said he was, somewhere, somehow there had been some trauma, some disgrace that had distorted his outlook, pushed him West, and slotted him abruptly into the small-time jobs he landed on failing dailies. There was loneliness there, perhaps, and bad sight and, maybe tragically so, the gradual, terrifying disillusionment of not being useful or wanted or even interested in all that means a newspaper.

Yes, I thought, maybe Birdie was killing you, Harvey. And maybe, in spite of what you say, you killed him.

❧ XXI

Although a small army of policemen kept browsing about the plant, passing Mabel Reitz's swiveling chair and other accoutre-ments with unnecessary frequency, I was amazed to see the *Dispatch* taking form by 3 P.M. The staff showed a real sense of timing in the last hours.

Jellinek had covered most of his local by telephone, partly out of pressure and partly out of warnings by Chief Laken and the accompaniment of three officers every time he went out. A rookie had stuck with Willy Dunkle as he did his rounds, and even the printers had a man with them when they took their break for coffee.

I was concerned about Kressnach's layout. Whether his rather emotional outburst of nostalgia for his Chicago days had been too much for him or not, I just didn't know. But he turned out a terribly ragged dummy. It was measured much too tightly and included headlines that didn't count out. I fixed it up as best I could. When Strong buzzed three times from the pressroom, giving his okay on the dummy, Kressnach seemed to offer me the hint of a smile.

"Not bad," I said, looking at my watch. "Five after. In spite of all the problems, I think we'll make it."

Mabel's headlines were the last to come in. She had two of the younger men on the police force flanking her as she maneuvered her way past Kressnach's desk like an Italian actress about to emerge from the rice fields.

"Here's the last, chief," she said. It wasn't a bad imitation, really, of Barbara Stanwyck. I could see the lawmen were impressed.

"Okay, sister," I replied, in my best Bogartese. "Okay."

Jellinek had dug up a good pair of mug shots of Caxton and Birdie, and Kressnach had located a large print of the *Dispatch* for below the fold. The exterior of the plant was clear, and it would make a good six-column cut—that is, two three-column plastic cuts juxtaposed, seeing as how the Swedish machine we had couldn't handle a six-column size.

I wrote the lead yarn short enough so we didn't have to jump it to an inside page. If I say so myself, that staff and I got a daily out with about the hottest local stuff you could handle, plus a reasonable balance in makeup and wire copy, in record time.

Even a twelve-pager has its headaches, and I was delighted when Willy Dunkle told me that his layouts were complete and, in fact, he had proofs ready to be checked by advertisers for the following day as well. "We *are* coming out tomorrow, too, aren't we?" he asked, with a grin.

"Yeah," I replied, "if we're still around." I threw down my straightedge and looked at the staff. They had really buckled down. I had underestimated them. We all pitched in on page proofs and wound up being only seven minutes late. Even Willy helped on the editorial proofs before starting his late-afternoon rounds with the next day's advertising proofs.

"Okay," I said finally, "let's take a coffee break while the printers wrap it up. This is National Friendly Week. Take a cop to coffee. I'm going to have mine here—without milk."

They all scrambled for the doors at the same time. I relaxed, made some coffee, and then sat back to review the situation.

Shirley's phone rang. I took it.

"Mr. Hadleyman?"

"That's right. Who's this?"

"My name is Brownlee, Mr. Hadleyman. James Brownlee. I'm an attorney—as a matter of fact, your attorney."

"Yeah," I said. "I've heard of you."

"I should imagine you have," Brownlee said, as though someone had just poured a stewed plum down his throat. "I was hired by Mr. Terrill to represent the *Dispatch* on occasion. Just local, you understand—Mr. Terrill, you must know, has a large legal team in the East."

"Yes?"

"Well," he said after a pause, "I thought we might get acquainted. Birdie told me that you were coming down, and since his—er—disappearance I've been quite disturbed."

"I can appreciate that, Mr. Brownlee. There have been a few disturbances around here, too."

"So I've heard," he replied. "Birdie left me some minor information that you should have, although I'm not sure it is really necessary now. I mean, considering the circumstances and all."

"What information?"

"Well," he said deliberately, "it's a bit difficult discussing matters over the phone. What would you say to meeting me later?"

"Fine. We have a deadline on our hands right now, as you know, and—"

"Oh?" he said with surprise. "You mean you're still going to *publish*?"

"That's what I came down here for."

"Yes, but . . . Oh, well. What do you say to six o'clock at the Nugget Lounge?"

"Right. Six at the Nugget. I'll be there."

I had a few minutes left before the staff returned, so I decided, remembering a look Shirley had given me earlier, that it would be a good idea to wash up. I got my kit from my VW out front and went back to the darkroom sink. When I was through, I realized that I had never really explored the large upstairs section of the building as I had promised myself I'd do, so I went up.

ॐ XXII

The arrangement up there was a pleasant surprise, to say the least. I had expected that part of the building to be as messy and grimy as all the rest. But when I entered the upstairs section through newly built—expensive—glass doors worked by an electric eye, it was like entering a James Bond setting.

In the first place, it was ideal for city-daily work—and I mean the kind of city daily that functions entirely on computers. The floor was completely carpeted with non-static material. The walls and ceiling were soundproofed, and areas were marked for air-conditioning vents. A series of swiveling heavy-duty desks designed to hold video terminals was arranged in horseshoe fashion, as though some designer from NASA had been called in to lay out the first space-traveling editorial office.

An elevator connection had been extended from the press-room, but it was incomplete, and several small, tubular rooms were seemingly still under construction. There was also the beginning of a complex of electrical fittings and outlets, as though someone were contemplating a computer and video terminal conversion away from hot metal.

That set me thinking. In those days, such conversions had not yet begun on a large scale in many American towns and cities on either side of the Mississippi. In fact, my own offset weekly was comparatively new on the offset scene, but it had been basically a kitchen-table-*cum*-garage operation. I had never seen anything so advanced as this layout.

A half-dozen light boxes were partially constructed. Some crates—the kind heavy camera equipment is shipped in, like enlargers—lined one wall. There seemed to be a mountain of cardboard boxes containing paste-up equipment.

No doubt about it, the *Dispatch* was obviously just this side of becoming a magnificently equipped, well-planned, and ultra-modern offset newspaper—this in the days when the New Journalism was still an infant incapable of muscle-building the kind of counter-journalism that would later dominate the American scene under the so-called slogan "interpretative writing." My days on the *Dispatch* were parenthesized by an era when the only Tom Wolfe newsmen talked about was the one who had produced a *roman à clef* in four gargantuan novels before dying at the age of thirty-eight, and when it was still fashionable for a reporter to get the facts right before going to press.

The pressroom was obviously the next step for whoever was doing the planning; the press conversion would be expensive. But now it was clear why the linotypes on the paper were falling apart. They were being phased out. Hot metal was cooling off fast.

I was about to go downstairs again when my eyes, now adjusted to the dark, focused on a bunch of wooden crates against a distant wall. I checked the contents of one of them. It contained small parts to what I figured would be a gigantic machine if it was ever brought in. Such a machine—obviously a monster of a gang-run offset press—would have to be fitted into the basement. I could tell by the manifest that it was the type you only find on very large dailies—double boom, added railings, extra parts for photo techniques, color runs, and all that. The parts were in cosmoline still, but I could hardly fail to notice that the manifest indicated *more than one* press was on order!

It was ludicrous! Before me was evidence of a planned operation costing millions. It would have made a big-city daily's expansion program seem penny ante. The graphic-arts section alone looked like the kind of dream a Walt Disney might have had while contemplating taking over the London *Times*.

But this was no Thunderer. The *Dispatch* wouldn't have even made a weak link in a nineteenth-century chain. With dailies folding in the East because half a million readers still couldn't woo advertisers away from television, what could a small Montana town have to offer? Crazy, crazy.

Behind the crates, which housed only the small parts of what I figured would be one of those high-speed Goss units, with inverted folders and shining, octuple operations built with automatic brakes and lovely, non-stop devices, there was a sort of caged room that swung to the left of the rear part of the upstairs. I pushed through the wire door, which was a bit stuck, and found a fairly decent layout for a newspaper morgue.

Several past volumes of the *Dispatch* had been bound and stored in there, which explained why I couldn't find back copies when I first came to the plant. As I strummed through them, I realized that quite a lot of work had gone into filing and clipping efforts, in contrast to the tossed-in-a-drawer system downstairs.

More out of curiosity than anything else, I began to piece together Caxton's story before Birdie Johnson had taken over. Caxton was the kind of person, obviously, who came in like a circus parade, and he had emblazoned his acquisition of the *Dispatch* across page 1 as though it had been the *Hindenburg* disaster. And in a way, it was.

Birdie, on the other hand, had scarcely mentioned his own takeover. He played up the Caxton disappearance for a few issues, then went back to normal. He even reverted to a more distant era in Montana journalism, restoring backcountry makeup, a folksy tone in the stories, and a frankly commercial approach to newspapering. I could see how the rumors of Caxton's skipping town had started. Judging from the paper's announcements, Terrill's repurchasing of the paper by sheriff's auction and Birdie's appointment by Terrill as acting publisher had received the town's solid blessing, abrupt though it was. I was beginning to think Caxton's disappearance had more to it than met the reader's eye.

The back issues showed that the handling of the news and features was pretty routine during Caxton's period: community affairs, economic optimism, opposition to taxes or change—things like that. I noticed one innovation: the series of articles, signed by Caxton himself, crusading on page 1 for a Wheat Research Agency to be built in Marksburg and financed as a "venture-capital undertaking"—the series I had seen back in Great Falls, when Caxton had circulated offprints of it. He obviously had a special crusade in mind. But I didn't see any other very spirited news articles or commentaries.

Only one item seemed unusual. It concerned Chief Laken's investigation into a shooting at Caxton's home during a party. Someone had fired through the window, but no one was hurt. That was all there was to it.

XXIII

I was still browsing around in the dust upstairs when I heard the staff coming back. When I went down, they were all present and at work except Willy Dunkle.

"Where is he?" I asked irritably. "He said he'd help us out on the last of the editorial proofs. They'll be up any minute."

"Search me," Jellinek replied. "He told the cop on his tail that he was going to hit a couple of places before coming back here. He had a page proof of Super-Thrift's, so maybe he went over there. The cop left him at the bus depot."

"Well," I said, lifting my voice above the pressroom buzzer, "we can't wait. Let's get at it. Here they come."

Now, I'm not saying that Marksburg's little daily would have taken a Pulitzer Prize for that issue, but I was pretty proud of those twelve pages when they came up in page proof. There's something exhilarating about the feel of proofs, anyway, with their crisp freshness offering first sight of all your work finally composed into a framework of drama and style. There's something about black on white in the printed word during a preliminary test run of a paper that hits a newspaperman the way a good sparring session affects a boxer before the big event. Those proofs were a little ragged, but the staff looked genuinely happy with the results.

"Now, I call that a story," Jellinek said, sitting back and looking at page 1.

I knew what he meant. He wasn't referring to my writing, but to the fact we had *news*—a scoop—on page 1. The disappearance of Birdie was headlined in the largest type we had. If we had had red ink, I wouldn't have run it, because somehow the blackness of the type, like Hamlet's motley, perfectly expressed the situation.

The double disappearance of Caxton and Birdie, I was certain, would evoke all kinds of speculation by readers who spent a great deal of their time whispering behind their squinting windows. Compounded by rumors already flying about Marksburg, the news on the front page would make the story irresistible. Chief Laken would be furious.

As soon as we rolled, I was going to remind Jellinek to phone the AP and UPI, as I had earlier suggested, but I learned he had already done so. That meant that the wiremen would be down sooner or later. Magazine writers would no doubt catch the scent soon enough, and I expected radio and television reporters to come in, too. Newsmen can't resist a story about their own, and I knew that this one would appeal.

What I had learned about a future operation of the plant upstairs, as well as the background stuff on Caxton, I would keep to myself for the time being. It would make a good magazine piece later. But the important thing from a news position was that this was the story of a newspaper, and the *Dispatch*, naturally, had an exclusive. Human life is the primary factor in any story, and when that human life is part of the life of a newspaper itself, there is the kind of angle that would have made Nellie Bly add a postscript to her memoirs.

The whole thing meant, really, that if I could keep the paper publishing for the next few days, it might gain national recognition. The potential in advertising and circulation was intriguing. Readers in the Northwest would be perusing the *Dispatch* as soon as we could get it to them. Each issue would be a collectors' item. Since there were no television or radio stations in Marksburg (thus no other advertising crew but ours walking the streets), the little daily could change overnight from a desperate rag in the final throes of bankruptcy to a prosperous, courageous—dare I say famous?—and very much alive newspaper.

I sensed all that and so did the staff. Even Harvey Kressnach put down his pipe and looked at the others with what might be described as pride. I know he felt some new emotion; his giggle was much higher pitched.

I looked at the large, blacked-out spaces where the two-column cuts were to go—one of Birdie and one of Caxton. The lower half of the page was blacked out as well, across six columns where the picture of the exterior of the paper's plant was to be placed. My editorial ran down the left-hand side of the page in boldface—brief as it was.

"The cuts ready on these?" I asked.

"They'll be up in a minute!" Mabel shouted.

That automatic engraver was a curse. It was an imported job from Stockholm that would deliver plastic cuts fairly quickly, but the shots came out pretty gray. They couldn't compare with hot metal.

"Too bad we don't have some good cuts," I complained. "I know it sounds morbid, but if we're going to use portraits of past publishers, at least they should be recognizable."

"Yeah," Jellinek agreed. Then he sat up. "Wait a minute," he added. "We'll probably have to use a plastic cut of Birdie, but I know that Caxton had a metal cut blocked of himself. Part of his routine, I imagine. It would be a double-column one."

"Good. Know where it is?"

"In the front office."

"Where?"

"Don't you remember me telling you about the front office?" Jellinek said. "That's where Birdie called me on that labor story. Remember? Well, I recall Birdie showing me a cut of Caxton just to point out what an egotist that guy must have been. It was in the desk up there."

I went up to the small room in front. It was large enough to hold a desk, a cabinet, two comfortable chairs, and a wastebasket. It would make a good conference room, at least for person-to-person combat.

The desk was locked. I got a screwdriver and pried it open. There was the usual stuff: checkbooks, some personal mail—that sort of thing. I found the cut in the second drawer and called Shirley in, telling her to run the cut down to the pressroom right away. I told her to tell Strong to roll, the proofs being okay.

I was about to leave when I saw a small folder in the top drawer at the back of the desk. It was marked "X-2." The missing confidential file. When I opened it, I was disappointed to find just a lot of bits and pieces—postage stamps, receipts, and the like. One receipt was from an ink company that was to forward a large supply of multilith ink for smooth-surfaced paper—further proof, I thought, of the *Dispatch*'s imminent expansion, since of course the paper currently used letterpress ink, and, occasionally for some job work, a bit of intaglio. Then I noticed a few typewritten pages underneath the odds and ends in the file, and as I read them, I realized why Birdie had kept them apart from the regular X-1 file.

The main thing was a confidential report on Willy Dunkle, obviously taken from police files. Dunkle had a criminal record. The report showed that he was actually a Canadian by birth, and he had been in trouble in Seattle. He had been jailed once for armed robbery and assault with a deadly weapon. He had served a year-and-a-half term in prison and had got out on probation. The record showed he had been in trouble again, in Wyoming—something about a stolen car—and his probationary status had been revoked. He had worked on weeklies throughout the West. A third note, written by hand (probably Birdie's), indicated that Dunkle had been involved in a holdup of a service station in North Dakota. The attendant had been badly beaten.

In the midst of the papers there was a clipping of an engagement announcement, obviously from a back issue of the *Dispatch*. The announcement contained a picture of a young woman of college age. She wasn't beautiful, but pleasant-looking, with a small, enigmatic smile that added to her looks. The clipping read:

Mrs. Ernst Koenig, Rte. 1, SW, Marksburg, announces the forthcoming wedding of her daughter, Renata, and William Lloyd Dunkle, formerly of Seattle, Wash., and current advertising director of *The Marksburg Dispatch*.

Miss Koenig, who attended local schools, is a graduate of Putnam Secretarial School in Ferdinand, S.D., where she also was a typist for one year for the Ferdinand Tractor Co. While there, she resided with her uncle and aunt, Mr. and Mrs. Martin

Koenig, former Marksburg-area residents. Martin now operates the original family farm east of Ferdinand.

The clipping went on like that about the Koenig family, but there was nothing more about Willy. It seemed strange to me that no one had mentioned that Willy was engaged or, even stranger, that the engagement had obviously been broken off.

There was yet another receipt attached to the report on Willy, and I wondered what it meant, because in addition to Birdie Johnson's name at the top of the receipt, the initials "W.D." were written in above a signatory line. This receipt was for an order of two 40-gallon carboys of ink products, which, combined with the multilith-ink orders, didn't really make any sense. It was tough to figure out why the *Dispatch* would need such an advance order of ink when, as I recalled Strong saying, Birdie was trying to economize on the stuff. The order was supplied by a commercial firm in White Sulphur Springs—a long way off. And although I knew almost all the wholesale outfits in the state, I didn't know of any large producer of ink products there.

Furthermore, I wondered, why hadn't Birdie destroyed the information concerning Willy's record? What had he planned to do with X-2?

I remembered wondering earlier what Willy Dunkle, obviously a hot salesman, was doing in Marksburg when he clearly could have been going places in the big city. At the time, I surmised that since he was the outdoor type, perhaps he wanted to be somewhere near good hunting and fishing. But this file changed things considerably. It was clear that I would have to ask Willy Dunkle a few questions, too. I wondered if Chief Laken knew what the file said. Birdie might have got all this from a hundred different sources.

"We're ready, Scoop," Mabel said brightly, sticking her flaming head around the doorway.

She stepped in then, leaning voluptuously against the paneling. Her eyes had a greenish glow in the dim light, and I noticed for the first time that she was taller, more slender, and even more provocative than she had appeared to be in that ridiculous *Perils of Pauline* outfit she wore just in case she was ever asked to carry a camera and strobe unit through a hotel lobby.

"Well," I said, starting to put the file away, "let's take a look at the final product. Nothing like a fresh page 1."

"Yeah," she replied slowly, not budging and meanwhile blocking my exit. "I like anything fresh."

"Yep," I retorted. "So do my wife and kids."

I took her by the arm, turned her around, and started toward the editorial area. But she remained still, looking at the file in my hands, apparently reluctant to move.

Although it was clear that Mabel was capable of flirting with anything that wore pants and walked, I detected now something else in her manner. It was as though she wanted to catch me alone to give in to a certain temptation to whisper something confidential: like the wife of King Midas, who had to shout a secret into the ground simply to get rid of it. There was an unease there—a spark of anxiety, I thought.

"Dunkle come back yet?"

"Not yet."

She was still looking curiously at the file, so I opened it and took out the clipping about Willy Dunkle's engagement.

"What's the story on this, Mabel?"

She glanced at it. "Oh, *that?*" she said. "That didn't last long. I'm afraid nothing ever lasts very long for Willy. He came on too strong, if you know what I mean. Rena's a good kid . . . and the funny thing, I think Willy really loved her. But she broke it off."

I heard the words, but the tone—and the knowing look in Mabel's eyes—said a great deal more. "We've got a minute," I said, going back to the desk and sitting down. "Tell me about it."

Mabel sidled over to the desk in a way that reminded me of Lauren Bacall going through her paces in *To Have and Have Not*. She sat down on the edge of it, and for a moment I could have sworn she was going to say, "If you want anything, just whistle," but she said, "To make a pretty short story shorter— well, Rena jilted him. For Caxton."

"Caxton?"

"Uh-huh . . . Mr. Smarm himself. He and Willy had one of those crazy projects of Caxton's going. Something to do with Rena's mom's land. She was a widow out southwest of town. The way I get it is that Caxton and Willy proposed a deal to Mrs. Koenig, who was reluctant, so Willy turned his attentions on Rena, at first to try convince her and her mother, but then he changed his mind when he fell for Rena."

"What kind of proposal?"

"Oh, I don't know, Steve. Some kind of land deal. Pretty big project, everybody said, at the time. Anyway, Willy was smitten and I guess he and Caxton had words when Willy said he thought it was a raw deal and no way to treat the Koenigs, and he backed out of it. I know that after that he and Caxton were pretty mad at each other. It got worse when . . ."

"When what?"

"Well, typical of Caxton, he moved in on Rena himself. Started waltzing her all over the place, and it didn't take long for her to fall for his big talk and easy money. She just up and jilted Willy. Broke off the engagement so fast Willy didn't know what was happening."

"I see."

"Caxton sooner or later moved in on all the girls—or tried to," Mabel said with a funny glance.

"Yes," I replied. "I do see."

"Poor Willy," she added. "He's a good-looking enough guy, but he—well, he just falls flat every time. He approaches a woman like he's stalking game."

"Must have been pretty humiliating, huh?"

"Yes," she replied. "Not that it did Caxton much good. He took off shortly after that."

"And what happened to Rena and her mother?"

"Oh, they went back to South Dakota—just as well, I guess."

"Why?"

"Well, the prospects for a girl aren't all that great in Marksburg, you know. And certainly Rena couldn't turn back to Willy Dunkle now, could she?"

I looked up at Mabel as I put the file away in the desk. She was studying my face. Her eyes smoldered a little and she gave me a slow smile.

It was time, I reflected, to get back to work.

❧ XXIV

We went down to the pressroom where the staff had gathered. The press bell rang three times, and I could hear the grumbling sounds of the beginning run as the rotary press started to turn over. It was like the beginning of the "Hallelujah Chorus" to my ears, since it meant that Strong had managed to keep the pieces together.

The first run of the first issue under my guidance as the editor and publisher of a daily newspaper was under way. It was a moment I had looked forward to since the days when I first served as a copyboy on my dad's weekly. It was a moment I shall never forget as long as I am meeting a deadline. It had nothing to do with success or failure, nothing to do with power or fame. It was between me and the newspaper business. It had everything to do with the challenge of getting a job done and seeing it done. I felt the hair rise on the back of my neck.

The job could have been much better, I told myself. I knew that the minute I saw the complete twelve-pager flipping off the mouth of the press and into the baler, where the ink-covered arms of the apprentice printers quickly seized bundles of papers and hoisted them onto the shuffling tables.

Strong stood at the mouth of the drumming press, ear-protectors over his head, selecting a paper every few seconds and quickly assessing the ink distribution on the pages. He would then reach down and flip a paper out of the moving series so as to mark the place in his assessment. He was all concentration, moving quickly back and forth, his ink-blacked fingers spinning dials on the presses. He saw me coming from the stairs and grinned like a minstrel man in burnt cork. He quickly scooped up an issue from the mouth of the press, handing it to me wordlessly as the press roared around us. Only then did I realize that for all of us this was a special moment. Everyone was surveying page 1 with pride.

I opened up the sheet and felt a pang, appreciating that it could have been a more professional job, indeed. My story looked a bit too hastily written, too dramatically trenchant. But at least it didn't jump to the inside. It fit well, too, with the two double-column pictures of Birdie and Caxton next to it, and the placement of the editorial down the left-hand side looked more professional now that the six-column, below-the-fold picture of the exterior of the *Dispatch* was in place. A bit sensational, perhaps—but it was still balanced makeup.

The concept that someone was trying to murder a newspaper, which was fighting for its life, came across well in the banner and other side stories written by Jellinek for page 1. Mine was the lead story, but Jellinek had the only byline on the front page and he beamed as he looked at it. I realized vaguely then that his byline had never appeared anywhere in the paper in the past, in spite of the fact that he must have done most of the writing for the sheet under Birdie.

"That's not exactly a prize-winning front page, Harvey," I said to Kressnach, "but it will pass for a daily."

The old man squinted at me and said nothing. But he went back to scrutinizing the makeup with thoughtful diligence and simply nodded approval when I suggested we keep aiming at balanced makeup in the next issue.

We were all discussing plans for tomorrow, standing in a huddled group around the press as though we were reluctant to leave the heartbeat of the plant. Strong kept the printers working, and even Leon Ermann seemed to have sobered up, doing what he could to help the apprentices complete the run. Then Chief Laken came down. Someone had handed him a paper and the pressroom walls seemed to vibrate as though a Brahma bull had got loose in the pit with a prickly-pear cactus tied to his cinch.

The chief glowered at me in disbelief, then shouted above the swelling roar of the press, "What in hell do you think you're *doing*? You tryin' to get everybody in this joint killed?"

"What?" I shouted.

The chief motioned up the stairs, and all of the editorial staff followed me as I traipsed after him. When we reached the editorial area, the chief turned on me angrily. I saw that he had doubled the number of police in the plant. He looked seriously alarmed.

"Listen," he said menacingly as he shouldered me into a corner and placed his red forehead close to mine. "Haven't you ever heard of *corpus delicti*? Until we find a body we don't have no murder! What's the big idea of this?" He backhanded the front page as though he wished it were my face.

I tried smiling. "Well, Chief, I don't see the word 'murder' anywhere. I simply described what happened when I came to town. It's all objective. Not even a byline. And you've got to admit—"

"Well, you *infer* murder!" he shouted.

"Actually, Chief, 'infer' isn't the correct verb. You mean 'imply.' One implies, but if someone infers . . ."

That only made him madder. "What are you trying to do, Hadleyman? Get the U.S. Marines in here? I want you to keep a lid on this thing until we can get some facts and—"

One of his rookies had come forward at that moment from the direction of the swinging doors. He placed a hand on the chief's shoulder and whispered into his ear.

"When?" the chief asked—all business now—a new wave of alarm crossing his brow.

The rookie whispered something more. The chief looked at me.

"Where did you say Willy Dunkle was?" he asked.

I looked at the staff.

"I think he's at the Super-Thrift or somewhere checking proofs for tomorrow's paper," Jellinek said.

"You *think!*" bellowed the chief. "Well, I'll tell you where he is. Right now he's halfway to Canada. Doesn't he drive the paper's station wagon?"

I looked at the staff again.

"Usually," said Mabel. "He uses it to do his rounds with the proofs."

"Humph! My men saw it roaring out of town over an hour ago. Dunkle was driving like hell. He made it across the county line, heading north. We've got an APB out on him."

"He can't get far, then," someone said.

"If he makes it to Canada, he can," the chief retorted.

I remembered that item in Willy's file. He was born in Canada and no doubt knew it well. I wondered why he had taken off, and was about to ask that question when the chief answered it.

"There's something else," Laken said, almost apologetically, looking at me. There was an eerie silence among the staff. "And I think it explains why Dunkle headed north."

"What is it, Chief?" I asked. The presses were rolling steadily beneath us now, a sort of throbbing echo pulsating throughout the plant like a bass accompaniment to the chief's husky voice as the run hit its high-speed stride.

"My men have found Birdie's body. Fished him out of the reservoir at the end of town. Apparently he was dumped in there only a little while ago. A kid spotted the body and one of my men recognized him. He'd been stabbed through the throat just as you said. The doc'll check him out, of course, but you'd better come down to the station later, Hadleyman. We'll need someone to confirm identification."

The chief turned abruptly and went out, not even giving me a chance to say, "I told you so."

We all stood stock-still, staring at one another.

"Not Willy . . ." Mabel muttered, looking away at Willy's desk.

But I wasn't thinking of Willy. My first thought was to ponder the chances of stopping the press run to get this latest newsbreak into the paper. Even a boldface box on page 1 would do the job. Jim Strong had come up the stairs with Leon Ermann, and Jellinek was telling them what the chief had said.

"What about it, boys?" I asked. "Can we at least get a box on page 1?"

"On any ordinary paper," Strong said, "there'd be no problem. But the run is nearly through and—well, frankly, we'd be takin' our chances gettin' started again and out on time and . . ."

"I see," I replied glumly. "Ah, well, I guess it'll hold. No one is going to beat us to Birdie's discovery by tomorrow anyway."

"Hee-hee," giggled Harvey Kressnach. "There isn't any shortage of news, is there?"

"No," I replied, sitting down at Birdie's desk, "and we might as well get at it for tomorrow's issue, even if we can't stop today's run. Without Willy it'll be tough enough filling the advertising spots tomorrow. We'll do as much as we can by phone. Mabel, I'll need you to do the rounds."

I glanced over at Strong and Ermann. Everybody was looking pretty subdued as the shock of the discovery of Birdie's body and the implication of Willy as a possible murderer sank in.

"We'll cut down to eight pages tomorrow," I added.

They all nodded.

"You're still going to come out, then?" Shirley asked dully, her eyes shifting from person to person.

I thought before I answered, which was unusual for me in those days. Then I stared hard at each of them.

"That's what a newspaper is supposed to do," I answered. I couldn't help thinking of Birdie either. Who, I wondered, would be next? "Let's get at it."

They automatically turned to their work, doubtlessly musing, as I was, about the way Willy Dunkle had skipped town. I made a firm decision. I went up to the front office and opened the X-2 file once more. The receipt for ink products that was signed "W.D." was topped with the logo and printed phone number of the White Sulphur Springs firm that had met the order. I picked up the phone and soon had a sweet-voiced secretary on the line. I gave her the receipt number and asked her to check on the contents of what had been ordered. She said she would call me back in a day or so.

While I was at it, I telephoned the post office—which had turned out to be a back room at the bus depot—and arranged to have a hundred dollars wired immediately to Maura back in Great Falls.

Then I got to work.

🐌 XXV

After the shock of Chief Laken's news, our first issue seemed more timely than ever, even without the latest bulletin. It was no time to rest on our oars. I had to keep the crew in action. Mabel didn't like the idea of going around picking up ad copy, but she did it. With the Super-Thrift spread already in and the next issue going down to eight pages, I figured we could get the jump on tomorrow's news copy.

Chief Laken's men kept getting underfoot, but the chief agreed to our continuing to work when I pointed out that that way we'd all be together where he could keep an eye on us. By now I didn't care if the town was filled with paranoids—and that's how it was beginning to look—I needed every person available in order to publish the next day. For all I knew, any one of the staff could have scared Willy Dunkle off right after lunch and still made it back to the office before I'd noticed anyone missing. I had been so engrossed in the morgue upstairs and in my discovery of the layout for a new plant that I hadn't been around to take note of who had come in when. All I knew was that they were all there but Willy when we began to check page proofs.

Maybe Willy was the killer-turned-scared, I thought, but in any case, with his skipping town my advertising sales had come to a stop. Whoever was trying to kill this sheet knew exactly where to strike.

Before storming out, the chief had assigned specific men to

each of us, to make sure no one else could skip off, whereas previously he had merely bogged down each person who left the office with an assortment of storm troopers. I felt sorry for whatever cop it was who had lost track of Willy. The chief also stipulated that the first person to get out of line would wind up in the jug. He advised us to go home right after work and stay there. Not having a home right then, I told him about my appointment with the attorney, Brownlee.

The chief was sore, but what could he do? He hadn't made an arrest, nor could he do so. He had to give us a certain amount of freedom, especially since I had pledged our cooperation.

I called over to Jellinek to see if there had been any response to our contacting of the wire services. He said not yet. The lead story, I knew, would be plenty for the AP and UPI. They'd want their own shots, of course. Good enough. I didn't tell Chief Laken what I thought would happen once the services got the story. He was mad enough as it was.

It was just after six when I reached the Nugget Lounge. The officer assigned to me was a rookie I had not seen before, an affable guy named Jerry. He seemed a little more civilized than the rest of the force I had run into the first night. I told him to have a few beers on the *Dispatch* and I'd sign for them at the bar. No sense making him suffer at my expense.

The rookie headed for the bar like an FBI agent trying to transfer out of Butte, and I went into a back lounge area appropriately called Prospector's Pit. It was clear that the Nugget was the cultural prize of Marksburg—it had real neon. The place had been built by privately donated funds under the auspices of a businessmen's club called the Marksburg Goldpans. The walls were lined with Indian relics and memorabilia of the Old West that were neatly arranged around a huge portrait of the president of the National Rifle Association.

A poor reproduction of a Charlie Russell mural lined the back wall. I had once seen the original at the Russell Museum in Great Falls before a millionaire had carted it off to some hideaway in the Southwest. The original had captured that violet-and-pastel-green twilight only to be found in central Montana as the heat of the day lifts off the high plains and the shadows of the Rockies drift out of the valleys. Even in a bad color reproduction, the artist's love of the smell of ranch coffee first thing in the morning, and the feel of leather on a saddle horn, somehow came through. I couldn't help smiling at what Charlie, whom most of Marksburg's citizens would have crossed the street to ignore in his barfly days, would have thought of the Nugget. It was too much of a professional man's hangout for anyone who had been branding cows all day, the kind of place where a newsman might go for a political tip-off, but never for a serious evening's drinking.

I was trying to peer through the cantaloupe-colored glare at the people seated in skunk-lined booths and at the bar, wondering if I was in a saloon or a bordello, when a phony type in his late thirties, smooth-shaven and as self-satisfied-looking as an assistant manager in a big-city hotel, came up to me.

"Mr. Hadleyman?"

"Right. Are you Brownlee?"

"Glad to meet you. Let's sit over there where we can talk. What'll you have?"

"Beer. It's a little early."

"Good-o. Harry, a beer for my friend and a ditch for me. . . . I see," he said, his eyes narrowing as he pedantically pushed his dark-rimmed glasses firmly against the bridge of his nose, "that you admire Russell. Great painter. Great painter. He loved the Marksburg area."

The beer was watery.

". . . a Russell Club that the kids could run," he was saying.

"What's that?" My mind had wandered. I kept registering on that expression of his, reminiscent of a college-fraternity man trying to play a sort of snotty-nosed Ariel in a bad production of *The Tempest*. I recognized the type. Brownlee was the kind of lawyer who, back in the Depression, would have got in there fast with bank directors and made a pile foreclosing on mortgages to small farms and private homes. He had eyes like the bit-ends of steel drills.

". . . I was saying that some of us in town are starting a Russell Club. Keep the high-school kids busy—you know, let 'em make and sell their own artifacts. Plastic tomahawks, fiberglass arrowheads, miniature Stetsons carved out of wood as paperweights or whatever. Touristy stuff. They'd do their own accounting—good business training. What do you think of the idea? Make a good feature in the paper?"

"Great," I replied. "Maybe you could talk some of my Blackfoot pals up in Great Falls into comin' in and teachin' the kids how to make bloody scalps out of rabbit skins."

Brownlee glared at me through his lawyer's lenses. "Well, *we* like it," he snapped. "And someone should do something to remind the people of Charlie Russell."

"Actually," I replied, marveling at the low quality of the beer, "Russell's paintings should be enough. Besides, he never set foot within twenty-five miles of this place and you know it."

Brownlee seemed to go into a sulk, but he snapped out of it by the time we had edged our way to an out-of-the-way table behind a pinball machine and a poker-dice table, where a drugstore cowboy and a girl togged in rhinestones had just risen to leave.

"You should try a ditch," Brownlee said, switching to what he no doubt considered his courtroom manner as the bar girl brought us two more drinks. "Beer can kill you, fella."

"At least I'd be in the running. Did you see our afternoon edition?"

Brownlee arched one eyebrow, like a B-movie actor. I never could do that.

"Yes. Is—uh—is Birdie's body still—well, missing?"

"Just heard that they fished his body out of the reservoir. Too late for our story."

"The reservoir!"

"Right. Laken is watching all of us as carefully as a Crow scout at Fort Laramie. That's my chaperone at the bar. The chief is letting us roll, but the staff can barely move around the office. It's going to be a struggle, Brownlee. Now with Willy Dunkle on the run—well, it takes time to track down ads."

Brownlee whistled. "Willy Dunkle? What do you mean, 'on the run'?"

"Laken thinks he killed Birdie."

Brownlee stared at me, then removed the huge rimmed glasses. Without them he looked naked.

"Poor Willy," he said, taking out a tissue and carefully polishing a lens, "Never thought he'd stoop to murder. Uh . . . did you know, though, that he had a record?"

I studied the attorney's face, wondering how much he knew—or, rather, how much he knew I knew. The steel-drill tips didn't flicker. He seemed peaceable enough—no .38 bulging in his pocket or anything, and I didn't see him slip anything into my beer. But it was getting to the point where I was suspicious even of myself.

"I found Birdie's confidential file this afternoon," I said. "There are a lot of things that don't add up."

"Such as?"

"Oh, lots of things. All I know is that Birdie must have given everybody in Marksburg plenty of motives for murder. I'm not so sure Willy Dunkle killed him. Maybe he was just plain scared and took off."

"I know what you mean," Brownlee replied smoothly.

And smooth described him. Perfectly tailored in summer colors that, even in the Nugget Lounge's garish light, well matched his pointed features and dark tan, he was clearly doing well as an attorney and a business power in the community.

"You might have had reason yourself," I suggested.

"What do you mean by that?" he asked. He put down his drink. The steel drills drilled.

"Jellinek told me about the labor and Merchants Association fracas. Seems to me you guys had Birdie under your thumb. I imagine you wouldn't have liked it if he'd suddenly developed a conscience."

"Oh, that." Brownlee chuckled, relaxing. "That was business. Anyway, can you imagine Birdie with a conscience?"

I had to admit he had me there. "Well," I added, "murder can be a business, too."

"Come off it, Hadleyman. What about yourself? With Birdie out of the way, you're a publisher now, aren't you? And there wasn't any trouble around here until you showed up."

"I wouldn't say that. What about Irwin Royal Caxton the Third?"

"He skipped town . . . just like Willy. That wasn't trouble. We're lucky to be rid of him."

"That word 'rid' covers a lot of territory."

"What are you getting at, Hadleyman?"

"Just this. Caxton had everybody in this town up in arms. He was in so far to the merchants, he had so many personal enemies, he was so much a cultural snob in the midst of a buffalo-chip way of life, that I'm not so sure he skipped anywhere. He was in the middle of some big plans when—"

"Don't be a fool," Brownlee snapped, polishing off his drink. I could see I'd hit a nerve. "If you had known Caxton, you'd realize that he could never have climbed out of debt. And, by the way, that headline of yours this afternoon isn't going to help matters, either. What are you trying to prove?"

"I'm trying to keep the Dispatch alive, that's all. Surely that's in your interest, Brownlee, not to mention the merchants'."

"Well, just between the two of us, fella, I think you'd be smart to close the doors, leave the worries to Terrill in New York, and go back to where you came from. Get a job in public relations or something. You have a hell of a personality for—"

"I'm sticking right here!" I snapped back hotly. "And, incidentally, the next time either your hatchet men or the unions try to rig a story in that sheet, as long as I'm publisher you'll both have to walk in the front door with your hats off."

"Hey, there—whoa," Brownlee said, changing tack. My voice had risen considerably. His was still as slick as an encyclopedia salesman's. "Don't get so wound up, pardner. Maybe someone in town does have it in for newspapermen . . . but I'm on your side. Poison and shears—that's pretty rough, even around here. But I didn't do it. Anybody on the staff look fishy?"

"They all do," I said. "Even Chief Laken seems to have some kind of special hate for the *Dispatch*. Anything's a possibility."

"Mmm, yes," Brownlee mused. "There *are* possibilities. It's not in his file, but I know for a fact that Leon Ermann was pretty sore when his wife ran off with your predecessor, the former editor."

"Yeah. Birdie said something about it to me on the phone."

"It *is* true," he added. "Everybody on the staff seemed to have some kind of gripe."

His eyes glittered for a full minute. I felt like a small trout dangling on a line. He was holding something back. There was a wry smile on his lips as he played with his whiskey glass.

"I was just wondering," he said idly, "about Caxton himself. I mean, what if he were not dead, as you seem to suspect. What if he hadn't skipped? Do you think he could still be . . ."

"As I say, anything's a possibility at this point."

Brownlee looked at his watch. "I've a dinner meeting," he said casually. "Here's why I called you. Birdie told me on the phone right after he had telephoned you in Great Falls that a new editor named Hadleyman was coming down. He said that I was to give you an advance check and the key to the house you'll live in while you're here." He took a check and a key out of his jacket pocket.

"Thanks," I said, taking the key. "Put the check back in the bank. I've already drawn my advance."

"Well, I'll be." Brownlee smiled at the check. "An honest newspaperman. You sure don't fit this town's motto."

"Whattayamean?"

"Oh, a couple of years back a group of us got together to form a sort of Marksburg historical committee. We were putting together a tourist booklet on the founder of the town, a character from Missouri, who platted the town in the nineties. I understand he was one of those circuit-riding judges or something—man named Blankenship. Anyway, he apparently considered himself a local wag and kept going around quoting Oscar Wilde or whoever about that famous bit on temptation. You know. As a joke, we made it the town motto: 'We can resist everything except temptation.'"

"That figures." I dangled the key. "What's this about a *house?*" I asked.

"Didn't Birdie tell you on the phone?"

"He said he had a place for me to stay, but that's all."

"You mean"—the eyebrow arched again—"that you haven't heard of Caxton's Folly?"

"Caxton's *what?*"

"That's what the cowboys call it. The *Dispatch* is currently the proud owner—or, rather, third mortgage holder—of the biggest mansion in the county. Caxton built a white tower, Southern columns and all, on upper Main. It cost somebody a small fortune. I thought everybody knew about it. Ever since Caxton skipped town, it's been standing idle. Nobody has even cleaned the place since he left. Furniture—everything—just as it was. Spooky joint. Birdie told me you would be staying there, since he'd promised you a place to stay. Cheaper than a hotel, but if you'd rather . . ."

"Naw, I don't mind," I replied. By this time, I was curious enough to wonder what more I could find out about Caxton. I looked at the key again.

"The plumbing work?" I asked. "I'm beginning to feel like one of the linotypes in the pressroom."

Brownlee chuckled. "It's your party. Frankly, I'd rather live in a tent, all things considered."

"I tried that last night. Believe me, one place is as good as another around here."

"You're probably right about that," he said, rising. "Well, good luck. If I learn anything, I'll let you know."

"Thanks. I'll call if I need a lawyer. Not the regular attorney," I added, echoing Brownlee's telephone tone. "Terrill has a legal firm in the East."

Brownlee forced out another chuckle and sidled away like a discouraged tomcat.

I discounted the idea of a third beer. Even watered-down brews had a weird effect on me since my operation. Number three usually meant my headlines would start to rhyme. Besides, I wanted to keep thinking a bit about this character Brownlee. After all, he was another suspect.

&a XXVI

Jerry, the cop, was finishing a beer at the bar when I paid the bartender. I told him where I was spending the night, and he walked back to the *Dispatch* with me so I could get my car.

The office was empty. I fooled around with a few stories, planned tomorrow's sheet, and then decided to have a pork chop at the bus depot before turning in. I was getting fairly exasperated at being the sole client in that cheerless establishment, and since Jerry had turned out to be a head above the rest of the population—and therefore an intriguing object of curiosity—I offered to buy him dinner. It was a good investment. As we ate, he repaid my hospitality with what scraps of information he had on the town, as well as the force, and it was clearly his own feeling that some sort of conspiracy was in operation. Mabel Reitz, for instance, knew more, he claimed, than she was saying.

"Even the chief has a protective attitude towards her," he said. "She's some number."

"A cynosure of all eyes, eh?"

"Huh?"

"I mean," I added, finishing my coffee, "her red hair is natural and everyone wants to date her."

"That's it," Jerry replied. "And that's *everybody*. Not just Jellinek and Willy Dunkle. Birdie took her out. And I think Caxton was interested in her, too. Every once in a while, you'd see that Cadillac of his out in front of her place. She's a popular gal. I have a hunch she knows something about his disappearance."

"That could be," I mused aloud. "Mabel seemed to know a lot about how Caxton moved in on Willy's girlfriend Rena."

The rookie peered at me. It was a sharp look, as though he were sizing me up. He lifted his coffee cup to tightly closed lips. I thought he wasn't going to say anything, but then he muttered into the cup, "What do you know about Renata Koenig?"

"I know that she and Willy were engaged and aren't now," I replied. "And I know that Willy must have been mighty mad after Caxton gave him the shaft. I gather from Mabel's story that Caxton had some crooked scheme going to get Mrs. Koenig's land, with Willy as front man, and then Willy, going soft on Rena, decided to chuck it all."

Jerry was quiet for a moment, then said deliberately, as though he'd just made a private decision, "Well, that would fit the kind of picture I get from the scuttlebutt around the station. The boys claim that Caxton had a history of shady deals all the way back to his college days. I'm told he once pulled off a bogus bonds maneuver with an offshore operation that got his family in Dutch back East."

"Offshore?"

"You know—offshore. That's when so-called businessmen who are low on cash want to maintain they have big accounts in foreign banks. Sometimes they go so far as setting up paper banks as fronts in foreign places, like the Caribbean, so they can claim to have foreign financing."

"Uh—is that legal?"

Jerry laughed. "Let's put it this way. Anything Caxton touched had a twist in it. And I guess he had all the right talk, like 'circumvention fees' and 'walkaways' and—"

"Walkaways?"

"Yeah—that's borrowing more than a discounted price of bonds purchased by an investor, then walking away with the difference between the bond price and the loan amount involved. I reckon that's how Caxton apparently got his well-heeled family in hot water. Local gossip—which travels around here faster than the speed of light—claims that Caxton's family sent him a comfortable retainer just to keep him west of the Mississippi."

"Where did you learn all that stuff—I mean, about bonds and walkaways, and all?" I asked, impressed.

Jerry shrugged. "Mostly I've just kept my ears open, the way you did about Willy and Rena. You probably have heard, for example, that Willy was Caxton's 'mechanic' in the crowd, so to speak. They worked lots of small operations, and I hear Caxton left Willy holding the bag more than once."

"So I gather," I said, although I hadn't really gathered anything clear, at all.

"Yeah," Jerry continued. "This town's still pretty sore about a lot of them—like the time Caxton backed Willy in setting up a loan agency and they skinned a couple of merchants. And one time there was a shipment of beef out of here—organized, as usual, by Willy and backed by Caxton—and when it was too late, some ranchers found that a pretty lofty fee was skimmed off the top. Caxton and Willy must have made a couple of thousand on that one."

"Didn't anybody try to prosecute them?"

"Well," Jerry replied, "Caxton was mighty smooth, and he was using that paper you're putting out to scare a lot of people. I know for a fact that one time he put pressure on a couple of councilmen to get some land rezoned on the edge of town. He and that guy Brownlee and some others had some money invested in lots out there and they stood to make a good chunk. I hear that Caxton first tried to scare the councilmen through the power of the paper. When that didn't work—well, I understand that Caxton had Willy lean on 'em a bit."

"Anything heavy?"

Jerry looked at me grimly and said, "What do you think? Willy almost did time for that."

"Uh—I was just wondering," I said after a moment. "Mabel told me that just before this Renata Koenig and her mother went back to South Dakota, Caxton was making a play for the daughter. Since she was Willy's girl, do you think Willy maybe scared Caxton off? I mean, it sounds to me as if he was jealous and mad enough to get pretty heavy-handed, and I wouldn't be surprised if he wanted revenge badly enough to apply shock treatment that would scare Caxton all the way back to the old folks at home."

The policeman merely shrugged and studied my face with an amused expression.

"But what I'm curious about," I added, "is where Birdie fits into all this. What did Willy have against Birdie Johnson? Scaring a publisher out of town is one thing—but stabbing one through the throat is another. I just don't get it. Here's Willy on the run now himself, with Chief Laken waving a murder warrant. And it does look as if Willy finally blew his top. But *why?*"

Again Jerry shrugged, then sighed and started to rise.

"Look," he said, "I've gabbed too much as it is. Besides, it's getting late. I'd better check in."

I could see he felt uncomfortable at having talked so much. It was okay to gossip a little about a past love affair everyone knew about, or to go over Caxton's background, as everybody else had done countless times, but it was quite another matter, I could see, for a man in this rookie's position to be talking to a stranger about a murder suspect who hadn't even been arraigned. There was no sense in pumping him, even though I felt, strangely enough, he had something else he wanted to say. The time would come, I thought, when he would say it. I knew this kind of man. He had a quiet way, like some of the cowboys I knew as a kid who used to give us free rides on the horses at the White Elephant Stables in Great Falls. They talked when they felt it was time, not before. They were individuals who did things their own way when they were ready. It's a trait I'm afraid I do not possess, but I've always admired it.

We drove up Main together in the VW toward my new residence. In that bucket of bolts, I felt like an Untouchable approaching the Taj Mahal.

The darkness of evening was just beginning to blanket the gaps between the mountains. A reddish-purple sunset fringed the distant hills and the town basked in a gauzy, summery hue that reminded me of the days when I was a kid, when we all played kick-the-can in the alley after dinner. The air was curiously soothing and vivifying simultaneously; it suggested the hour of promise before darkness. To look up Main toward Caxton's place, to see the last of the day reflecting in appliance-store windows, to wait for the old streetlight to work itself into green in its lazy, erratic manner as a few citizens strolled slowly past the Spanish-American War cannons—all reminded me of those joyous August evenings and of small-town peace long before I had ever thought of deadlines or wire services or the nerve-wracking demands of getting presses in operation. Not to mention murder.

Modern pressures suddenly seemed a lifetime away, and a calmness in the atmosphere, the kind of atmosphere that must have intrigued the apparently restless founder of Marksburg, filled me momentarily with a longing to rush down to the creek that hushed its way sleepily through the heart of the town, and just sit among the willows with nightcrawlers on a line, hearing a hose running somewhere, or the smack of a screen door, or chunks of ice rattling in a frosted pitcher of lemonade. Real lemonade.

Jerry watched me looking at the cannons. "Marksburg is the only town in the state, I reckon, that didn't give those up for scrap metal in World War Two."

I laughed. "It doesn't seem like such a bad town, though, Jerry—that is, if you don't count the people. Who'd ever think that this placid, evening sort of place could give birth to a bloody, macabre act of violence like—like Birdie's death?"

"I don't know," Jerry answered. "People can really foul things up, can't they? I mean, it's like when you go fishin'. You find a great spot, a place where you'd think no human being had ever set foot, where chipmunks skitter all over the place and deer tracks give you a sense of being a pioneer—and then suddenly there's a big clutter of beer cans on the creekbed just where you want to cast a line."

"Yeah. I know what you mean."

"Still, it's funny," he went on. "This ain't like any other town in Montana. I was born and reared over in the Madison Valley where there's a few towns this size, but they're a lot different, know what I mean? Yes sir, there's something—well, I hate to sound like a silly kid, but something *evil* about this place. I mean, I've only been here a little while, but the town *does* something to you. It—well, it sort of corrupts people, I think."

"Come on, Jerry. People and towns are pretty much the same anywhere."

"Well, maybe they are and maybe they ain't."

"And maybe it's your imagination."

"No," he argued. "I mean it. I can sort of smell it. There's an atmosphere or something. Call it what you like—greed, narrowness, something. Maybe hatred."

"How about provincialism or inordinate pride?" I offered.

"I dunno," the rookie said in a brooding, almost sulky manner, as though he had something on his mind that he was trying to muster up courage to remove. "But once in a while I get a whiff of it. Sometimes it's in people's faces—like that Brownlee guy you were talking to. He's as crooked as a coyote track, believe me. And—well, maybe I shouldn't talk about it to you, but even the chief—well . . . and then there's that creepy character, Kressnach." He shuddered.

I knew what he meant. I wanted to push a bit, since Jerry obviously had something more he wanted to tell me, but I sensed again he would have to unburden himself in his own time.

We stopped at the corner and I could see Caxton's Folly jutting out of the boulevards and the surrounding weed-filled lots like a gigantic block of chalk. Blasphemous as the analogy might seem, it reminded me of pictures I'd seen of Canterbury Cathedral, the way it shoots out of cluttered and minute evirons—square, Gothic, and as powerful-looking as the mailed fist of some medieval giant struggling to break through from beneath the surface of the earth. In spite of its state of disrepair, it had a sort of static energy combined with an appearance of belonging to the earth itself. It put the old bank building across the street and the gas-station kitty-corner from it in a modern, fifth-rate category. There was no doubt about it, Caxton's Folly was *the* thing in Marksburg. No wonder the town hated it.

Jerry climbed out of my car at the corner, giving it a contemptuous look, and announced that he guessed he'd done his duty. He told me that patrol cars would be doing the rounds of everyone's house that night, so I'd better not go wandering. It was almost dark. We said good night.

"That's some theory of yours," I called after him, with a chuckle. "I mean, about this being a Jekyll-and-Hyde town."

But Jerry didn't feel like opening up, obviously. He simply wandered off in the direction of Main's streetlight with a deprecating wave, as if to dismiss his own qualms. But I thought I heard him mutter, "We can resist everything except temptation."

I wondered if that included the temptation to murder someone like Birdie Johnson. It was hardly a comforting thought as I drove on a few yards and parked by the curb in front of Caxton's Folly. I hated to admit it to myself, but I felt more than slightly hesitant to get out and approach that cold, forbidding white mansion in the dark alone.

XXVII

To associate Caxton's Folly with my Uncle Gamaliel's rehearsals for his periodic piano recitals may seem, in retrospect, a bit fanciful. But I had good reason to connect the dark interior of that immense whited sepulcher with the haunting strains of Rachmaninoff's Prelude in C-sharp Minor—especially the shadier movements in the bass clef so somberly rendered by my uncle.

It happened this way. As I approached the place, I realized it hadn't been built simply from the ground up, but had been put together part by part, like the Frankenstein monster. Apparently, one financially ruined dreamer after another had added his random, grotesque whims—one alabaster symbol of indebtedness after another—to the wide-winged house. I subsequently learned that Caxton had acquired on some nebulous legal pretext the remains of the old stone structure (first erected, according to rumor, by the town's founder, Judge Blankenship) and given it a new lease, as it were, on death.

It looked more like a mausoleum than a home. One moment it gave the impression of an overweight tombstone about to sink another foot into the earth, the next it evoked a paradoxical sense of gargoylean lightness, as though it occasionally defied the law of gravity.

Caxton had, seemingly, put more of other people's money into the grounds and crushed-gravel driveway than most people in Marksburg earned in a year. After having the house's exterior painted a sort of Deep South white with a Doric-columned façade and spacious verandah attached, he had made it—depending on how one might interpret the phrase—the showplace of the state. The governor had been his first guest, no doubt unaware that his archrival had never paid the contractors, painters, furnishers, and carpenters.

The garden had been badly neglected. The lawn had grown to weeds higher than the porch steps. Perennials, some dry hollyhock stalks, and ubiquitous wild roses had arched their way uncontrollably up the sides of the porch. A dried-up ragweed smell hinting of decay arose from the foliage and mingled with the miasmatic haze of summer's dusk; the weeping willows seemed laden with dust, bending their spidery branches low over the driveway as if to obscure my approach to the porch steps.

A swastika had been painted crudely by some indignant person on the front door. Someone else had obviously tried to rub it out with a faulty detergent, leaving an ugly yellow Teutonic scar on what was probably the largest and thickest oak entrance in the state. A Georgian fanlight, beautiful in its simplicity, had had its dignity punctured by a rock that had shattered a triangle of colored glass. I tried the key. The heavy door swung open easily. Well made. I could hear my footsteps echo on the tile flags as I entered the shadows of the hallway.

The light fixture in the hall ceiling didn't have a bulb. Just my luck, I thought. The fact that all shutters had been drawn, and curtains after them, contributed to the dismal silence that pervaded the interior. But even in the melancholy darkness, as I pushed through the second door that separated the hallway from the rest of the house, I could understand how Caxton had impressed everyone; clearly this was an exalted, if somewhat bizarre, bachelor shrine.

As my eyes adjusted to the dark, I could make out a wide stairway with a balustrade ascending into the umbral void. To my left were partially opened French doors leading into what must have been the living room. On the right was a study, a bit blocked off from my sight by a half-opened sliding door, but I could discern shelves covered with volumes, the spines of which shone dully in the pale light that seeped in from the street through the study drapes. Beyond this area I couldn't make out a thing. I decided to try the lamp in the study.

I was crossing from the hallway entrance through the study door when I thought I heard a noise, a sort of tumbling sound, like someone's foot bumping something. I stopped. No—just silence. I tried the lamp and it worked. At least the electricity was on, even if there was a shortage of bulbs in the house.

My first impression of the study was enough to convince me that Caxton was—or, at least, had been—a man of mixed appetites who enjoyed squandering money. And it became progressively difficult to understand how he could leave what I saw around me. Not that there was any consistent taste—just the opposite—but clearly a great deal of planning had gone into the room. But even if Caxton could abruptly leave all this—voluntarily, that is—he was beginning to take shape in my imagination as the type of hedonistic individual who did not get involved in fortune-hunting, and all the self-indulgent pleasures that questionable pursuit arouses, for a lark. High stakes were demanded. Somehow he struck me as the type who, contrary to what Brownlee had suggested, would cling to material things with frantic stubbornness, the diligent type who could have climbed out of any mess—unless he were physically deterred.

His taste ran (one might say, jogged) along the border of William Faulkner's mind, with occasional sallies into the labyrinthine chambers of Edgar Allan Poe's psyche. The study was designed for comfort, relaxation, and intellectual diversion. It reminded me of Thomas Jefferson, with its beautifully treated wood, wine-colored velvet drapes, and leather-and-mahogany furnishings. Yet all this would be suddenly interrupted by a melodramatic touch of the macabre. It was the kind of study one would expect to find in some overdone, romantic Bavarian castle. The room—and indeed, as I found out later, the entire house—reflected the personality of a man who loved art for its symphonic qualities, but who could not draw a line between the harmony of pleasant surroundings and the jarring perversities of excess. The study did seem to have a statement to make: that it was completely removed from the crass Bauhaus false fronts and jerry-built cracker-box structures of Marksburg's Main Street. But if it was an oasis in a wasteland, one had a feeling the dates on the palm trees were rotten and the beckoning pool filled with non-potable water.

I was aroused now to want to make the grand tour, but I could not resist browsing through the excellent collection of volumes on the study shelves. There were first editions and some fine bindings, but once again the oddness of taste intruded on the senses with a startling tension, the way one might discover in a greenhouse of orchids a Venus flytrap. Amid the sets of Dickens and Zola, for example—sets beautifully bound in leather with marbled endpapers (and pages, I might add, uncut)—a gruesome-looking paperback illustrated by what appeared to be a gothic nightmare and bearing a title in flaming figures, *Satan of the Newsrooms!*, stood slightly forward, as though recently read. Lying open and upside down on a reading table next to an overstuffed chair was a well-worn comic book entitled "Tales of Terror."

Such a paradox of taste, however, left my mind when I perceived something much closer to the morbid realities of contemporary society. The drapes, I noticed, had two holes in them, no farther apart than cat's eyes, that looked ominously like bullet holes, though the panes in the window behind them had obviously been recently replaced.

I remembered that small item I had seen in one of the back files of the *Dispatch* in the upstairs morgue. It had referred to a shooting incident in Caxton's house during a party; the paper was dated just before the publisher had disappeared.

I studied the two holes more closely. If someone had fired from outside—say, out on the quiet street along that side of the house—and through the window . . .

I went outside and around the house to study the area. Although it was now getting dark, I could tell easily enough that a person could park a car in the deserted street and, by standing on the hood of the car or the back of a pickup or something, fire a rifle at window level, dead-even with the holes in the drapes. I went inside again and stood by the window, estimating the level of entry of two rifle slugs. Unless the missiles' flight were interrupted, they would hit the bookshelves lining the wall just opposite the window. I examined the shelves on that side of the room, behind and above the overstuffed chair and the reading table. Almost immediately I found a patched hole. The wood putty that filled it up was fairly fresh. Someone had obviously tried to varnish it over, but there was a shade of difference in color. The hole was in a shelf just beneath books at the level of my head. Yet there was only one hole. I carefully measured the holes in the drapes and then estimated where I thought the other hole should be from the second slug.

It didn't exist.

That meant only one thing. The second rifle shot had been interrupted. Or, put another way, it had found its mark. No doubt it had lodged in something between the window and the bookshelves. And that something could well have been a person in the room . . . someone who, perhaps, while seated and reading, had been startled by the sound of the first shot overhead and had then risen quickly, just in time to catch the second shot at head level. Judging from the height of the first slug's hole in the bookshelf, that person, if about my height of approximately six feet, would certainly have been killed. (Caxton, I discovered later, was six feet tall.)

I looked uneasily around the room. A record player, gathering dust but still open (as though someone had been listening to it and, without turning it off, had got up and left) had the needle arm resting on a record. I looked at the label: Rachmaninoff's concertos. And that's where my Uncle Gamaliel comes in.

One of my earliest memories dates back to the infant years of the Depression when Uncle Gamaliel came to live with us in our big, troglodytic house on the south side in Great Falls. He was Dad's only brother, not unlike Dad but perhaps representative of the more eccentric side of the Hadleyman family. Mom insisted on calling him "Major Hoople," though never in his presence. I remember a tall, dark-haired but slightly bald, kindly gentleman whose eyebrows seemed to take on lives of their own whenever he was anywhere near the opposite sex. He had his own room upstairs where my brothers and I would spend hours examining his bicycle clips and Sigma Chi cuff links, and pictures of himself performing for the Chicago Symphony Orchestra in years gone by. One brochure particularly intrigued me. It advertised Uncle Gamaliel's tone poem "in the tradition of Liszt and Pratt," entitled "Chronicle," and described as a symphonic blending of the music of the spheres with the throbbing rhythms of the rapidly growing newspaper domain in America—or, as my dad described it, "a cosmic tribute to journalism." Clearly, the association with printing not only confirmed in my young mind the credibility of Uncle Gamaliel's status as my father's brother, but also gave the composer an excellent opportunity to employ to the fullest the liberality and power of his left hand.

In any case, one time my older brothers were caught red-handed in the basement pilfering a supply of Santa Claus suckers Mom had been hiding for the holidays. She had correctly guessed the cause of subtle susurrations and clumsy movements in the basement, calling down the stairs that she had a hairbrush in her hand. The basement was so designed to lead up to the kitchen, but forked off at some point in limbo to a backstairs toilet where I seemed to have spent the bulk of my fifth year of life. The boys sought refuge with me, knowing that a window in the toilet led conveniently outdoors.

Mom, of course, was not to be outrun. She went out the back door to head us off at the pass, so to speak. I, naturally, was caught up in this fracas, joining my brothers in terror and flight even though I was guiltless. The three of us scrambled around to the front, hoping to make our escape over the small hedge that outlined the front yard, but just then our two sisters, preoccupied with chalk and hopscotch on the front sidewalk, looked our way, alert as ever to even the remotest possibility of putting the three boys in a bad light with whatever authority reigned at the time.

We dashed into the front of the house; my brothers disappeared magically in the nether regions, and I dived under the huge Mason & Hamlin grand piano. This precious black instrument, dominating an entire corner of the living room, was more than mere forbidden territory; it was Uncle Gamaliel's religiously private domain, the final vestige of his association with America's musical capital during the first quarter of the twentieth century. Before hard times drove Uncle Gamaliel westward to take up lodgings with us and to accept a quasi-remunerative position of enriching intermissions between films at local cinemas with dexterous performances on the organ, he had reached the apex of his prodigious concert career on the ebony Mason & Hamlin. To approach it, not to mention diving under it, was to invite Dad's gravest expression, Mom's hairbrush, and the kind of rage from Uncle Gamaliel that could be matched only by the wildest portions of his ecstatic performances.

I cowered beneath the piano for hours, terrified into paralysis as dinner passed and darkness drew on. Finally, I fell into a sort of coma in an area most removed from sight.

Now, it was the habit of my uncle to practice for his recitals after the children had been put to bed. My mother and father would usually read or listen to the radio or edit Dad's galley proofs in the dining room while Uncle Gamaliel worked over his scales and arpeggios and whatever pieces he might be preparing for one of his Grand Opera House concerts. In the final stages of rehearsal, he would unfailingly turn out all the lights in the living room except for a single wall lamp (he called it "playing to the muse") and roar away—especially when the piece was by Rachmaninoff. The shadows helped him, he claimed, both to evoke the somber mood of torment on the Russian steppes and to stimulate his memory while playing "blind."

On the occasion of the Great Sucker Theft, after my brothers and sisters had been soundly thrashed and hustled off to bed, whimpering, even before the streetlamps were alight, Mom and Dad went out to comb the neighborhood for me. Meanwhile, Uncle Gamaliel, being in the final stages of preparing Rachmaninoff's Prelude in C-sharp Minor, entered the living room, turned off the lights, and undertook one of his more tempestuous rehearsals. Unbeknownst to anybody in the family, of course, I was sleeping soundly in the corner, almost directly beneath the bass strings of A-sharp and G-flat so emphatically commanded by Uncle Gamliel's left hand. No sooner did he crash down on the keyboard with the opening three explosions of the thunderous prelude—Dthumm! Dthumm! *Dthumm!*—than I was shocked into a traumatic waking state that was forever to register in my haunted psyche.

The fact that the piano, my cosmic uncle, and I were the only occupants of the immediate vicinity did not help to reassure me, being, as I was, only half aware that I was alive and horrendously frightened that a three-footed giant was trudging my way to devour me like some vulnerable, bleeding Santa Claus sucker. Since those impressionable years, I have always had a particularly nervous reaction to the Russian composers in general and to Sergei Rachmaninoff in particular.

As I noted before, it may have been pressing coincidence a bit to find that particular recording in the study of Caxton's Folly, but, whatever the cause of its presence, my nerves definitely soured the sweetness of reason. A stifling sensation developed in my chest. The house suddenly grew menacing. Yet somehow the act of movement under the self-deception that I could investigate other rooms had a calming effect, and I busied myself by removing a bulb from a lamp in the study and inserting it in each socket as I moved from one part of the mansion to another.

The dining room, expensively furnished and still intact (even some mail rested unopened on a mahogany sideboard, and a man's hat lay in the corner), was protected by various ghostly sheets to prevent dust, but as I went through one of the doors leading off that room, I found myself in a large kitchen that told quite another story. Here dishes and cutlery were scattered about, some even unwashed. A half-empty quart of milk, which smelled fresh, was on a bare table in the middle of the room, adjacent to an open box of cornflakes. It was as though someone, I thought with a slight chill, were still *living* there.

I checked out the second floor. There was a certain grisly, almost sacred silence up there, although occasionally I could have sworn I was hearing small, loathsome sounds.

After I'd fixed the bulb in a socket in the master bedroom—Caxton apparently having taken "master" seriously—I received yet another culture shock. There was a lamentable contrast of taste: built-in stereos, walled-in chairs, Danish-style coffee table versus an ancient four-poster and a Victorian chest of drawers adorned by a baroque gold-leaf-and-enamel clock that didn't work. In addition, there was that same sense of order and messiness. The room was clean and properly arranged: Caxton's expensive golf clubs and vast supply of suits and sports clothes filled a wardrobe with sliding doors, and a college annual containing a graduation picture of him as president of his university scroll club lay neatly beside a pen and notebook on a side table; yet a sliver of soap in the messy soap dish in the shower, a pair of shorts hanging on a towel rack, and a sock on the floor hinted of an unknown presence.

In fact, there was more than a hint. On a dressing table that looked as though it had just been polished, there was an ashtray with fresh-looking cigarette butts in it. Beside it, there were some keys, a few dollar bills, and a bit of scattered small change, as though someone had emptied his pockets last night before going to bed.

I could not help feeling someone was living in that room—right now—who would step up any moment to admire once more the various framed pictures adorning the dressing table. There wasn't a speck of dust on them. The pictures were all of young women, whose images certainly reflected Caxton's circumspect taste. They ranged from the high-school-cheerleader type, all bobby sox and bubble gum, to the svelte, sultry-eyed sophisticate. Most of them meant nothing to me, but I did recognize the faces of Mabel Reitz and Shirley Weaver.

One photograph in a cardboard foldout frame caught my attention. It was of a rather pleasant, familiar-looking brunette, signed: "To Irwin—with all my love and then some. Rena." I recalled the clipping in Willy's file. Sure enough, the picture was the same one used for the engagement announcement, and on the back of the photograph I found an inscription in a woman's handwriting: "Renata Koenig, Marksburg." The date beneath it indicated that the photograph had been signed shortly before Caxton disappeared.

I looked around the room and suddenly felt very lonely—very anxious to see Maura, to be with her. I didn't belong here. I belonged at home.

A cold little chill rippled over my shoulders as I wondered why, if Caxton had left voluntarily, even rapidly, he had not packed some of his clothes. I couldn't shake the feeling that someone had slept in the room recently—a feeling that made me jump with a start when I caught my own image in a door mirror.

Was someone else there—right at that moment? Or were these details merely evidence of a disordered mind? Or, I thought reluctantly, could it be both?

Maybe that was it. A disordered mind in an unsound body— more Hyde than Jekyll. Somehow the thought rang true. Wherever signs of life could be observed in the house, there was a certain rage for chaos. Haste and leisure were curiously blended. That shelf of paradoxical reading material in the study had described it perfectly. An adult reader who strolls through the leaf-fringed atmosphere of Hawthorne's Brook Farm or Thoreau's Walden one moment and apparently takes up a copy of some kind of horror comics the next—unless he has critical motives—would intrigue any psychologist.

I went to bed that night in an understandably nervous state. Between the house, my late thoughts, and the events of the last twenty-four hours, I could not convince myself that this was just another house in a small town and that I was just another twentieth-century newspaperman with a case of nerves. Even though it was after eleven and I was jaded, I hated going to bed.

I left the light on in my bedroom, if the truth must be known. But I had good reason.

I had picked the smallest and most remote bedroom in the house—apparently a small guest room. I had undressed reluctantly and climbed into the bed only after looking under it. I spoke out loud to myself the whole time. I had considered reading a little Robert Benchley book that I'd picked off the shelf in the study between the tales of Brockden Brown and Mark Twain's shorter works, but once in bed, all I could do was stare at a painting on the bedroom wall. It was of a great river that wound its way into a vague horizon of water and sky. On the river was a raft and what looked like a wild-eyed, crazed boy poling it toward oblivion and waving goodbye to the viewer.

I was still staring at it, trying to make peace with the night, when it happened. Like a thunderclap it happened . . . familiar, but nonetheless as startling as three giant steps pounding down on the floor of the heavens—three rumbling booms that rocked the bed like an earthquake that would have awakened—or perhaps been caused by—Uncle Gamaliel: Dthumm! Dthumm! *Dthumm!* Rachmaninoff's Prelude in C-sharp Minor!

I nearly jumped out of my pajamas. I ran down to the study and there it was, roaring away. The record had seemingly started up by itself. I finally reasoned that it had been on the on switch, and after I'd placed a bulb in the socket of Caxton's bedroom upstairs, perhaps I'd also flicked on some second while examining all the fancy stereo equipment up there or something. But that didn't calm my nerves any. I switched off the record player, went back up to my bed, and finally got to sleep.

I was so exhausted that even the genuine presence of Uncle Gamaliel wouldn't have awakened me. I was plunged into oblivion. For more than nine hours I slumbered dreamlessly. But, as I said, I left the light on.

❧ XXVIII

Things were badly delayed at the *Dispatch* the next morning, since I arrived very late. First, I overslept. Then, when I finally did rush out of the house, unshaved (the water had been turned off in the house, which vaguely registered as a puzzle in my mind, since the soap in the shower in the upstairs bedroom had been wet), a black-and-white police car was waiting at the curb in the streaming light of a sun-gold Montana morning to take me to see Chief Laken.

"Let's stop at the plant first," I said to the taciturn policeman behind the wheel, who had said nothing when I asked him where my usual chaperone, Jerry, was. "I have to check in."

"Okay, but snap it up. Chief wants you to meet him at the morgue to identify Birdie Johnson."

"Morgue? Does the police station have a morgue?"

"Naw. We use the Boynton Funeral Home. Chief's there with the doc now."

It was a horrible prospect, having to identify Birdie's mutilated body on such a heavenly morning. But I knew the chief would be a stickler for official identification; I had reported the murder, after all, and as I probably knew Birdie as well as anybody did, I figured there was no way out of it.

The Boynton Funeral Home was on the other side of town. After I checked in with Shirley Weaver to make sure that the staff had instructions, the cop drove me over.

At least the paper was getting started. Jellinek was already checking his rounds by phone and Mabel was to circulate among the merchants to pick up advertising copy and proofs. Kressnach would start the inside page layouts—I hoped.

I was just thinking about the lead story for the day—the identification of Birdie Johnson and the latest developments concerning the missing Willy Dunkle—when we approached the bus depot. I stopped for a cup of coffee and doughnuts to go, not exactly what a dietitian would prescribe for a nerve-wracked newsman recuperating from an ulcer operation that had resulted in removal of two-thirds of his stomach, but then the bus depot's breakfast menu was hardly *cordon bleu*. Besides, I knew I was already delaying the chief, whose scowl was even darker than usual when I arrived at the morgue.

"I hope you're satisfied," he growled. "The whole town's talking about Caxton again, and now this business about Birdie Johnson . . . Well, you've opened some pretty old sores in Marksburg, y'know."

I didn't say anything. I was learning. The doc was standing behind the chief, visibly shaking, although whether such vibrations were the result of a heavy night before, a breakfastless morning, or simply the intimidating presence of Chief Laken was hard to say.

The doc led us to a side door of the funeral home, which was a large, converted private house. I was surprised to see a fairly up-to-date laboratory installed where the kitchen and dining room had once been.

"Incidentally," the doc said, looking at his shoes and pausing in the middle of the room, "we identified the poison in the milk that was used on that cat at the newspaper office. You were right about that, too. Strychnine. Enough to kill a man."

I whistled.

The chief shuffled his feet restlessly at the doc's use of the word "too," and mumbled something. Without further preliminaries, the doc went to a tiled wall, slid open what looked like an oven door, and pulled on the handle of a huge drawer. It rolled out easily to reveal the outline of a body beneath a white sheet. The doc pulled the sheet back and there was poor Birdie looking more peaceful than I had ever seen him.

From what the chief had said—and from my experience in the past covering the occasional drowning—it was clear that Birdie could not have been in the reservoir for very long, since the body, exposed from the waist up, showed no signs of decomposition. He was all too easy to recognize. Up until that moment, I somehow had hoped that the disappearance of Birdie's body had made it possible for this entire experience to take on the proportions of a nightmare from which I would eventually awake; but it was not to be. I shivered.

One of Birdie's cheeks was slightly swollen and bruised. The purplish scars on either side of his throat were visible, but amazingly small, and his face was a ghastly, sallow color. The way his hair had been combed with a hickish part down the middle, and the way his head was tilted so that you could see the hint of an artificial, rather stupid smile on the waxy lips, I sensed a touch of black comedy about it all, but the strain of the past hours was too much for me. I turned away.

"That's Birdie, all right," I said in a low voice. I could not help adding, "What a waste. He was a talented guy."

The chief merely grunted and the doc slid the drawer back in. Then we went out for some air.

"Funeral's tomorrow," the doc said as we stepped into the sunlight. "Thought you might want to tell the people at the *Dispatch.*"

The chief offered me a ride, but I was still affected by the sight of Birdie lying dead in the morgue. That first night in Marksburg came back to me with a shock. The strange flashes of lightning in the shopwindows just as darkness had settled on the glistening streets . . . the sound of the wire-service ticker clicking, clicking . . . those shears and that spindle . . .

I shivered again. The chief nodded at me as he and the doc drove off. Too late I realized that the black-and-white had also left. My VW was still down at the house. It was infuriating. I had to walk across town and I was already late.

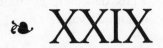 # XXIX

By the time I hurried up Main Street toward the office, it was going on eleven. I would really have to hustle, I thought, if we were going to make the deadline. But that was the least of my problems, as I quickly observed.

A block from the *Dispatch* office I could hear the sound of murmuring. At the same time, I was aware of a crowd on the sidewalk up ahead, and an alarm went off in my brain as I realized that a lot of people had gathered in front of the office! I started to trot, increasing my pace until I was in full sprint as I noticed with a panicky feeling that smoke was rising from the back of the building.

Police cars were in front. I could hear a siren somewhere.

"What is it? What's going on? Let me through!"

A few people stared at me and then stepped aside while I elbowed my way toward the swinging doors. My heart seemed to constrict as I saw the cause of the commotion.

The place had been attacked. The front right window was shattered. I could see an old brick lying amid shards of glass on the floor inside the building. The other display window, the one that housed the front conference room, was still covered by venetian blinds and remained intact. But someone had printed on it with a spray can of red paint: R I P.

The crowd milling around in front of the office kept murmuring something about a bomb. Shirley Weaver and Van Jellinek came into view at the swinging doors, which they had locked, attempting to keep the crowd at bay.

"All right!" I shouted, my back against the door as I challenged the curious faces. "Go home! It's okay! Just a bit of a racket."

No one budged.

Shirley and Jellinek let me in and snapped the lock behind me. Several cops were hurrying past us from the pressroom. One of them held a small wooden box delicately in front of him, as though he were carrying an antique vase.

"Make way," he ordered.

"What happened?" I asked Jellinek.

"It was a bomb," he said excitedly, his eyes sparkling. "Come on, I'll show you."

The back part of the editorial section was filled with a heavy gray mist, and I was really worried when I saw smoke rising from the pressroom.

"Oh, no!" I groaned as Jellinek headed for the stairs. "Not the presses! Anybody hurt?"

Some of the men were coughing and I could see Jim Strong standing between the press cylinders, bent half over and looking up. He came out a moment later, wiping his hands.

"What happened, Jim?"

"I dunno for sure. Somebody planted a bomb in the back room—back by all that old equipment and that vat of ink. You know—where we keep the extra rolls of paper. The press is okay. Just a lot of noise and smoke, really."

I looked around. You could barely see. Our eyes watered from the stench of charred rags and burnt paper mingling with the smell of the huge quantity of thick old ink sludge in the open vat, plus all kinds of printing chemicals.

"Open some of the floor-level windows," I ordered. "Somebody check the paper rolls. We can't take a fire in here, not with all those chemicals and that debris in the back room." Jellinek and one of the apprentice printers went off.

"Everybody okay?" I asked again.

"Ermann's hurt," Strong replied. Then, seeing the alarm on my face, he said, "Oh, he's okay. Broke his leg. No one was hurt in the blast. In fact, no one was down here except Leon. It was about five minutes before any of us arrived. He was drunk. I think he must have slept in here last night or something, because he was lying down between the rolls of paper. That's how he broke his leg. The blast dislodged an upper roll and it crashed down on his leg."

There was a look on Strong's face that struck me as odd at the time, although I understand it now in retrospect. It seemed to have a touch of alarm in it, but more, I should add, concern—concern for Ermann. I remember being slightly surprised, because there seemed to be little love between the two printers.

"Where's Ermann now?" I asked.

"A squad car ran him up to the hospital a little while ago. We . . ." Strong paused and studied my expression, "We were all sort of wondering where you were."

"I was with Chief Laken at the morgue. Had to identify Birdie's body."

Strong nodded. Jellinek returned and said there was no trace of fire. He explained that Mabel was out picking up ads and that Kressnach, seeing the mess when he came to work, turned right around and said he would be at the bus depot, pointing out disgustedly that no one could work in that confusion.

"How are you?" I asked Jellinek as we started up the stairs.

"A little shaken," he confessed. "That crowd out there has been milling around ever since the explosion. Not a soul was around when I came on at nine, and Strong and I were the first here—except for Ermann, that is. He must have spent the night downstairs with a bottle."

"I know. Strong told me."

"What'll we do now?"

It was *the* question. We were in real trouble, and I knew it. The looks on the faces of the apprentices—and, not counting Ermann and Strong, they comprised the remainder of the printing staff—told me they were plenty scared. I doubted if Strong could keep them working for long. I could count on him, I knew, especially since none of the machinery was lost. And Ermann's being knocked into the hospital was not all that serious, since he was about as useful as a shot flashbulb anyway, being half drunk most of the time.

But the serious problem was the delay that all the confusion had caused. In about three hours we had to have a paper up, and practically nothing was done. I felt like packing it in.

The explosion was more demoralizing than anything else, and I was wondering if I had any right to ask anybody to keep going—including myself. I had a wife and family to think about. And what did it matter, anyway? Jellinek was a crass young climber who, to use his own words, which I had over-heard, would probably sell out the first chance any decent offer from another paper came his way; and as for the rest of the staff—well, Mabel had spunk, but she didn't know the business; Ermann was a write-off; Shirley Weaver had proved unreliable; and that guy Kressnach—well . . .

The crowd was beginning to disperse and I saw Shirley up front, sitting at her desk with her back to me. Her shoulders were trembling. She had been picking up the large shards of glass, like someone moving in slow motion, and dumping them in the wastebasket, but now she just sat there shaking all over.

I went up to her. "Take it easy, Shirley," I said, putting my hand on her shoulder. "It's over now. Nothing too serious. Maybe you should go home and get some rest."

I was solicitous, but I didn't really want her to leave. We needed everybody at work. But she took me at my word, picked up her purse, put her suit jacket over her shoulders, took one more glance at the shattered window, and then looked back at me, dabbing at her eyes with a handkerchief. Her mouth went up at one side in a sort of snicker, and I suddenly realized with a mild sense of shock that Shirley had not been crying but laughing.

"Good idea," she said airily, making a motion with her right hand as she brought her purse up toward her chin that I would have interpreted under other circumstances and with perhaps a coarser type of woman as a rude finger gesture. "Damn good idea."

She walked out the door and up the street. It took me a few moments to realize that there are some things about women I shall never understand. This time, in any case, I was pretty sure my circulation manager was gone for good.

‏‌ XXX

I was just trying to decide if I should run after Shirley Weaver when the phone on her desk rang. It was Maura calling from Great Falls. She wanted me to come home.

"I heard on the radio about some kind of explosion in Marksburg—at the paper. Are you all right?" she asked.

She sounded wonderfully sane and stable in contrast to the ambience of the *Dispatch*'s newsroom and composing section. I heard the kids' voices in the background and suddenly felt a great desire to be back home.

"Everything's okay," I lied cheerfully. "Except that the cook at the bus depot could take a few lessons from you. You wouldn't believe this place. Lots of work, Maura. But I'll be up this weekend."

"That's marvelous," she said. "What's Marksburg like?"

"Well, it's different, I'll say that for it."

". . . drift chops," I thought she said.

"What's that?"

"Thrift shops. Does Marksburg have any good thrift shops?"

"Oh . . . uh . . . I doubt it."

"Are you eating regularly? How's the stomach?"

"Fine, fine. Still have the small bandage on, just for safe measure. But I think I could take it off now. I'm really okay, Maura. How are you and the kids getting on? You should see the house I'm staying in. Uh . . . did I ever tell you about Uncle Gamaliel's rehearsal when I—"

"I called the *Tribune*," she interrupted. "It had a story here about . . . about the disappearance of Birdie Johnson. Wasn't he the man who rang up here? What's going on down there? You aren't mixed up in something dangerous, are you? The *Tribune* said something about your trying to keep the *Dispatch* publishing, and there was an item on television on the national news about it. I think you'd better come home."

I explained as best I could on the phone, keeping it all light. But she didn't sound convinced.

"Did you get the money I wired?" I asked.

"Yes, but—"

"Look, Maura. Things will be okay. There's just some crank down here with a small-town grudge. You know the kind of thing. Happens on newspapers all the time. There *was* an explosion, but no damage."

"Come home."

"I'm okay. I'll be up on the weekend."

"Steve," she said softly, "we all miss you a lot already. You won't take any risks, will you? It sounds kind of scary."

"I'll be careful, Maura."

"If there was an explosion," she continued, then paused, "I mean, can the paper still come out? What can you do? Write it in longhand?"

It wasn't until that exact moment, when Maura's voice put it that way on the phone, especially when I recalled my defunct weekly, that I made my decision. Call it vanity or stubbornness—I don't know—but all I knew at the time was that after the *Independent*, after a year of deadlines and after getting the taste of a paycheck coming in, the least I could do was to give it a good try. After all, I'd only put out one issue. When Maura made that comment, it suddenly occurred to me that there was a way I *could* keep going. In that same droll way, Maura had said once of the *Independent*, trying to encourage me just after the printer had closed his doors, "Why don't we write it in longhand?" She didn't give up easily.

"You know, Maura," I said on the phone, "you've given me an idea. The paper will still come out, but it will be smaller. We're still rolling. I'm cutting down to six pages today."

"Six pages—for a *daily?*"

"You watch, Maura. They'll be collectors' items one day."

There was a pause on the other end of the line. Then Maura laughed lightly and said, "Okay, Steve. Go for it."

"Right!" I replied.

When she rang off, I went straight to the pressroom and told Jim Strong we were dropping to six pages instead of eight. He looked at me as if I'd just said the St. Louis *Post-Dispatch* had been converted into a comic book. From a printing point of view, he said, there isn't much difference between six pages or eight pages as far as time and production are concerned. I rebutted that it was a matter of getting editorial matter down and set; I wanted to cut every corner.

Then I returned upstairs. Jellinek was already on the phone. I told him to go down to the bus depot and get Kressnach. We would fill in the inside pages with contract ads, wire stuff, and boilerplate. The back page would run whatever ads Mabel brought in wherever we could place them. The point was to meet the deadline.

And we did. Kressnach got the dummies down in record time, such as they were. Mabel came in with a few ads and reluctantly agreed to help on circulation. We all read page proofs. The second issue of the *Dispatch* under the new management, breaking the story of the discovery of Birdie Johnson's body, with obit and funeral announcement, was on the streets on time, although I noticed only half the usual number of newsboys had shown up. We also played up the explosion story with a shot of the front window.

During the reading of the proofs, Harvey Kressnach had looked myopically at Jellinek's story on the explosion, his pipe arrested in air. "I didn't know Ermann was injured," he commented in a surprised tone.

"Yep."

"Well," he commented dryly, "that's a stroke of luck."

"Hey," I replied, looking up from a page proof, "that's no way to talk, Harvey. Where's the luck in it?"

"Well," he replied, with that high giggle of his, "you know what they say in the business when you want good luck: 'Break a leg.'"

"Very funny," said Jellinek.

❧ XXXI

I would have good reason in the future to remember Harvey Kressnach's remark about good luck, but it did seem for the moment that with the publication of the second issue of the *Dispatch* the wheel of fortune was turning in our favor. In spite of the fact that our circulation operation was clumsy, we sold out. Our run had been 5,000, counting the mailers, and the kids that did come to sell them on the streets returned six or seven times.

It may have been only a six-pager, but everybody was buying four or five copies. I decided then that even if we lost all our newsboys, we could drop off as many as a hundred copies at several points: the bus depot, the drugstore news counter, the hotel and motels, the bars, and so on. They were really moving. We could run an announcement stating that anyone on the mailing list who didn't receive a copy through the post (just in case we couldn't get the mailers out) could drop in and pick up an issue if he wished to do so.

The advertising also surprised me. Merchants were coming in from their shops with orders filled in. There was more than we could handle in six pages, since we had to honor contracted stuff first. But the point was that the *Dispatch* had suddenly become a vital and important newspaper to the community, which had had little good to say about it up to now.

Even Clarence Vilger, proprietor of Vilger's Sporting Goods Store, came in with an ad. I remembered Willy Dunkle complaining at our first meeting that Vilger had vowed he would never read the *Dispatch* and had kicked Willy out of his store, in spite of the fact Willy was one of his best customers during hunting season. Now here he was with an ad form in his hand, hoping to place a two-by-six on page 1. Throughout my entire career I had been opposed to running ads on page 1, and, in fact, never gave in to such commercial pressures during the sparest days of the *Independent*. But I could not resist this chance to capture the business of Marksburg's most truculent merchant. I took Vilger's ad with enthusiasm and charged him two bits extra per column inch.

Phone calls kept coming in all day from out of town. There were requests for a thousand papers in each of Montana's major cities, like Butte and Helena and Billings and Bozeman, and after the *Tribune* in Great Falls had publicized my role as a former *Trib* reporter now in the hot seat in Marksburg, there was a request for over five thousand copies alone up there.

The only way we could meet the demand would be to cut down to four pages until more newsprint came in. But that was only the glowing tip of the proverbial economic iceberg. By six o'clock that evening, we had received phone calls from the wire services and television networks. *Time* magazine and *U.S. News & World Report* were sending down stringers, and a photographer from the Washington *Post* rang to ask how he might charter a plane from Great Falls to Marksburg once he arrived in the state.

The *Dispatch*, if it could keep printing, was becoming a national item. I was beginning to feel like Ben Bradlee carrying on an epic battle against the White House.

I mulled all this over in my mind as we locked up the paper for the night, everyone going home with his personal police escort. Jerry, the rookie cop, accompanied me to the bus depot for dinner again. He simply strolled silently beside me as we started off. I was deep in thought.

I suppose I should have been thinking about the various incidents that had occurred and worrying about the future dangers, but my mind was in a turmoil about the paper. I had come down to Marksburg on a Monday night, and so far we had published a Tuesday and a Wednesday edition. That meant there were two to go for the week, since the paper didn't come out on Saturdays and Sundays. I figured that if I could keep going Thursday and Friday, like an alcoholic who faces only the immediate task before him, I might make it. I would have almost a week under my belt, even if I was down to four pages for Thursday and Friday. And a four-pager would be rough enough, especially if the apprentice printers walked out. We would take time out for Birdie's funeral in the morning, of course, and I felt personally we should close our doors for a day out of respect. Still, Birdie would have wanted to have the paper come out, I felt sure, especially under the circumstances.

"Here we are," Jerry said.

We ate in silence. When I finally emerged from my brown study, Jerry looked pretty depressed himself.

"You're looking a bit peaked," I said.

"Yeah. The chief had us up half the night. We ain't gettin' nowhere."

"Anything on Willy Dunkle?"

"Naw. And this bomb thing has Laken on the ceiling. He thinks you're outa your nut."

"I will be if I have to spend too much more time in that house of Caxton's. Ghosts all over the joint. But if I can just hang on . . ."

The policeman stared at me over his meal. He had one of those faces you come across sometimes in Montana's mountain country. There was a friendliness, a real concern there. It was an expression you could count on. Some time back, the literary and social critic Leslie Fiedler wrote, quite justifiably, about a certain type of "Montana face," the type that involves a hickish stare, country manners, and a sort of rustic deviousness. But perhaps he did not see enough of the other kind—the kind that, though hardly cosmopolitan, is sensitive to mankind at large, or, as Bud Guthrie would put it, the genuine article.

So far, all I'd come across in Marksburg were examples of Fiedler's "Montana face." It was a pleasure, therefore, to meet another expression in this young cop's eyes, an expression as solid as the pioneer tradition that led from the early-nineteenth-century jump-off point at St. Joseph, Missouri, to Bowker Gap in the shadow of Montana's lonely Hollow-Top Mountain.

"I guess it's true what they say about newspapermen," Jerry commented with a chuckle. "There really is such a thing as printer's ink in the blood, huh?"

I laughed. "Something like that," I replied. "Newspapers go a long way back in my family. My dad was a reporter for the *Daily News* in Chicago years ago. That was before he came West and started a weekly in Great Falls in the Depression."

"Chicago?"

"Yep. Good newspaper town. You'd be surprised how many Montana newsmen came out of Chicago in the old days. Even old Harvey Kressnach did a stint there with the INS."

"Kressnach?"

"So he told me."

"That's funny," Jerry said thoughtfully. "I ain't been in Marksburg much longer than you, as you know. But I was here when Kressnach came, and I remember well Mabel Reitz telling me he was from California. Said she knew him down there."

"Well," I replied, "he's no spring chicken. Probably came West, just like my dad."

We talked for a little while about our folks. It turned out that Jerry had come from Norris, a small mining town in south-western Montana, which was quite a surprise, since my mother was born in Pony, near there—up in the hills—and he had even heard of that side of our family. By the time we had walked back to Caxton's Folly, I felt—for the first time, really—that I had a friend in Marksburg. But he had reiterated that it wasn't a town for him. He told me confidentially that his job on the force was not what he'd expected, and that probably he'd go back to the Madison Valley or maybe join the state highway patrol in the capital headquarters at Helena.

I suspected there were bad feelings between him and the chief, by the way he talked, and though I caught him staring at me more than once, as if there were something that had been on his mind since I had first come to Marksburg and been roughed up at the station, he didn't seem to want to elaborate. It was as though he knew something but was waiting for the right moment to reveal its "proper" meaning—no doubt, what it means to any honest policeman: clarity of facts based on hard evidence. Anyway, again I didn't press him on it; I had my own problems. And they weren't long in making themselves obvious.

 # XXXII

When I went to bed that night in the guest bedroom of Caxton's Folly, that painting of the river made me restless all over again—and all over again, I had trouble sleeping. I went down to the den, using a flashlight that I'd borrowed from Jerry, and picked out a book of tales by Edgar Allan Poe.

It wasn't a happy choice. I suppose I picked it out because I'd been talking to Jerry about my mother's family. Mom loved Poe's work, memorizing it by rote when she had worked in a pea factory after Dad died, or reading it aloud sometimes to me when I was a boy.

As I read, I could see her dark eyes moving over the pages, her voice rolling sonorously over the ululant sounds of Poe's syllables. My brain was tired, and I dozed in bed, the funereal tones of "Ulalume" seeming to float around the bedroom in a way that restricted my breathing. I felt a sort of snapping at the back of my head, the way a person who is overtired sometimes does when dozing off. The air was filled with the momentary domination of black, although the light still was on. I reminded myself that I must remember to bring more light bulbs back from town in the morning.

I went off—then woke again. I looked at the book in front of me. The pages fell open to "The Fall of the House of Usher." Appropriate, I thought. I recalled a poem in it, and as I read it again, the words seemed to pulsate in my mind with the rhythm of a heartbeat:

> And travellers now within that valley
> Through the red-litten windows see
> Vast forms that move fantastically
> To a discordant melody;
> While, like a rapid, ghastly river,
> Through the pale door,
> A hideous throng rush forever,
> And laugh . . .

I dozed off again, but I seemed half awake. My mother had gone somewhere and I was alone in a great house. It didn't seem that I was dreaming. I kept telling myself I was awake.

But the house was now suddenly far away and, in the distance, the face of the house was like an old-fashioned portrait, now of Oscar Wilde—only twisted and grotesque and perverse as the picture of Dorian Gray—now of the puckish boy on the raft in the bedroom picture, grinning maniacally at me, beckoning me with his wild-nature eyes. Then the windows of the house grew huge, resembling hollow eyes, red-litten with blood-colored drapes. The drapes—or, no doubt as Caxton would have called them, draperies—had holes in them, and light gleamed out of the holes in a greenish, phosphorescent manner, like cats' eyes. The door now was solid, now turned into a maw of oozy darkness, now a gaping mouth as I entered it—or, rather, saw myself floating through it. I heard the pounding of my own heart, which the house echoed in crescendoing tones. . . .

I sat up with a sharp cry. My mouth was dry. I *had* to sleep. This was ridiculous. My nerves were getting frayed. I turned out the light and shut my eyes. But I couldn't shut off my imagination. I would doze off and wake up repeatedly. I was beginning to sweat. Then I seemed to go off for longer periods, only to be awakened by the sound of my heart's ga-thump, ga-thump.

I sat up in the dark. In half-slumber it had *seemed* like my heart. But it wasn't. There was definitely a noise. I listened, and a moment later there it was again—no small, coincidental creak, no imagined inkling: a definite noise. I listened, holding my breath; a moment later it recurred, even more distinct than before.

It was coming from downstairs. I remembered the Rachmaninoff incident, which I had momentarily attributed to chance. But this was humanly caused, no doubt about it. There it was again.

I decided not to turn on the light. Instead, I got up, putting on my pants and trying to get control of my nerves. I felt for the flashlight.

Why, I asked myself, didn't I turn right around that first

night in Marksburg after I saw Birdie's body, jump in my VW, and head straight back to my wife and family?

Gradually, as I became accustomed to the darkness and heard nothing more, I fortified my nerves. I was alive, after all. Someone has to fight the darkness, and not by whistling either. Even disorder and hatred and murder can be straightened out, overcome, rectified. This whole business had to be faced and stopped. So did the twisted mind that I was now convinced was behind it all.

I was halfway down the stairs when the thumping started again. It was below, all right. Far below.

I made it to the kitchen. I found a butcher knife in the cabinet drawer and slid it into my belt, waiting for the noise again. For a moment, I considered the possibility of a door swinging in the wind or something falling outside against the wall of the house. Then I heard the noise again. I hated to admit it, but I knew this time I had definitely located the sound. Muffled as it was, so distant-sounding and so far below, it had to be coming from the cellar.

I found the old cellar door opposite the pantry. Being one of the older houses in Marksburg, Caxton's Folly did not have a regular basement, but a huge, dank, lopsided, half-earthen, half-cemented cellar, probably used in the old days for everything from repairing machines to storing preserves. It was larger than any modern basement, divided into several rooms, with the heating plant, plumbing, and electricity converted to modern use. A whiff of underground dampness wafted over me as I started down the rickety wooden stairs. I beamed the flashlight downward and, holding the knife ready, decided I might as well go the limit.

The thumping started again, this time clearly and loudly in the cellar. I almost collapsed on the stairs. I wasn't sure, but I thought I heard other sounds, like movements, too. The thumping sound stopped abruptly as soon as the beam of the flashlight hit the bottom of the stairs.

"Who is it?" I called, hearing the fear in my own voice. "Who's there?"

My blood tingled as I saw a definite, dark movement across the gravelike room. I turned the beam in that direction. An L-shaped streak of yellow brightness flashed in the darkness in answer to my light, as though someone had opened a door a crack and then closed it again. Blackness. I beamed my flashlight around the main room quickly. Nobody. Then I flashed it back against an old door at the other side of the room.

I stood absolutely still and listened. Cobwebs swayed slightly in the tiny breeze coming from some underground opening. Junk was littered everywhere in the main room, its eerie shadows providing a sordid *frisson* right out of a Broadway suspense thriller. I swallowed and gripped the knife anew, stepping forward slowly. My foot hit a box. I ran the flash down. An old trunk, piles of newspapers, and a half-inflated balloon filled the light.

Instinctively, I crouched low and turned off the flashlight. I wondered briefly if maybe I was still having a nightmare and simultaneously wished that my heart would stop making such a racket. It was all too true. Someone was on the other side of the darkness, just beyond a door that, for all I knew, could lead to practically any corner of hell.

I worked my way gradually forward, like the FBI men in those notorious two-reelers of the late thirties. Although there had been a yellowish light behind the door, no gleam of it shone out beneath the door now. It was a huge, roughly made barrier that looked as though it led to a tunnel that would allow whoever was on the other side to escape in the night.

It had to be done sooner or later. I held my breath and yanked it open. Darkness. I crouched low again, waiting. I must have stayed in that position for a full minute.

"Okay!" I shouted. "I've got a gun on you! Come on out!"
Nothing.

"Come on or I start blasting!"

I picked up a piece of junk next to my knee and threw it in, hoping I could stir whatever was in there the way you might stir a rat out of a woodshed. There was a sudden flurry of movement. Something knocked me backward, sending the flashlight flying. A form rushed over me in the dark, a boot or heavy shoe catching me on the elbow as I tumbled. I was stunned by the weight and swiftness of the blow. Whoever it was, he was moving like the wind.

I scrambled to my feet, spitting dirt and groping for the flashlight. I couldn't find it. By that time I heard someone bounding up the cellar stairway. I caught a glimpse of shadow and substance, but hardly enough to discern size or shape. All I knew was that there was a sort of demonic, animal speed about the way it had overcome and leaped past me. I heard a clatter of furniture being dragged from the kitchen, and before I could reach the top of the cellar stairs, whoever my attacker was had wedged a chair or table against the door from the pantry side. I tried to open it, but it wouldn't move.

To tell the truth, I was just as happy to have my adversary out there. Aside from a sore elbow and a rather coppery taste in my mouth, I seemed all right.

I went back down to look around. There was no sense in trying to budge that door; I'd have to find another way out of the cellar.

I finally found the flashlight. The lens was broken but it still worked, and the full glow from the naked bulb made the main room of the cellar seem even more like a dungeon of horrors.

The debris down there was incredible, additional evidence that wherever Irwin Caxton had gone he obviously couldn't take it with him. Empty luggage was in one corner; in another, sports equipment, the box of an old flash camera, and newspapers and magazines were strewn about, exposed to the dampness.

When I explored the small room where my assailant had been hiding, it did not take long to conclude that he had been in that earthen cubbyhole for more than one reason. The bulb

·152·

on the flashlight suddenly failed. I struck a match, realizing that the L-shaped beam of light I had first seen coming from this area must have been from the attacker's flashlight, since the socket in there—like most sockets in the house—was bulbless.

I stepped into the room a little farther and felt my foot sink in soft earth. I struck another match and looked into what resembled a tiny grave. Next to my foot were a small pick and hand shovel, which explained the thumping sound I had heard. Someone—no doubt the same someone who had come flying out at me like Washington Irving's Brom Bones—had been digging. I peered at the pit and discerned with a shudder the alligator-skin jacket and emerald-colored scarf Mabel Reitz liked to wear. Something else was beneath the half-buried scarf and I was reluctant to explore further, expecting to find Mabel herself. Fortunately, the object was less pulpy in substance, but nonetheless ominous. It was a fresh envelope with the stationery stamp of the *Dispatch* on it. Printed across it in irregular, hastily scrawled letters were the words "So much for Women's Reitz."

The match burned my finger and I dropped the envelope with a shout. I lit a third match. The meager light showed a few objects around the freshly dug pit and my glance fell on something in the corner. It was just a flicker of a shadow of something that barely registered on my consciousness. I was understandably preoccupied with the prospect of unearthing Mabel's lovely form at any moment. Suddenly a shuffling noise above me, apparently from in front of the cellar door leading from the pantry, interrupted my thoughts.

The third match went out. I had to get out of that darkness. Half-nauseated, I stumbled back into the main room.

"Anybody down there? This is the police!" The voice, as welcome as air to a drowning man's lungs, was Jerry's. He had been removing whatever it was that blocked the cellar door from the other side. I came up squinting.

"It's me—Hadleyman."

"What happened?" he asked as I emerged, dusting myself off.

"I was just pulling up to the house for a routine check when I spotted somebody running out the back way like greased lightning. Couldn't get a look at him in the dark, but he was sure moving. You all right?"

"Yeah," I said shakily. "He locked me in down there when I came on him all of a sudden. He'd been digging, believe it or not. With a pick. I'll tell you about it later, but I think you should get hold of Chief Laken."

"Laken? Why? What's wrong?"

"Someone was burying some stuff, including Mabel Reitz's coat and things. Don't ask me why . . . unless—well, unless he was burying Mabel, too."

"Mabel! Down *there?*"

"I—I think so. I found a note."

"Mmm . . ." Jerry paused, looking toward the cellar steps. "I guess we'd better get hold of the chief, all right, and get a squad up here. Laken's home in bed now. You'd better come down to the station with me."

"Okay," I said, taking a deep breath. "But break the news to the chief easily. I think he's kind of fond of Mabel. And anyway, if I recall correctly, he doesn't much like being disturbed in the middle of the night."

❧ XXXIII

By the time we reached the station, the dispatcher had already phoned the chief. Laken had immediately gone into action.

He left a message for Jerry to go straight back to Caxton's

Folly and cordon off the area, making sure nobody touched a thing. He would meet Jerry and a squad of men there. As far as I was concerned, the dispatcher added, I was to remain at the station until the chief arrived.

Quoting the chief, the dispatcher put it a little more cryptically: "Tell that horned-toed, disjointed nosy bastard to keep out of sight and sit tight or I'll throw him and the rest of that newspaper crowd into the bull pen and leave 'em there!"

Anyway, while I was waiting for the chief to return to the station, I grew distinctly uncomfortable. The night shift comprised mostly the same collection of heavies who had, to use a polite euphemism, interrogated me my first night in Marksburg. Both the Swedish Angel who had slapped me across the mouth and the vengeful-looking deskman whose toes I had trod on were on duty.

The police gathered around me like a crowd of mastiffs threatening a wounded weasel. They stared at me as I shifted uneasily in a hard chair, trying to light my pipe. Nobody said anything. As I seemed docile enough, the group soon tired of hovering around and withdrew to various corners of the room.

"How're things with the Klan?" I asked, hoping a little levity might relieve the tension a bit. It was apparently the wrong approach, because the tension in an atmosphere dominated by a glaring light just above my head did not lift.

The Swedish cop's trenchant reply more or less clarified matters: "Shut up."

I studied my nails. The bare light above the simple deal table where I sat grew warmer. Four or five policemen passed back and forth in the shadows. No one said anything. Even the hostile dispatcher sort of faded in the distance, putting his feet up on the booking desk and pushing his cap low over his eyes. Those eyes, I thought, were studying me, but I couldn't see past the glare of the naked light bulb.

The scene from my point of view reminded me of a movie based on a story by Dashiell Hammett or Raymond Chandler or somebody. I think it was Dick Powell playing Marlowe. I saw myself in the role momentarily, possessing something of the Powell-Marlowe cool—even cynical—*savoir faire* that gives heroes grace under pressure. I tilted the chair back, put the thumb of my left hand through my belt, and looked down at the tabletop, puffing sagely on my pipe a few times.

"You know, guys," I said with a feeling of camaraderie that I believed would establish just the right tone for sharing confidences, "I've got a theory about this crime. Wanta hear it?"

Silence.

I told myself that these boys must recognize the internal perspective a newsman on the beat can acquire in his nightly rounds amid the underworld's shadier districts. Of course, it was true that I hadn't been on a crime beat for some time. But I figured that my theory would hold them spellbound. The silence in the room, it seemed to me, was tacit acknowledgment of respect for the kind of acumen a crime reporter must command in moments of intensive investigation—indeed, even in crises.

I hunched my shoulders a little and removed the pipe from what Dick Powell would call the straight line that was my mouth. I cleared my throat.

"The way I see it," I said crisply, squinting into the brightness, "is that we have here a classic case of schizophrenic paranoia. The psychodynamics are macabre enough, right? And what psychology books would describe as violent exhibitionism is certainly involved in this case. A sort of—uh, atavistic *Sturm und Drang*. You know, repressed primitivism and all that. In short, we've got a psychopath on the loose."

I felt that was a nifty opening. I wasn't sure just what elements in Marksburg made up *Sturm*, or exactly what a *Drang* was, and I was hoping nobody would ask me what I meant by atavistic, but it sounded grand.

I continued: "Now look, fellas, the perpetrator in this case is obviously suffering from all kinds of traumatic experiences in his—or her—or even its—childhood. Oh, I know, I know—the police always think it's a simple case of the good guys versus the bad guys. But is it? I mean, if someone swipes an old lady's wheelchair or something, you probably figure he's just plain mean. But maybe he's just paying the world back for the time someone stole a candy bar from him when he was twelve."

I paused and puffed on my pipe, realizing that I was frowning. Actually, my example wasn't the best. That *is* pretty low—swiping an old lady's wheelchair. Also, it reminded me of one time at the Emerson School when the Polson gang took away my squirt gun during recess in the sixth grade. I guess they were sore because I told Miss Carson they were smoking Wings cigarettes again in the boiler room. But that was mean, taking away my squirt gun, and especially when they filled it with ink and shot it at me during our school Thanksgiving morality play. It was bad enough that Ollie Polson got to play Pilgrim with Donna Mae Ingebritzen as his wife, Purity, while I had to play—as usual—the Tree of Apathy. But they didn't have to go and squirt ink all over my brand-new WPA overalls.

I sighed, recalling the last time I had seen Ollie Polson's face. It was a one-by-three cut, head-and-shoulders mug shot, which the *Tribune* had run on page 1 several years back under a headline indicating that Ollie had crossed one state line too many with one withdrawal too many from one federal bank too many in which he unfortunately had no account.

Then there was the time Ollie's brother Alvie bet me a nickel I couldn't knock out one of the front lights of a Plymouth parked by the school with a piece of playground gravel. How did I know the car belonged to the principal? And I never got the nickel, either. . . .

"Come to think of it," I muttered almost to myself, "there *are* some pretty mean people in this world."

But, tempting as it was to warm up to the subject, I interrupted myself. These men, I reckoned, must be anxious to hear my summing-up.

I assumed a direct, no-nonsense manner. "In any case," I said, "consider these facts. First, I come to Marksburg on a dark and stormy night to find Birdie Johnson murdered and no one believing me after I get assaulted, right? In the morning, someone slips strychnine into the milk for coffee. I alone take milk, and apparently *the murderer knows that.*

"How—I put it to you—just *how?* I have had coffee so far only at the bus depot, right? The waitress there may know that I use milk, so I cannot rule out the possibility that she may be an accessory before the fact. Knowing the conversational pattern of waitresses and that everyone in Marksburg, apparently, passes the time, day or night, at the only real coffee shop in town, I figure she could be a communicant of information, wittingly or otherwise, to the killer in our midst."

I crossed my legs, conscious of a heavy frown stretching over my brow. That *was* a problem, really. Not only was the waitress clearly uninterested in anything criminal or otherwise in life beyond the periphery of her own working counter and personal cosmetic bag, but she also was so nondescript I couldn't recall what she looked like.

That line of thought seemed to lead toward a mental cul-de-sac. I backed up and shifted gears.

"Then, too," I mused, "it's possible someone could have checked my habits beforehand, or simply guessed that a person who has recently had an operation for a duodenal ulcer would probably be on orders—as I am from the doctor—not to take coffee straight, but to dilute it with heavy doses of milk or cream.

"Anyway, the plan, as Robert Burns would put it, has gone agley, however well-laid it might have been, and the cat got the poison by mistake. Frustrated, our killer next scares off the one and only real advertising man available to the *Dispatch* since the killing of Birdie Johnson: our own Willy Dunkle. The reason, I suspect, that you have not been able to locate him or the paper's station wagon, which he used for his abrupt departure, must lie in the fact he has been scared off permanently. That is, I believe he has lit out for parts unknown and will one day be discovered in some city as ad manager for a big daily.

"Now," I continued, piecing things together in my mind, "the killer is further frustrated, so to speak, when he sees that in spite of the running away of the adman I am determined to carry on, even though I must reduce the size of the paper and must send Mabel Reitz out to collect ads. He must be furious that I have decided, in fact, to capitalize on his attempts to stop me by publicizing such criminal activity as front-page news."

I couldn't restrain a little chuckle at this point. "Imagine," I said, "the killer's reaction when he or she realizes that I've actually increased the circulation and potential advertising linage in the first issue! Furious, the killer tries a frontal assault on the paper, placing a bomb in the plant, smashing one front window and painting the other with a morbid 'Rest in Peace.' All that is obviously meant to force us into a position of not being able to print—nearly removing the press itself, which is vital to the operation. The printers are frightened . . . but the culprit fails and the second issue comes out anyway.

"Of course, Mabel Reitz, whom I must send out for ads, is next. Poor Mabel. A game girl. Maybe her column could have been a bit more—well, a mite more professional, but she *did* try hard and was actually bringing in a few ads.

"And what happens? It's the latest and perhaps the most satanic ploy our killer is to use so far. I wouldn't be surprised, gentlemen, if when the chief returns we learn that the freshly dug trench in Caxton's Folly that I peered into only a short time ago turns out to contain much more than Mabel's jacket and scarf. I'll bet anybody here a scoop of beer that beneath that loose soil lies *the lovely body of Mabel Reitz herself!*"

I paused a moment, trying to gauge the effect that my intonation had at that point upon my shadowy audience. A chill seemed to permeate the atmosphere. You could have heard the proverbial pin—or is it penny?—drop. Still, something seemed to be left out in my calculations even as I spoke. There had been something else in that basement room near the pit that had vaguely fixed itself in my mind, but I couldn't call it up.

"Anyway," I continued, straightening up a little in the hard chair, "what do these facts point to? What motive lurks in the distorted brain of this homicidal maniac? What consistencies might we observe in his or her *modus operandi*? What person, on all of the occasions to which I have so far referred, might have had the opportunity to carry out such a violent and diabolical series of actions?

"The answers," I answered myself, "point in one direction only. All the evidence suggests that someone has a deep and lasting grudge against this newspaper. A grudge that has driven him or her to go on a rampage against the *Dispatch* as a personality. The killer is trying to destroy more than a staff, more than a physical plant. It is the newspaper business itself that is to be the ultimate victim.

"The reason I have not been killed yet, although I was savagely attacked the minute I entered the circle of the *Dispatch*'s operations and almost poisoned to death before I could even get an issue out, may be attributed firstly to the fact that I am a survivor with Lady Luck still on my side, and secondly to the possibility that I was not yet well enough known to the killer to be considered part of the *Dispatch*'s personality. Nor was I expected to survive the shock of Birdie's death or to be capable of continuing at the helm once the advertising, circulation, printing, and—no doubt—editorial departments had been decimated, even obliterated.

"But now that it is clear that I *shall* continue, what remains? . . . Right!" I retorted. "My death remains! Such a grudge—a ridiculous vendetta that fits in well with my theory of the paranoid delusions of a deranged avenger with a split personality—must include the removal of the new editor and publisher.

"And who would hold such a grudge? Who has reason to hate the paper so much? Is it Van Jellinek, the frustrated young journalist whose capacities have been held back by the *Dispatch*'s stern adherence to the commercial laws of Main Street? Is it Harvey Kressnach, the formerly prominent Chicago newspaperman whose career in a remote Western town seems headed for a cruel form of attrition—a gray dead end? Is it Jim Strong, the capable and loyal printer who, in the opinion of some, has been foiled in his ambition to publish this newspaper himself? Is it Leon Ermann, bitter over his uxorious problems caused by a lecherous preceding editor and inassuageable even by alcohol? Could it be Shirley Weaver, soft-spoken, shy, quiet Shirley, who was clearly overworked, underpaid, and obviously at the center of things?

"Could I really dismiss even people associated only indirectly with the paper like the attorney Brownlee, whose power in this town is obvious, or, for that matter—and, gentlemen, I say this with all due respect—Chief Laken himself? Admittedly, the chief would probably carry out any tendency to violence in a more overt fashion—something like .44s blazing from the hips in a Main Street shoot-out at high noon—but his view of the newspaper world, it seems to me, isn't without its prejudices.

"So who could it be?" I asked loudly.

There was, of course, no answer. I perceived that all ears were, if I might blend such a metaphor, hanging on my lips.

"I'll tell you who. It was the one person who from the start had reason to hate this newspaper . . . the one person who had nurtured a grudge from the seed of hatred to a monstrous, poisoned plant and who had infected his own mind with macabre details and uncontrollable avarice."

I paused dramatically, rather pleased with my precious diction at the moment, and removed my pipe and placed it gently on the bare table, the way, I imagine, the orderly and fastidious Lord Peter Wimsey might have done in his confrontation with conclusive facts. In truth, I did not know what I was going to say next. I had no one in mind, but I felt my calculations were leading me directly toward the identity of the Marksburg killer, and scarcely had I registered such a feeling than a name, an identity, a solution sprang into my mind.

I almost stood up, so clear and penetrating was the revelation, as I exclaimed into the glaring light, "That insane killer has to be none other than the one person who had the motive, the means, and the opportunity to perpetrate all of these crimes in rapid succession: *none other than the missing publisher, Irwin Royal Caxton the Third!*"

I felt that my words must have thundered down on the hearing of the baffled police, who no doubt had been stunned into silence by the mystifying power and infallibility of sheer logic. My summary, I felt, was not unmasterful, and at first the silence around me seemed almost like applause as I pictured each law-enforcement officer there mentally arranging the crystalline facts in place and forming the inexorable conclusion to which my summation had led them. But, in fact, I must admit to a slight disappointment at that conclusive moment—a disappointment perhaps like that felt by a prophet unrecognized in his own country, or by Lincoln after his speech at Gettysburg.

Unfortunately, no one seemed to be there to hear me. All the police had apparently slipped out of the room. All but one, that is. That was the dispatcher at the booking desk. He was asleep. Furthermore, I noted irritably, he was snoring.

❧ XXXIV

I was dozing in the hard chair when Chief Laken arrived. He shook me roughly and told me to clear out. I was half asleep as I tried to rise, but his anger had an impact, especially when I felt his huge hand on the back of my suit jacket, ushering me toward the door.

He was muttering something about Mabel Reitz being snug in bed at home and the earthen pit I had seen at Caxton's Folly being nothing more than a recently dug sewer hole. I mumbled something in return about Mabel's jacket and scarf, which the chief had described as "just one more harebrained Hadleyman hallucination."

I tried to remind him that Birdie's death was all too real and that there would be nothing hallucinatory about the burial service in the morning, but the chief merely slammed the front door of the station and I found myself trying to keep my balance in a mud puddle in the dark. Understandably, I was not inclined to return to Caxton's Folly at that hour, so it was back to the *Dispatch* advertising counter for another fitful sleep.

I awoke long before nine. Perhaps that was just as well, I thought, since there would be a lot to do, and the staff would be late showing up, what with Birdie's funeral scheduled to take up the first hours of the working day.

Besides, my mind was now filled with contradictions. Some of the hairs with which I had woven the warp and woof of my hypothesis of the night before concerning Caxton-as-lurking-killer were afflicted with split ends.

Chief Laken's revelation that Mabel Reitz was all right, for example, still left her, as far as I could see, as a suspect. Then another mystifying thing happened. Just after I had washed up and was preparing to leave for the funeral service, I received a long-distance call from the manufacturing firm that I had previously phoned at White Sulphur Springs.

It was the same sweet-voiced secretary I had spoken to before. "We sent a large order several months ago," she said.

"I see. But what exactly was it? And why to W.D. at the *Dispatch?*"

"Our records show that a large order of products was sent to a Mr. William Dunkle, president of the Dunkle Chemfact Company, sir. I don't know anything about the *Dispatch.* Our records show the receiving address simply as the bus depot in Marksburg. The materials were to be picked up there, sir, and I'm fairly certain they were, since they were signed for and since I sent on the receipt myself."

"You sent the receipt after you received payment?"

"Of course."

"You didn't request payment in advance?"

"No, our policy—"

"And you also sent the receipt to the bus depot?"

"We . . ." She was obviously turning over some pages at the other end of the line. "Oh . . . umm . . . why, you're right. The receipt was mailed to W.D., care of the *Dispatch*. A notation here indicates the products were to be used in Marksburg for making ink, which we don't produce here, of course."

There was a pause. "Still, sir, I'm sure everything is in order. Our policy is never to send such a large quantity of highly potent material to anyone who is not qualified to use it for commercial purposes."

"Potent material? Commercial pur—" I stopped short. "Did you say Dunkle was president of—of—"

"Dunkle Chemfact, sir, that's right." Another pause. More turning of pages. "Yes—here it is. Mr. Dunkle placed the order first by telephone. Now I remember. He said something about his new factory not being ready and that we should send on the chemicals for pickup. Two carboys—forty gallons each—of chamber fluids. It was signed for and the receipt was sent. Is everything all right, sir?"

"Oh . . . yeah . . . thanks. Uh . . . but what are chamber fluids?"

"That's just our trade term for the chamber process of treating chemicals, but you really should talk to our chief chemist about that. Shall I connect you?"

"Actually, I'm in a bit of a hurry up here," I replied. "But thanks. I'll call later when I'm free. You've been a great help."

"You're welcome, sir," she replied sweetly, then added, using a tone suggesting she could be of further help. "You might send for our catalogue. It goes into detail about our entire range of products, including those that involve ferrous sulfates and other chemicals we use in the chamber processing of H_2SO_4 and all that. But, as I say, our chief chemist should be available later and—"

"Thanks," I said, hanging up. It was getting close to nine.

I knew that some chemicals were necessary for the engraving and stereotype operations in a hot-metal plant, and still others for multilith and offset operations—although exactly what, I was not sure. But eighty gallons? I figured it all had something to do with the conversion to a new technology, but for the life of me I couldn't see where Dunkle would want to start a manufacturing company to deal with ink products.

 # XXXV

I was just going to dig up an encyclopedia to find out more about H_2SO_4 when I heard a rapping on the front doors. It was the rookie Jerry again. He wasn't in uniform and I could see his own car, not a black-and-white, idling at the curb.

"Thought you'd like a lift to Boot Hill," he said affably.

"Thanks. I could go up in the VW, though."

"Come on," he said. "Somebody seeing that dying armadillo might try to bury it at the funeral as well. I want to talk to you, anyway."

He drove me over to the cemetery. There was no need to go

to the Boynton Funeral Home, since there would be no formal service. Jerry looked a bit glum, I thought.

"Did you know Birdie well?" I asked.

"Hardly at all," he said. "In fact, I haven't made many friends in this town. That's one reason I'm clearing out. Do you know that you're the only person in Marksburg who ever bought me a beer?"

"Clearing out?"

"Yeah," he said. Then he added quietly, "Besides, I've been fired."

"No joke."

"That's right. The chief gave me the sack. That's why I really wanted to talk to you."

"What happened?"

"I dunno, exactly. The chief said I was becoming too chummy with you. After you left last night, I tried to back up your story—I mean, about the ruckus in the basement and all. I told the chief about seeing someone running out the back way, but he just told me to stick to parking tickets and speeders. Well, I sort of blew up and told him I thought something funny was going on in this town and he spun around right there at the desk like he was gonna slug me. He sure is hot-tempered. He sort of checked himself, though, and said I'd better think about new employment—now."

It was hard to figure. The rookie had seemed to me like a good cop—in fact, one of the best. He hadn't been in the station that first night when I was roughed up, but I had a feeling that if he had been, he wouldn't have liked the third-degree approach anyway.

"What are you going to do now, Jerry?"

"I'm headin' for the Madison Valley," he said, pulling up through the gates of the Marksburg Cemetery. I saw the chief's car ahead. Jerry stopped when he spotted it.

"I'd better not go any further," he said, looking anxious to leave. "I just wanted to let you know before I pulled out that something smells pretty bad down at the station. I think I'll mention it in the capital on my way home. I have to go through Helena anyway—might as well kill two birds with a single shot, right? I don't know what's wrong exactly, but I think you might be pretty smart to go back to Great Falls. Anyway, I believe, like you, that there is more to that incident in Caxton's Folly than the chief wants to admit."

"Well, thanks for your help, Jerry. . . . Sorry you're leaving. I could use someone around here—a person I can trust."

Jerry peered at the horizon where the pine trees fringed the cemetery and almost glowed in the morning light. "I've gotta make a living," he said apologetically. "And, as I say, Steve, there's something—something strange about this town that sort of eats at you, y' know? I can't explain it."

"You mean like all of that Caxton tomfoolery—con games and Willy roughing up council members—that kind of stuff?"

"That and more. I didn't tell you everything I've heard about Willy and Caxton."

"Yeah—what about that?" I asked.

Jerry took a deep breath and studied the horizon again. "Can't hurt now, I guess," he muttered. Then he said, "You see, for a while Caxton was happy enough with small deals, but then he got that brainstorm about a Wheat Research Agency. Maybe you remember his news stories about it."

"Sure. Seemed ordinary enough to me."

"Oh, yeah, sure," Jerry chirped. "Real ordinary. Montana's quality of wheat is probably the highest in the nation, and research—especially in the university system and through various official agencies—has played a big part in all that. The trouble is, Caxton obviously didn't give a hoot about any real agency. Far as I knew, he never once contacted the Farmers' Union or the Montana Grain Growers Association or the Farm Bureau or the university or anybody else. He just kept drumming up enthusiasm for the establishment of a privately owned and operated agency right here in Marksburg."

"Well, it may be a lot of baloney, Jerry, but what's illegal about it?"

Jerry smiled then. "The *illegal* part of it," Jerry said, "was what he planned to do to set it all up, if he had been around long enough to do so. You see, it sort of came to a head when Mrs. Koenig's troubles developed. Old Ernst Koenig, before he died, built up a pretty good spread southwest of town with his brother Martin. Martin sold out to Ernst and went back to South Dakota to mind the old family place. And when Ernst fell over from a heart attack one day, he left a nice bit of real estate behind him. Unfortunately, he left it to a sick widow and her daughter Rena."

"How sick?"

"Bad lungs. She and Rena couldn't work the place, of course, although they could have hired plenty of good help. But that's when Caxton saw his chance. He made Mrs. Koenig an offer that must have made him look like Gary Cooper leading the cavalry to the rescue. First, he gave her a song and dance about how hiring help and trying to keep things moving would be a losing proposition, what with her ailing and all. Then he told her he and a lot of the local ranchers were planning a Wheat Research Agency. The whole county had been talking about Caxton's editorials calling for one, so she must have felt she was on the inside of something big. Anyway, I get it that Caxton suggested she put her place at the disposal of the agency. She could be on the board of directors or something, and her land would be used by local farmers and ranchers as a testing ground for advanced agronomy, and so on."

"And she went for it?"

"Not at first. He proposed that the agency would pay her an annual fee and she wouldn't have to lift a finger. I'll bet Caxton made it all sound mighty attractive, like promising that she and Rena also would share the profits from experimental farming. Plenty of security. No risk. A future for Rena. Perfect for the widow in her weakened condition."

I shook my head. I could see Caxton rubbing his hands together.

"Mrs. Koenig was still unconvinced," Jerry continued, "so then Willy went to work on Rena. The plan was to get Rena to convince her mother to sign an agreement that stipulated Caxton would act on her behalf—following regular board meetings and all that, of course—mortgaging the land to help create the agency's facilities, buildings, and the like. It was a typical con man's line. Caxton had claimed to have backing from the Coast, and even his family back East, and that he needed an option to buy the Koenig land or a loan based on a mortgage to provide enough cash up front—'venture capital,' he called it—to attract really big money for a really big project."

"Would an agency be *that* big?"

"Caxton would make it sound like Kellogg's Cornflakes. But what Mrs. Koenig didn't know she was signing in the deal was a clause stipulating that if she reneged—or died—Caxton could move in and take over the property . . . lock, stock, and barrel."

"But wait a minute, Jerry," I protested. "I know some ranchers and farmers in this state, and I don't know a single one who doesn't have a lawyer. Surely, Mrs. Koenig . . ."

"Oh, yeah. The farmers around here have lawyers, too. And most of 'em smelled something funny and soon advised their clients to pull out. The agency never really had a chance of becoming anything more than hot air. But at first there was plenty of enthusiasm among a lot of people who hadn't wised up, and before she knew it, Mrs. Koenig was ripe for signing on the dotted line."

"But didn't her attorney warn her?"

"No," Jerry replied, shaking his head. "Not *her* attorney."

"Don't tell me . . ."

"You guessed it," he said. "Her attorney was Brownlee."

"Well, I'll be . . . But, then, what went wrong?"

"In a word—Willy. You see," Jerry added, stretching and enjoying the narrative, "Caxton made a slight miscalculation about people—the kind of miscalculation the bunco artist often makes. He was so sharp he cut himself."

"How was that?"

"Hard as it is to credit, Willy fell in love. I'm pretty sure he went for Rena in a big way. My guess is that he told Caxton the deal was off. He couldn't blow the whistle on Caxton because he was in pretty deep on a lot of projects. Furthermore, as you know, he has a heavy record. But he must have decided to pull out anyway. I figure Caxton, seeing that he almost had Mrs. Koenig signed up, decided to move in on Rena himself. He had to keep the Koenigs in his good graces for the time being, anyway. That must have poured salt on Willy's wounds, because Rena fell for Caxton and jilted Willy. And Willy, in addition to being humiliated, must have been even more furious when he couldn't convince Rena that Caxton was phony."

I thought that over a moment and whistled. "What happened to the Koenig place finally?"

"Mrs. Koenig wasn't naïve," Jerry said. "She was dazzled, all right, but she had the sense to say she wanted to check things out on her own. In the process, she got sicker and decided the best thing to do was to go to South Dakota to her brother-in-law's place. Anyway, I figure she also wanted to talk to Martin Koenig, who would guide her right. Smartest thing she ever did."

I recalled Mabel Reitz saying the same thing.

"Anyway," Jerry said, "I thought I might as well fill you in on what I've learned before taking off. No sense my hanging around here. Maybe you should hit the trail, too, Steve."

"Nope," I replied. "I'm sticking. That paper's gotta roll. And you know something? I'm still mighty curious as to why Caxton took off so fast. And why Willy would do Birdie in."

"Well, you'd better watch your trackin'," Jerry warned. "Maybe you've noticed that the more answers you try to come up with the more you find questions. Instead of things getting clearer in this neck of the woods, they just get murkier. And I have a hunch there's a mean grizzly bear out there in the dark timber. Be careful."

"I'm beginning to know what you mean," I replied, getting out of the car.

Just before I swung the door closed, Jerry leaned over in his seat and said, "One other point, Steve. I was curious about what you said at the bus depot. I mean, about that character Kressnach, and his bein' from Chicago and all that. I queried the Pasadena police in California right after I left you. That's another thing. Chief Laken was furious. Most forces would praise you for showing initiative. He just bawled me out for interfering with the case and for using the telex machine to contact California. Anyway, I got an answer."

"What was it?"

"No record on Kressnach. He was workin' on the West Coast for years, but never as a newspaperman. He was in the trade-journal business for theatrical publications. Sort of part-timing character who hung around studios a lot. The police recognized my description right away. And one thing's certain."

"Yeah?"

"He never worked in Chicago. Far as I could find out, he's only been out of California once—and that was when he came here."

Jerry drove off then, leaving me with still one more odd-shaped piece in an incomplete puzzle.

৯ XXXVI

By the time I reached the grave site, quite a crowd had gathered in the cemetery. In fact, the whole town seemed to be there.

Chief Laken stood with the doc near the open grave, where a mechanical table device held Birdie's coffin for lowering into the earth. Van Jellinek, fidgeting and restless as ever, was with Kressnach; Jim Strong and the three apprentices stood just behind them. Leon Ermann was there, too, on crutches, his leg in a cast, and I could see Shirley Weaver standing alone, off to the right. They looked like the mutineers on the *Bounty* about to set Captain Bligh adrift in an open boat.

To my relief and considerable joy, there was Mabel up front, flanked by a prosperous-looking man and a grim-faced woman, whom I guessed to be either her parents or the original models for *American Gothic*. He looked mighty familiar. She looked like the corpse that ought to be buried that morning. Mabel, on the other hand, never looked more alive—sort of like an updated Lois Lane just clutched by Superman from the jaws of death. I waved at her. She wiggled her fingers at me covertly, stopping abruptly as her father frowned. I remember feeling surprised that in spite of all that had happened in the past few days and nights, everyone locally connected with the paper was there—except, of course, Willy Dunkle.

It was a glorious morning for a funeral service. Too bad the coffin was closed, I thought; Birdie would have appreciated the turnout and the way the air sparkled and beams of sunlight streamed down on us through huge elms amid shimmering aspens and cottonwoods. The distant pines soughed in a slight breeze, and as Chief Laken nodded to the doc, who began to speak, the crowd closed in to hear his words over the chorus of sparrows, kinglets, and robins.

"As you all know . . ." the doc started.

"Speak up!" someone shouted. "Birdie can't hear you for the birds."

I was horrified at the laughter that followed.

"As you all know, Birdie Johnson didn't have time to tell us how he'd like to be put away. Fur's I rec'lect, his people are from upstate, an' I don't know what church they belonged to."

"Wouldn't make no diffrunce in Marksburg," someone called.

"Anyway," the doc went on, "we thought just a simple ceremony would be what Birdie wanted, so I . . ." (He looked nervously at the chief, whose lip movements seemed to me to mutter something like "Wrap it up, Doc.") "That is, if someone wants to say a few words . . ."

A few words! I felt ashamed when no one seemed willing to step forward to say anything. It was wrong, I thought. Yes—wrong, wrong to let down a fellow newspaperman, no pun intended, like this. Not one of the staff made the slightest gesture. Jellinek, I noticed, was stifling a yawn, for heaven's sake! Birdie was a man who had climbed to a station in life, after all, with the diligence of Horatio Alger. I thought of the self-improvement almanac of life that Benjamin Franklin had set down so meticulously for himself in his youth. I was reminded of F. Scott Fitzgerald's Gatsby, whose gaze had been so fixedly set on the green light of success across the harbor of the American Dream. He deserved better than this! I could understand the feeling of hostility by some toward his memory. I didn't really know him all that well, and I must admit we didn't always agree, but this unseemly haste—without services—was a disgrace. Of course it was important to get back to business, but there hadn't even been a hint here of a eulogy. The whole town was treating it like a joke!

"Doc," I said, stepping forward, "I want to say a few words."

I thought I heard Kressnach give a little moan. I looked around and saw him standing there for all the world like a half-melted snowman. I was just thinking, after what Jerry had told me about his never having been in Chicago, that we would have to have a little talk, when he did a curious thing. A ray of sunlight beamed through the fork of an elm tree and across his face. Kressnach squinted back at the light through the thick lenses of his glasses and then, with a little smile and a seemingly unconscious but nonetheless dramatic movement of his head, adjusted his tie with his left hand. You'd have thought *he* was about to give a speech.

"I—I just want to say, folks, that, well . . ." I searched my mind frantically for the right words.

The crowd murmured impatiently.

"C'mon!" the chief muttered in my ear. "Say yer say an' let's git a-gittin'."

"Uh . . . well . . . Well, it looks to me like Birdie Johnson has met his last deadline. I just want to say that as a fellow newsman, although we had our differences, I, for one, will do my best to make sure the *Dispatch*. . . . Well, uh, in the words of the great Richard Harding Davis . . ."

The crowd was dispersing fast. Chief Laken made an anxious motion and two gravediggers in the background came forward and started lowering the coffin into the earth.

I changed my tack. "It may be thirty for Birdie," I added in a moment of inspiration, raising my voice a bit to try to overcome the sound of scraping shovels that threatened to drown me out, "but the presses will still roll and . . ."

The gravediggers were shoveling in earnest now, and the crowd was practically gone. Someone behind me mentioned Kelly's Southside Bar & Laundromat and there was a hurried exodus of most of the remaining mourners.

After a moment, still talking, I was aware that I was alone by the grave. But as I turned to leave, Mabel Reitz's father, well-dressed, portly, and florid-faced, stepped forward. Mabel and her mother stood far back, watching warily as he approached me. Well, I thought, now someone was finally going to show a little propriety. A decorous word or two from at least one Marksburg citizen, and an influential one at that, could serve at least as a token tribute to a publisher's memory.

I couldn't get over how familiar he seemed. Maybe we had met before, I thought, or was it just that he reminded me of the actor Edward Arnold in one of those tightfisted business roles he used to play?

"Mr. Hadleyman," he said with considerable force, "I want you to know that, as of now, Mabel is no longer working for the *Dispatch.*"

I looked at Mabel in surprise. Even at a distance she seemed to have that alluring I've-got-a-secret expression in her eyes. I couldn't tell if she was trying to smile or simply peer off somewhere beyond the tops of the trees. Her mother held her arm as though she might float away without an anchor, and, strange as the situation was, I thought she was remarkably attractive—Mabel, that is—in the morning light. The little scarf and jacket that I had last seen in the earthen pit of Caxton's Folly only hours earlier were as fresh and crisp as the morning air; in fact, they never looked spiffier on her. She suddenly flashed a smile in my direction. Yes—very much alive.

"Are you listening to me?" her father demanded, taking off his glasses and polishing them with a fresh hankie.

"I should think," I replied, "that Mabel is now old enough to make such a decision for herself."

"Well, you should think again, then," he said, with a snort. "This whole thing has gotten out of hand. Until this business about Birdie Johnson's death is cleared up, I don't want any of my family mixed up in all this publicity, is that clear?"

"If it's about last night . . ."

"Last night had nothing to do with it, except that I think maybe your imagination is running away with you so you'll have more copy for that rag of yours. Chief Laken told me all about your crazy story about Mabel's clothing in that—that cellar. You can see for yourself she's wearing her usual, melodramatic outfit and I can assure you that she was home all night last night. You've gone too far this time, Hadleyman."

"But . . ."

Mr. Reitz peered at me, then put his glasses on. "Look, as far as that crummy sheet of yours is concerned, you don't have to worry about the Marksburg Central Bank. We have a contract with the paper that we'll honor, and Terrill has told me he's given you support for the account. So I won't renege on that. We need a paper in Marksburg. But I don't want Mabel hanging around there anymore." He turned abruptly then and started to leave.

A strange thing happened to me in those few seconds. I needed all the help I could get at that paper, and Mabel would be handy in collecting ads and giving the effect, at least, of being the member of an active and busy staff. But I needed the bank more. For a moment, I thought of a little professional persuasion, some sort of highfalutin talk about needing Mabel's colorful astrology column and news coverage of women's events and the like. But her father probably realized Mabel wasn't another Simone de Beauvoir. Then I thought about running up to him before he got away and telling him off, the pompous ass. When I was a young reporter, perhaps that's what I would have done.

But the strange thing was that whereas at first I was tempted to tell Reitz to take his bank and stuff it, as I might even have done that first day in Marksburg, now I was suddenly eager to assure the banker that his talk of money and backing the paper was my kind of language. I wanted to *thank* him; I wanted to be on the side of power in town. His reference to the Central Bank's continuing support of the paper had gone deep.

So I clamped my mouth shut. The ad was the thing, I told myself. You pound Main Street for the big ones. You go for the advertising linage and the contract. H. L. Mencken's sarcastic gibes at editors who can count better than they can spell and who suffer from the fear of ideas were the kind of barbs that I would cheerfully have echoed in an *Independent* editorial before coming to Marksburg, but now they seemed like so much Baltimore sage for newspaper turkey dressing. When an important advertiser is also the bank where your Eastern supporter has lodged the barrels of gold, you don't start running around in circles declaring your independence—not in Marksburg, anyway. You genuflect and tell the Mabels of the rag to forget it. That's the way I found myself thinking.

I hadn't thought that way before.

How I had got hold of such an attitude I can't quite recollect. At the time, I felt it was a vital viewpoint. It is possible, of course, that it had developed in me over the past few days independent of events. But frankly I'm skeptical about giving so naïve a rationale to my rapid adoption of it. There was more sense to the idea that I had been susceptible to external influences. In retrospect, I realize how powerful such environmental forces are, because I had suddenly found myself thinking like Birdie. And, instead of resisting such thoughts, I was actually welcoming them, above all relieved to hear that the money— no matter what—was coming. I would have fired Ernest Hemingway if Mr. Reitz had demanded it.

It brought to mind, briefly, Jerry's recent comment about feeling corrupted. I knew then that Mr. Reitz and the rest of the town could call the *Dispatch* any name they wanted to. The important thing was to survive. I was so preoccupied with that thought that I almost forgot something else, which flashed through my mind just in time.

"Uh . . . Mr. Reitz!" I called.

He motioned to Mabel and his wife to keep going and turned to stare at me, clearly ready for an argument.

"Mmm . . . tell me," I said, "have you ever heard of the Dunkle Chemfact Company?"

He looked at me as though I had a dripping nose, which, in fact, I had. "No," he said gruffly, although his eyes hinted at some other possibility. "No such company of that name around here."

"Are you sure?"

"Hadleyman," he said impatiently, "I'm as sure of that as I am sure you're a first-class, blue-ribbon, prize-package jerk."

He stalked off with the last word, but I couldn't help wishing that he could hear my last thought, courtesy of Rod Steiger in one of those great mystery roles of his: "Well! That doesn't make you a bad *person*, you know."

I started to head back to the paper then, once more without

a ride. At the cemetery gate, Harvey Kressnach was waiting for me. He, too, was walking, so we set off together. He waddled along beside me like a sort of distressed, flatulent cocker spaniel. His cheeks sagged and he said very little. When I brought up the business about his never being in Chicago, he grew downright morose. As we approached the front doors of the paper, he fumbled in his coat pocket and took out a piece of paper.

"I meant to show you this," he said. "I found it in my pocket just after the funeral."

The note, printed in those same irregular letters that I had seen on the note in Caxton's Folly, stated: "You're next, Fatso."

"Ah, ignore it," I said, starting through the swinging doors. "There was a note for Mabel last night, too, but it didn't come to anything. Someone's just trying to scare you off."

"Well," replied Kressnach, failing to follow me through the doors and turning decisively as he started, flat-footed, right up the street, "he's succeeded."

XXXVII

As much as I wanted to question him about his past, not to mention his immediate future, I knew there was no use in trying to call Kressnach back. I watched his hunched-over figure rolling away. His shoulders said everything. He wasn't coming back. This was getting mighty serious.

Shirley Weaver wasn't at her desk when I went in, either. I

had meant to talk to her at the funeral to try to convince her to stay on, because she looked like someone who was planning a long nervous breakdown in some luxurious and remote sanatorium. I phoned her house but she apparently wasn't answering any calls. Alarmed, I looked around the editorial area, noticing that Jellinek's desk was still clean.

There were noises coming from the pressroom, at least, so I hurried toward the stairs, only to meet Jim Strong coming up. He had a kit of tools under his arm and a serious look on his face.

"Jim—what's going on?"

He went right past me and I caught up with him as we were passing by my desk. "I guess it's all over, Steve," Strong said, finally stopping and putting down his kit.

"Whattayamean—all over? We have a paper to put out."

Jim Strong sighed. "It's no use. The staff won't be back. Mabel's been blocked. Jellinek told me that he's been phoning around the state for a job and apparently this morning he lined up a reporting spot, since he told me at the funeral he wouldn't be coming in—ever. Ermann can't work—never could. I saw Kressnach heading for the bus depot when you were coming in and apparently Shirley Weaver is out of touch. But that isn't all, Steve."

I waited for the blow.

"Seeing everybody else going, the apprentices just announced that they aren't coming back to risk another bomb."

That did it. I knew that Strong wouldn't stick around without the apprentices.

"Can't you call 'em back?"

"Not a chance."

"You mean to tell me," I said, looking around, thinking of Kressnach's departure, "that you and I are the only people left?"

Strong picked up his kit. "Not quite," he said quietly. "Just you, Steve," He started to leave.

"But look, Jim," I pleaded, catching his arm, "we can't give up now. We've only got today and Friday to worry about. If we can come out for two more days, we could get other people in to help us—I know we could. What do you say?"

"It's no good," he replied, looking up at me with a solid, professional look that told me he was used to looking reality squarely in the pocketbook. "You gave it a healthy try, Steve. But I can't let the apprentices down. Don't you see? By walking out, they're making a union issue of this. If we brought anyone in, it would be scabbing. Our boys have never been treated properly, except for that bonus you gave 'em the first day. As I told you before, it was me who once talked 'em into donating part of their wages so we could keep on printing. They stuck by me and the paper all the way. But that explosion did it. I can't ask the men to come back after that. And as foreman, now that Ermann has been injured, I can't stay on my own or call in other men without letting them down. They stuck by me—I have to stick by them."

I couldn't think of any answer to that. He waited for my answer, but when I said nothing, he shrugged and turned to go.

"Okay," I said bitterly. "Clear out, then. Why not? The ship's going down."

Strong paused.

"Go on," I jibed. "It's only a newspaper."

"Sorry you feel that way about it," Strong said, not unkindly. "But the men . . ." Then he left.

✍ XXXVIII

I slumped down in the chair at my desk, looking around the deserted plant. It was almost eleven, four hours before a deadline, and no one had even bothered to turn on the ticker.

It was slow death, I thought disgustedly. One by one the staff had trickled away. I supposed that the funeral was the last straw. Kressnach was scared witless. And Jellinek's taking off without even a by-your-leave . . . Well, whoever was trying to kill the *Dispatch* sure knew the right psychological warfare.

Anger began to rise from deep within me. My stomach bandage started twitching. I'd had nothing but grief since I arrived—nothing but problems. I got up, kicked a wastebasket, and took a swipe at a desk lamp on my way over to flick on the ticker. It started to chatter away, like some old crone nagging me.

I shouted back at it, "Four lousy pages! That's all! Just four pages! If I could have rolled today and tomorrow, I *know* I'd have licked it. Four stinking pages!"

Whatever about the battered equipment in the pressroom, I had a potential fortune in printing equipment upstairs, but it was all useless to me without men to run it. If only, I thought, I could work that rotary myself.

The ticker chattered back at me—nag, nag, nag—as though answering my complaint with a remonstrance composed by the newsmen of the world. I was like a drunk on a street corner having an argument with a parking meter. The sound of the ticker amused me in a masochistic sort of way.

"Look," I said, starting to imitate its chatter, "this isn't fair. I've already lost one sheet. My own weekly. My weekly. For two cents I'd print the thing myself, if only I knew how to get that rotary going. Man, I don't even know how to work the folder! Four lousy pages!"

I don't know if it was the thought of the folder or just some zany whim that came to me as I stood in front of the ticker, watching wire copy rattle away as though a message were being sent to me from some divine press bureau of the Fourth Estate, but suddenly I was struck with an idea. It was farfetched, but not impossible. Maybe the equipment upstairs was too complicated for me, and maybe the paper's rotary presses in the basement were also too much of a challenge, but . . .

I ran downstairs to the pressroom and back by the boiler. The mess was still there, even though Jim Strong had said the men would clean it up. There was still that broken-down router, the stinking vat filled with sludgy ink, and, beyond all that, the old Babcock press I had seen during my first tour of the plant.

I may not be able to work a big rotary press, I thought, but I can sure work that. It was ancient and dusty, but it looked something like my dad's old outfit; and I remembered Jim assuring me that in an emergency it could be used for posters and whatnot. I recalled how he had started it up during my chat with him and how we had both been pleased at its slow but nonetheless definite operation.

Well, if ever there was an emergency, this was it.

Four pages! Four pages nothing! . . . I could never get the folder working and put out four pages, too. But, I thought, it was just possible I could roll a front page.

Why not? A one-page issue. Why not?

"Why not?" I shouted, my voice echoing throughout the pressroom. "Okay, you—you newspaper killer, you printercidal maniac, whoever you are! Come and stop me!"

I raised both my fists in the air, shaking them at the ceiling. My voice seemed to ricochet off the walls. I made up my mind. I went over by the linotypes and pulled the main switch so they would have power and the lead pots could operate. Excitement began to stir within me as I heard the current start and felt the heat beginning in the pots.

I was going to print the *Dispatch* myself. I could work a linotype, couldn't I? I could handle a Babcock. Well, sort of. Somehow I would get it all out, if I had to carry every copy to every house in town myself. The idea was to go to press.

I heard myself laughing as I rushed up the stairs. I locked the front doors. Then I looked around frantically for copy paper. I went to my desk and bashed out a lead story, giving an account of the incident at Caxton's Folly and the funeral of Birdie

Johnson, and, to pour salt on my own wounds, the determination of the editor to keep publishing. I gave myself a bold quote. I also wrote a side story on the bombing of the plant and the departure of the rest of the staff.

It didn't take long to figure out how to operate the Swedish plastic-cut engraver, which enabled me to make a cut out of a picture of Caxton's Folly that I found in our background file. I also typed up copy for a boldface box announcing that this one-page issue of the *Dispatch* was complimentary and that the paper would soon be back on a normal scale, but meanwhile it was imperative that the paper not miss an issue.

Then I grabbed a bunch of wire copy—the noon roundup—to fill the rest of page 1. I would make up the page as I went along.

It was almost one-thirty before I realized that I hadn't had any breakfast. I was starving, but I didn't dare stop working. The phones had been wailing like banshees, but I didn't answer any of them. I thought I could hear people banging on the front doors. I stayed in the composing area and pressroom.

Trying to work the linotype by memory took some experimenting, and for a while I thought I might have to give up. But it is remarkable how things come back to you. At 2 P.M. I had managed to set the main story, with the lead paragraph of it in caps—more by accident than intent—and some of the wire material. I checked the overmatter drawer and found about a column of type already set, most of which would have to do.

Then I tackled the hard part: the stonework. The fact that I had operated a linotype a few times as a kid helped me get through that phase reasonably well, if you don't count all the errors, but I had never composed columns in lead before on the stone and I knew I would have to rely on past observation of compositors. Fortunately, I had spent a lot of time working with compositors, since one of my jobs back on the *Trib* had been to make sure the paper went to bed before I locked up at night. But I didn't really know how to tighten a turtle frame, and only after several experiments did I finally figure out that basic step. I made up the page with lead then, and it didn't look half bad, really. There was a hole on the left-hand side that I was saving for an editorial, which I composed right at the linotype machine. I explained to readers and advertisers that all contracted advertising would be run in a future issue, compliments of the paper, but that meanwhile a front page was all that I could manage.

I tried to make it sound as though everything would be back to normal by the following week, but just getting out the paper this day without even daring to think of the next was task enough for me.

I was in a heavy sweat by 3 P.M. Deadline for page 1 was three-thirty and I knew that whatever newsboys were left would be showing up soon. There would be no mailers, of course. I still hadn't begun to print yet.

In fact, I wasn't even sure that the casing I'd used for my page 1 would do for the old Babcock press—I'd just have to chance it. At least there was no stereotyping for a rotary to be done anyway, since this was a flatbed operation. So first I got some matting and placed it over the metal page frame of type. Then I pounded it all even with a mallet, doing it carefully two, then three times—although I didn't know why—recalling the many times I had seen compositors do that. Then I locked the frame tightly, put a leather-and-matted pressboard over it, and pounded it all over again. When everything seemed as snug as I could get it, I slid the metal page onto the bed of the press. I'd have to forgo any page proof for this issue. I was about to start up the press when I remembered with a sort of panicky shock that I'd forgotten the ink.

I couldn't find any! I checked the ink distributor on the rotary, but although that press had a little in it, I wasn't even sure how I could get at it. Then I had an inspiration.

I remembered the vat full of sludgy, oily ink near the boiler. When Strong and I were talking that first day, he had told me that Birdie had tried some economy plan and was figuring on using up all that old ink. The smell alone would put you off, but I recalled that when I said to Strong, "Well, let's use the stuff anyway to get rid of it," or something like that, he had not protested. That meant the stuff must at least be usable!

I hurried into the back area. Lugging empty gallon tins, I toted the stuff, foul and thick as it was, to the old ink trough on the Babcock. I was bathed in ink by the time I pushed the button on the press, but, sure enough, she started up like a trouper—or like some ancient clock with a few parts askew—the rhythmic motion as slow as a disjointed pantomime artist, yet smooth enough.

I inked it up first, and then, locating the cut paper, I lined up a stack, pressed the suction button, and fed a few sheets into the mouth of the old crock. The first dozen or so came out looking like burnt blotters. But then, after a few minutes of the run, the front page began to take shape. The ink distribution was horrible, but I managed to thin out the sludge by mixing whatever I could find that resembled linseed oil (we never did get a new supply), and the page came out cleaner every twenty sheets or so. I was scattering paper everywhere, up to my knees in it as I stood by the press, adjusting valves, stirring the ink in the trough, and trying to realign the paper.

It was a terrible mess. I couldn't keep ten sheets steady at a time. No matter how hard I tried, too, the blotchiness and unevenness of distributed ink would not go away. By 3:30 P.M., I was covered in a second coat of ink and so was half the pressroom.

Then, miraculously, the press suddenly settled down. It sort of purred, like an old lion, and each sheet came out looking consistently inked. It was still uneven, but in spite of the bad registration, it was clearing up and was even quite readable. I stepped up the run. Now the sheets began to come out one a second, each one beginning at last to look like the front page of a paper. I figured there was enough cut paper left for about three thousand copies.

I had to smile as I looked at the page. My editorial, which I had intended to run down the left-hand side, actually ran down the right, since I had forgotten to compose the sheet in reverse order.

"It will have to do, Jake!" I shouted exultantly, laughing at the top of my voice, remembering how my dad used to call up to his old printer, Jake Rimple, at the beginning of a run, "Let 'er roll!"

The press throbbed on, that great, rolling rhythm ending in a swishing-out of the front page of the *Dispatch*, one after another. I was almost delirious at my success.

"Roll on, page 1, roll on!" I shouted. I jumped up and down around the press, laughing and smearing my face with ink. In the midst of a sort of ritual dance, I remembered how my dad had watched me after his paper had rolled the first time I'd ever helped him as printer's devil.

"Greatest sound in the world," he had said to me.

I now knew what he meant. I felt so triumphant that I failed to see a series of small faces peering fearfully at me from the edge of the pressroom. Finally, when I turned around, I stopped in embarrassment. Staring at me were the seven or eight loyal newsboys who had not given up on the *Dispatch*. They had come to the back door to pick up their papers.

"Grab as many as you can, boys!" I shouted. "Spread them around—free. Give everybody one. Drop a hundred off at the hotel, two hundred at the depot . . . hit every house."

"But what about our sales?" asked one enterprising boy.

"What do you make a night?"

"About two bucks."

"Right. I'll give each of you five dollars . . . but get going!"

The five dollars was the right tonic. I piled copies into their arms and they took off. They were soon back for more, curious at the odd appearance of a one-page newspaper, printed on one side only, brandishing a banner and a lead story full of typographical errors, but a paper nevertheless.

"This sure smells awful," said one kid, sniffing at the fresh ink on the page.

"I know," I said, with a laugh. "And you obviously have a nose for news. Now go out and peddle your papers."

PART THREE
Headline

ళ XXXIX

By the time the last of the newsboys had disappeared, I was almost too exhausted to clean up. Still, it had to be done. I remembered Jake Rimple, a Bull Durham cigarette dangling coldly from his pale lips as he leaned on a long-handled broom almost as dirty and skinny as himself, telling me that a clean pressroom after a run was one of the most important things in the business. Now I knew why. Paper was strewn all over, the walls were spattered with ink, and the press itself was a gummy mess—it all had to be cleared if I were to repeat the performance the next day, something I dreaded thinking about.

One day to go. If only I could roll again on Friday, I thought, I'd have finished out the week. There might be a chance of getting some help in over the weekend. Somehow it had become an *idée fixe* with me. The thought of only one more day helped me to screw up enough energy to clean the press.

The thing I could not seem to do was cut paper. I had often seen the pressmen working the cutter—no easy task, even though it appeared to be simply a matter of stacking it and measuring it. But I was so tired I had trouble even reading the worn measuring edge. The lack of sleep the night before, the series of traumatic events, and the pressure of deadlines, more than the actual physical or mental work, were beginning to take their toll, especially in the area of my duodenum.

Still, I finally managed to cut up what I thought would be enough for three thousand single sheets. As far as the extra copies for other towns and cities were concerned, they'd have to wait.

I dragged myself upstairs sometime after 9 P.M., startled to hear the telephone still screaming away. Several requests for papers had been arriving in Marksburg from all directions during the hours since I'd started working in the pressroom.

Now that the paper was out, I figured that an avalanche of photographers, wiremen, magazine reporters, and newspapermen from points east and west would be ready to break down the doors. The stories that I had asked Jellinek to send out on the wire (not that he had needed any prompting) had begun to cause a regional, even national, reaction.

But I needed food and sleep. The rest of the world of the media would have to wait, too. I was about to crash.

I slipped out of the office by the back door, locking it behind me, and went down the alley to the bus depot. It was crowded with strangers, easily identifiable as newsmen of various shades. One photographer had equipment strapped around his body like an automaton in search of a recharge. Through the window I saw a pile of little notepads on a table also cluttered with decks of cards and poker chips. Two different television-company vans were parked in the back lot. The place was bedlam. No wonder the newsboys had been excited when they came back for more papers. The tips were fantastic, they said, and all motels and the one hotel in town were jammed to the windowsills.

I was too fatigued to face all that, in case someone spotted me, so I walked over to Kelly's Southside Bar & Laundromat and ordered two steak sandwiches, french fries, and coffee to go, then headed straight for the paper's back door. It would be senseless to go to Caxton's Folly. No doubt newsmen would be keeping a hawkeye on that place, too, so I settled on the advertising counter with an extra supply of cushions and slept solidly.

I awoke at dawn feeling terrific. The work hadn't killed me, after all, and somehow the idea of getting the *Dispatch* out this last day of the week excited me. I'd face the following week when it arrived.

I had barely turned on the ticker and phoned the bus depot for coffee (a mistake, because the call alerted the newsmen, who had swum into the place for the night like a school of piranhas) when the floodgates did, indeed, open wide onto the paper. Moments after I was observed working in the plant, a wave of photographers and wire-service men came gushing through the swinging doors.

The place was deluged by every conceivable type of media man and woman. Radio reporters followed on one another's heels with microphones waving like suckered tentacles. The television people were already setting up lights and stringing innumerable cables, while others with strobe attachments to the portable cameras on their shoulders were pacing around the room studying angles and testing light meters. The paper looked like some huge aquarium full of weird deep-sea monsters darting about in electrically charged waters. One could recognize the wire-service reporters by the way they crabbily clawed at each other, trying to get to the center of action—namely, myself—as I attempted to climb on top of my desk, shouting for order.

Should this keep up, I thought, I'd never be able to get even a one-pager out. I finally grabbed a phone and got hold of Chief Laken. If the *Dispatch* was going to get nationwide coverage, I was delighted, but I wanted to be certain the paper at least had enough protection to function, even if it took the Vigilantes.

Within moments the advertising, circulation, and editorial areas were filled with reporters, stringers, film men, photogs, and general, all-round free-lancers. It reminded me of a political convention in a phone booth. A man from *Time* corraled me and the AP and UPI men interrupted. Strobe lights were flashing from all directions; I remember being curiously surprised when a small man with a huge beard came up and said in a polite voice that he was from Agence France-Presse.

It was an embarrassing moment, as well, since the UPI representative immediately elbowed his way to my other side, his toothy grin like that of a mint-chewing used-car salesmen. His manner suggested that he and I were on closer terms than others there, seeing as how UPI provided the only wire service for the *Dispatch*. He did not mention that the ticker tape was coming C.O.D.

The Agence France-Presse man remained marvelously *de rigueur* throughout the UPI man's monologue, which contained mainly innuendos about special sidebars for his service alone. Being flanked, as it were, by these internationalists, I welcomed the intrusion of the head of the AP bureau in Helena, whom I'd known in Great Falls. He was a foot taller than any of us and spoke like Sterling Hayden. He grinned in a knowing way and quipped, "Looks like you have us all on the spike, Steve."

"Not quite," I added, looking around. "Reuters hasn't shown up yet."

I sat down at my desk and stared, dazed at the melée as the police arrived and attempted to restore order. In a sense it was a victory. Even if I put out a mimeographed piece of 8½-by-11, written, as Maura had suggested, in longhand, if I called it the *Dispatch* it was still going and it would not close its doors. Not now. It had a future. Clearly, too, Marksburg was on the map.

ಜ XL

While the police were busy, I wrestled the phone away from some radio fanatic from upstate and called the *Trib* in Great Falls. The way I figured it was that, of course, the *Dispatch* should and would break any story concerning its own survival and the attempts by anyone to murder it, but, after all, it could only run the sketchiest of stories in its limited form. So I felt that the *Trib*, no doubt the best newspaper in the Northwest and in many ways my alma mater, should get an exclusive.

The editor of the *Trib* was tickled. He told me he would send a man down in a few hours, but an exclusive from me would be even better. It was when he added that he wished he were free and he'd come down and give me a hand himself that I had a brainstorm.

After I hung up the phone, I clambered back up on my desk. Things were reasonably quiet now, so I called for attention.

"Anybody here have a Typo card?" I called out.

There was a thoughtful silence, the question no doubt evoking a few suspicious thoughts in the minds of the electronics people, but then a Polish-looking, middle-aged reporter called up to me, "Yeah—I can handle hot metal. Why?"

"Wanta give me a hand with an old Babcock press?"

The man smiled. Some of the older reporters laughed and the AP bureau chief gave me a broad and, what seemed to me, knowing grin.

"Go ahead, Ralph," someone else called.

"Why not?" the man called Ralph replied. "It would be fun to work a press again."

"Do you need a wire-desk man?" someone else said, joking.

I spotted him. He was from one of the national newsmagazines.

"I'm serious," I said. "I have a three-thirty deadline. Anyone who pitches in on this one issue gets a story."

There was a pause—you might call it a caesura in a symphony of thought—and then, amid a series of jovial comments and catcalls, such as "What's your pay scale?" and "Let's face it—it's a good angle," and whatnot, the whole crowd broke into good-natured, if somewhat cynical, approval. It would liven up their afternoon, anyway.

I quickly had volunteers from a group of some of the most talented newsmen you could find, especially when I promised the whole crowd an old-fashioned press party after we rolled. At first there was pandemonium, but soon I had several of the men and women in the crowd gathering around the editorial desk, swapping ideas. The radiomen were delighted, giving an on-the-spot report on national newsmen working to save a small-town newspaper's life. I let the TV men go ahead and start to set up a studio right in the plant, promising camera interviews as soon as we went to press.

The police were going crazy, but I didn't care. The cooperation of the media, working to salvage one of their own, was a national story in its own right.

It took a bit of shouting and organizing, but pretty soon I had a semblance of order in the place. The AP chief helped me there. His very presence spoke authority, and I noticed that he was well organized and cool, cannily reserving a telephone at the back for his special connection to Helena. I found out sometime later that for all of that, the UPI man was faster, but made myriad errors, while the AP man was much more accurate, sacrificing some haste. The Agence France-Presse reporter never picked up a phone and merely spent his time conversing with all of us, occasionally studying odd bits of *Dispatch* equipment. Ultimately his was the most thought-provoking and philosophical story of the lot.

Meanwhile, I was busy giving orders. I had a *Time* stringer and a feature writer from the *Christian Science Monitor* handling wire copy. A Chicago *Daily News* man, fired up with a chauvinistic angle when he heard my dad had once been a reporter on that paper before moving West, took over the makeup. A Denver man and a reporter from the San Francisco *Chronicle*, with some character from the Milwaukee *Journal* (the *Chronicle* man had been born in Marysville, Montana, and the *Journal* writer told me that the Milwaukee paper's managing editor had once reported for the *Trib* in Great Falls, and therefore snapped an order to "get out there for a taste of pioneer journalism!"), kept busy writing some nice color stuff. A *Kiplinger Newsletter* reporter did a short piece on the economy of a dying daily suddenly resuscitated (forecasting, I am happy to say, a financial boom for the *Dispatch*).

What amazed me was the efficient and professional manner in which every person slid into the fun. It was all just for a lark as far as they were concerned, but the work was absolutely down-to-business. It was newspapering, no matter how minute—and newspapering was something everyone there took seriously and did to the best of his ability.

My main problem, in fact, was that I had a mountain of quality produced with only a molehill in which to place it. There was too much for one sheet printed on both sides. Ordinarily I could have gone up to as many pages as I liked, of course, but in spite of all the help, I didn't want to mess around with that folder. It was such a complicated mess, I figured no one could fix it in time, either. And it was getting late.

So we all argued on what pieces we would cut down to a paragraph or two, what we would leave out, what we could merge. I reached some kind of high, I think, when the correspondent from the St. Louis *Post-Dispatch*, who had already agreed to write a three-sentence, torrid guest editorial on freedom of the press, stuck his head up over an antiquated Royal typewriter and said in a loud voice, drowning out the debate by a dozen people over the choice of what stories should run, "Hell, Steve—you're the editor. So edit!"

When the paper came out—one sheet on two sides with the best makeup, writing, and presentation of the news since Dana published the *Sun*—everybody in the place seemed to have had a hand in it. When they weren't pitching in to get the paper printed, they were busy on the phones sending off their own stories. It turned out that the man called Ralph also knew how to cut paper properly, and he stacked up enough for a month to come. Everybody cringed when I showed the crowd the huge vat of stinking ink that we had to use, but it did the job all the same.

Producing that Friday edition involved mass confusion, but the excitement itself seemed to buoy up everyone, and a sort of pride floated through the plant as Ralph and I finally held up a front page to a loud cheer. The photographer from one of the wire services, who had constantly been picking off shots during the entire process, successfully used our primitive darkroom to develop a series to be sent off on his portable radiophoto kit, and he had given me a few extra prints of a team of about a dozen national newspapermen working away on the *Dispatch*. One of them made a beautiful three-column, page 1 shot, although the paper's plastic engraver didn't do it justice.

I was concerned at one point that perhaps some of those newspeople could get in trouble with their own papers or services or magazines for participating in the publication of another paper, but nobody in the bunch turned a hair over that. As Ralph put it, there wasn't an editor or a publisher in the business who wouldn't have wanted to be there.

I was proudest, I believe, of the lead story, which came out mighty solid-looking under an eight-column banner with the following bylines:

By Simon Feldberg,
Staff Writer, *The New York Times*

Howard Citress,
Washington Post Special Features

and

Steve Hadleyman
Editor and Publisher, *The Dispatch*

❧ XLI

Once the citizens of Marksburg had copped on to all the ruckus at the *Dispatch*, they flocked to the office, of course. I ordered that the doors be kept locked, but once the paper had rolled, I opened them up. A couple of volunteers handed out copies of the paper at the doors.

The newsboys brought their friends, and most of the old crew of boys came back, too, so the *Dispatch* was well on its way. Additional volunteers carried off bundles to the various distribution centers, including bundles for other Montana towns and cities. As soon as we ran out, we simply rolled some more, and to tell the truth I'm not sure how many issues we printed that day. But circulation didn't matter that much at the moment—getting out at all was the main concern.

Two magazine writers offered to pick up stuff I'd ordered from Kelly's Southside Bar & Laundromat so we could celebrate. They brought back three cases of whiskey, a couple of barrels of beer, eight dozen sandwiches, two bottles of pickles, two jars of mustard, a quantity of olives and potato chips, and a large Coke for the guy from the *Christian Science Monitor*.

The party was a huge success, with all the newsmen autographing a copy of the *Dispatch* for me, since I decided on the spot to start an album. Others began interviewing the various citizens of the town, remembering—as befit their profession— that the story they had been assigned to cover concerned the murder of Birdie Johnson and an attempt by someone in the town to stop the printing of the paper. I noticed with no small sense of irony that not one of the editorial or printing staff of the *Dispatch*—not even Strong—was around.

One of the television people reminded me of my earlier promise about television interviews, so I ordered the doors locked again and the camera crews went into action. But the party was in full swing, with so much whiskey flowing you'd have thought it was St. Patrick's Day in Butte. I should add that I hadn't been used to anything stronger than beer since my stomach operation, and the drink plus the heat from the klieg lights, or whatever they're called, made me feel a little dizzy by the time someone jostled me into a small arena of television activity where the crews had set up battery equipment.

An interviewer who looked like a model for a men's clothing advertisement in one of the sportier glossy magazines approached me, removing horn-rimmed glasses the size of pancakes. I could tell by the way he walked that he'd already undergone a serious amount of drinking. I was feeling a bit merry myself.

"We're not on yet," he said, with a friendly nudge of the elbow. He held a paper cup half full of Johnny Walker in one hand and a testing mike in the other. The whiskey seemed to have affected him even more than me, although when he handed me a neck mike and told me to clip it on, I got it a bit tangled and fastened it so that the mike went down my back. While I was rerigging it, he stared seriously at his thumb for a moment and said, "Uh . . . I'll give you the high shine . . . uh, sign, okay? Better fix him up, Dolores."

Dolores, a young, bosomy brunette in cute little overalls, readjusted my mike and dabbed at my face with a powder puff. She brushed my hair. I thought she looked like a young Zsa Zsa Gabor in a black wig.

"Howja like to be in moom pitchers, sweetheart?" I said with a Sam Spade leer. She gave me a deadpan look and the interviewer returned.

"So you're Steve Higleyman, huh? Watkins is the name. Just relax. Act natural." He seemed to be thinking over his words. Then he added, "Well, anyway—act."

We both laughed as we shook hands. His palm felt like a slab of wet soap. I felt relaxed—maybe too relaxed—but he didn't look so well. I suggested another drink.

"You should put some whiskey in that water," I said, sounding, I thought, rather hilarious. "We call that a 'ditch' in Montana."

"A ditch, huh?" He peered at his drink curiously, then poured a liberal amount of liquor into it. "Don' mind if I do." It was a bit alarming the way he could knock that back, tossing the paper cup over his shoulder.

The cameras were rolling on someone else, who was holding up a copy of the *Dispatch* and talking away in a deep monotone.

"Now, in a few seconds," the interviewer Watkins said to me, his lower lip protruding with what he must have considered a grimace of confidence, his head bobbing up and down with assurance, "the lens will swing our way and the little red light'll go bleep-bleep-bleep," (chuckle, chuckle) "an' then stay on, the l'il devil. 'S our signal, I'll jus' ask you a few quimple sessions. 'Kay?"

"'Kay!" I snapped. His horn-rimmed glasses seemed to have a third lens between the regular two. "Say," I added with enthusiasm, "didn't I see that girl, Dolores, in that movie 'bout . . ."

The red light blinked—then stayed on. There was a shadowy motioning going on behind the camera.

The interviewer's lugubrious voice suddenly started a long narration. At first it was marvelously clear, but after a few phrases it seemed a bit garbled to me as the lights got hotter and the glare stronger. People behind the camera seemed to be moving about quite a bit.

Suddenly the interviewer turned to me and was asking me something about the Korean War.

". . . wounded during the attack on Old Baldy?" the voice said.

"Who?" I asked.

"You," he repeated, studying my eyebrows as though they were infested by insects. He seemed out of focus. "I said I believe you were in the Korean War."

"Naw," I said. "Some other guy. I never got out of Roberts. Hey, did you know Camp Rot . . . Roberts hash larges' p'rade groun' in the whole world an'—"

The interviewer interrupted me with a query about Birdie Johnson. I couldn't quite follow him, the effect of the whiskey now making my head spin, but I looked past his shoulder once and waved at the camera.

"Hi, Maura," I called out, giggling. "Hiya' kids . . ."

The interviewer smiled at me benignly, although there were frantic motions in the distance. We were both dripping with sweat. He managed to stifle a laugh as he turned toward me again, his voice now overserious.

"Tell me honestly, Mr. Hodleyton," he said, his voice deepening, "about the murder of—of—"

"Johnson. Birdie Johnson."

"Uh . . . yeah. Birdie Johnson. Tell me, weren't you pretty scared when you discovered his body?"

"Naw," I said, grimacing, I'm sure, like Humphrey Bogart in *Casablanca*. "What of? An imsame killer?"

"Well, what did you do then?"

"I bought a bus ticket home."

I thought that was a great line. I was feeling terrific. I giggled again, and this time the interviewer also giggled, putting his arm around my shoulder.

"Seriously," he said, spluttering a bit, "when did you deshide to keep on pub'shing?"

"Yup!" I replied.

"Yup?"

"Yup!"

"Whatcha mean, 'yup'?"

"Ohhh," I replied, my mouth remaining open as I nodded happily at several people behind the camera whose waves at us seemed out of control, "jus' . . . yup."

"Hmm," the interviewer replied. "Why not? Good's any answer. Yup?"

"Yup."

We both chuckled a lot at that.

"An' I unnerstand thish was incident somewhere here or Cassock's Bollocks, there, 'coursh, 'boutaglidd 'n Mabel Rice's jashet inna hounded hoss . . . uh, haunted housh . . ."

"Yup."

"Wassat all 'bout?"

"Well," I said, focusing my eyes with difficulty, "I foun' thish hole inna cellar, see. The poleesh are lookin' into it. Tee-hee!"

This time the interviewer simply lowered his mike and half folded over in a convulsion of laughter. I couldn't stop laughing and collapsed into my swivel chair, my legs shooting up in the air so that I almost fell over backward.

I remember thinking that the crowd of TV people behind the camera must have thought we were as funny as Laurel and Hardy themselves, since they seemed to be having convulsions of some sort, too.

"Uh—uh," the interviewer stammered at last, "tell me somepin'—are we live or on tape here?" He was asking me the question seriously, I think, but his tone was still full of good humor, the effect of which was all the more stimulated by the way his face was bent close to mine. He had somehow managed to work his tie up to one of the lenses of his spectacles, giving him a sort of jaunty, piratical expression.

I said, "Yup."

That last "yup" broke us up again, and as an announcer reached across both of us, waving an arm in front of the camera, there was some kind of break in the action. I wasn't clear on the matter, frankly, but I recall being a bit disappointed that the fun was over, because I was sure it would be a good time to tell everyone about my theory concerning the killer of Birdie Johnson. Somehow, in my mind, I had managed to link the whole thing to the White House and a scandalous revival of Murder, Incorporated.

But the camera was peering in another direction and someone was talking about a deodorant. Dolores, looking unbearably pert in her tight overalls, was telling someone else she thought we'd better do the rest of the program later. The last time I saw Watkins, the interviewer, he was sitting behind the UPI ticker having a discussion with his microphone.

ᔕ XLII

For the next few hours, I had a brief nap down in the press-room. When I came back up, Dolores was very helpful. She had a flask full of hot coffee and my head was much clearer. In fact, I was feeling pretty sober, because a lot of the TV people were upset about the interviewer, Watkins, who had now wandered off. It was my guess he had joined most of the party, which had deserted the premises.

"Where's everybody?" I asked.

"One of the newspapermen said something about moving the party on to a place called Kelly's Laundromat or something. Anyway, we'll be joining them there. Maybe we can get an interview later, right?"

"Sure," I said, shaking my head. "Sorry about the mix-up. I think it was the whiskey and those lights and all that."

"Here," Dolores answered soothingly, handing me a cup of coffee. "Drink this. You'll be fine." An official-looking man came over and said that it would all work out okay. They had plenty of stuff for their broadcasts, and we could handle the interview anytime.

All things considered, they were pretty good sports about it, and Dolores ultimately broke out with a laugh. "Ah," she said, "that's show biz." She walked over toward a camerman who was packing up equipment and smiled at me over her shoulder, adding, "Break a leg!"

Something clicked when she said that. It startled me and made the taste of the coffee strong in my mouth. I swallowed and asked her to repeat it.

"What?" she asked, picking up a mike wire.

"What you said just now."

"Oh, anyone can garble a shooting. Forget it. We'll try it again later."

"No—no!" I said excitedly. "I mean that other thing—about a leg."

"Break a leg?" asked Dolores. "Oh, that's just a show-business phrase. I thought everybody knew that. It means good luck."

"Break a . . ."

I jumped up then. The effect of the whiskey was now completely gone. I couldn't have been more sober. I felt a shock go through my nervous system.

"Of course!" I shouted. "Show business! Break a leg! Break a leg! That's it! I've got it!"

"Got what?" someone asked.

"I think he's still drunk," the official said to Dolores.

"Quick!" I shouted to no one in particular. "I've got to check something. Let me out of here!"

It was coming to me fast. That was the expression Kressnach had used. "Break a leg." He had said, "You know what they say in the business—break a leg." But he did not mean the news business, naturally, since he wasn't really a newspaperman. He meant *show* business. He had worked on the California theatrical trade papers and had lived on the Coast, not Chicago, Jerry told me. And I recalled how that funny little man had stood in a beam of sunlight at the cemetery, unable to resist nature's spotlight to make a dramatic movement of adjusting his tie, upstaging even a corpse.

Kressnach was no wire editor. He was an actor! No wonder he had never really come from Chicago. He was out of show biz by way of Pasadena! The extent of his headline training was probably *Variety's* "Hix Nix Stix Pix." Now it was clear why he couldn't dummy up a news page. Probably the closest he had ever been to a news office before coming to Marksburg was on a studio set in Hollywood, and that was where Mabel Reitz had known him. All that melodrama about jumping a contract with INS, and so on—pure bad script.

I wondered why I hadn't put it together before that moment.

Thinking of Mabel had reminded me of that pit in the cellar, too, and that's what I had to check on. Now I knew what I had seen out of the corner of my eye by matchlight. I had been too distracted by the shock of seeing Mabel's jacket and scarf for it to register properly. But the power of sobering up from the whiskey, the black coffee, and Dolores' casual remark, strangely enough, had brought the past events sharply into focus.

"I'll be back!" I shouted at the few remaining TV people as I scrambled over debris and ran toward the front doors. Almost everyone had gone over to Kelly's Southside Bar & Laundromat—everyone, that is, but Chief Laken. He was sitting in his black-and-white in front of the *Dispatch*, hanging over the steering wheel like a huge, red-faced vulture. When he saw me rush out, he jumped from the car, moving very quickly, and caught me by the arm.

"What's going on, Hadleyman?" he demanded. "Don't tell me you're joining that motley crowd at Kelly's?"

"Chief!" I exclaimed. "I think I'm on to something. Kressnach—break a leg! Don't you see? Kressnach is an actor, and I think—"

"Never mind what you *think*," he growled. "You just stick to this paper. Leave the mystery to me. You may be the only staff member left on this sheet, but my job is to keep an eye on you."

He was a big man, Chief Laken, the kind you don't easily push aside. But I was too excited to stop now.

"I've got to check out something in Caxton's Folly," I said impatiently. I pushed past him abruptly and started up the street.

He caught up with me and said gruffly: "Then I'm coming with you. I'm not letting you out of my sight."

We got in his black-and-white, and he agreed to drive me up there, short as the distance was. He kept giving me odd looks, but I was too excited to explain, too anxious to put things together, in too much of a hurry to get to that pit in the cellar where I was certain I would find the solution to the mystery. It was no time to start a long argument about the power of a few drops of whiskey and black coffee with the chief of police.

ᴂ XLIII

When we pulled up at Caxton's Folly, Chief Laken asked me as he flicked on his radio mike, "Is this something that's going to call for reinforcements?"

"I don't know," I replied, bounding out of the car. I could

hear him calling the station as I hurried toward the front door. By the time I had rushed inside and reached the top of the cellar stairs, the chief had caught up with me. I asked him to lend me his flashlight.

"No need," he replied, turning on the lights. "I ordered bulbs put in all over this place after last night."

The cellar wasn't half so large or menacing-looking with the electricity working, although a single bare light hung down without a shade over the central room. I hurried to the small cellar room where I had seen Mabel's things. The half-dug pit was just the same, but not as deep as I had first thought.

"It was somewhere around here," I said, looking about.

"What?"

"It—in the corner of my eye I saw something—over here, I think."

I got down on my hands and knees and sifted the earth. Then, with a small thrill, I felt my hand strike an object. I wiped the earth away and pulled it up triumphantly to show the chief.

"Look!" I said proudly. "The murder weapon. I *knew* I had seen something . . . well, something that flashed at the back of my mind, like a subliminal advertisement on TV, but which I could not quite recall, since in a way it was out of context— you follow?"

The chief was staring at me, the wisp of a smile on his thick lips. How unusual to see him smiling at all.

"Look," I said again, dangling the object in front of his eyes. "Do you see how it works?"

The chief said nothing. I showed him.

The object was a pair of shears, but not an ordinary pair. They were editor's shears that had been filed in half at the point of juncture. The blades were separate from the handle and had been welded together and attached to a thin wire, the handle grips also having been welded into a fixed position. Thus the blades dangled from one end of the wire and the handle from the other. Something red-colored was smeared all over the blades. I examined the apparatus for a minute, then fit it around over the back of my neck like earphones, my hair obscuring the wire. The result was that the shears appeared to stick in one side of my neck and out the other.

The chief still stared at me, wordless, as I scratched around in the earth some more. A few seconds later I had located the phony spindle, too. It had been clipped off, and a little wax tip with powerful spirit gum attached to the end of it. I knew that if I had placed it on my head it would look as though it had been driven directly into my skull—one of the oldest magic tricks in the game! Now, a little chicken blood trickling from my forehead, Hollywood style, some more "blood" smeared over the back of a ripped shirt, I thought, and I'd look just like a very dead newspaperman.

I stood up, taking off the apparatus, slightly annoyed at the chief's sluggish response. He scratched the stubble on his jaws indifferently, chewing thoughtfully on the flesh on the inside of his left cheek.

"Do you mean," he asked dully, "that you think Birdie was just wearing this stuff and pretending to be murdered when you showed up?"

"Right."

"But why?"

"I'm not sure—yet. But I have a feeling Harvey Kressnach could tell us."

"Kressnach? Why him?"

"Because the preparations, the makeup of Birdie's appearance at the editorial desk—even the lighting—were all so theatrical. Kressnach was familiar with theater. He knew all along that—"

"But," interrupted the chief, "how would you explain our identification of Birdie's body at the Boynton Funeral Home and the funeral itself and all that?"

"Well," I answered, warming up to the discussion, "if you think about it, Chief, it was the same song, different verse. I mean, all we had was a quick glimpse of the body—just a few seconds, the way I had only a look at Birdie lying dead in the editorial office. Again, at the funeral home, it all could have been cleverly applied makeup—the pallor of Birdie's face, the so-called bruises, the morgue's atmosphere. If he held his breath while he was lying on that slab and while the doc slid open that big drawer, Birdie could have fooled anyone for a few seconds anyway. Man, I only looked for a moment and turned away. Maybe you did, too. And as far as the funeral is concerned, the coffin was closed. I'll bet you ten bucks that if we took a good look, we wouldn't find any Birdie Johnson six feet under."

The chief sauntered into the main room of the cellar and sat down on a crate. He looked at me with a slow, deliberate movement of his head as I followed him. He seemed to be thinking over his words carefully.

"You're forgetting something, Hadleyman."

"What's that?"

"My men said they found Birdie's body out at the reservoir. That means they'd have to be in on something. And the doc would have to be involved in some kind of plot, right? You're suggesting that he musta helped in rigging up a phony identification and all that."

"Well, maybe—yeah, I guess so. That's something you'd better check into. And I wouldn't be surpr—"

"And one more thing," the chief continued, shifting uneasily, "I know everything my men do. I keep close tabs on the doc, seeing as how he drinks so much. You should know by now that nothing gets by me."

The way the chief said that, slow and definite, each word punctuated by that heavy, thick-lipped way of his, as though syllables were chunks of rock candy he was carving with his teeth, was rather ominous. The way he sat there, his well-padded shoulders hunched over like some pensive fullback watching the losing end of a game from the bench, his heavy brow seemingly lowered by the weight of his shaggy head, made it hard for our eyes to meet. His huge right paw rested on his thigh close to the .45 automatic in its holster, curiously menacing in that quiet, remote, earthen place.

I swallowed. "You—you knew. You and Doc . . ."

The chief stared at me.

"You and Doc and . . ."

"That's right."

The voice saying "That's right" was not the chief's. It was higher in pitch, a sort of whining tenor. It came from behind the chief, near the cellar stairs, artificial-sounding, the way a synthesizer might imitate the human voice, the kind of tone you would expect from an escapee from a madhouse simulating speech.

I blinked. I knew right away. My heart flipped in my chest like a wounded sparrow. The chief seemed to be staring a hole in me. I thought the silence would last forever. I can still visualize it all in my mind's eye: the shadow on the stairs, the lack of any motion, the feeling of cold sweat on the back of my neck.

Then the silence was broken. "That's dead right," the voice said. "The chief and Doc and *me*."

I looked up then in wide-eyed surprise, even though I knew the source of that voice. It came out of the shadows.

"Hello, Steve."

"Hello, Birdie," I replied.

❧ XLIV

The penumbral light of the small room seemed to be closing in on me with a steady, almost suffocating movement. It was as though the walls were breathing, and Birdie's shadow, growing first small and then large against the vacillating motion of the bare light that swung on the eddy's heist of a cellar draft, grew apart from all reality as well. It turned into a gray-black haze that filled the room like some noxious odor of rotting organic matter.

It had to be a nightmare. I would awaken any minute now, surely, and find the children pulling the covers off me. Maura would be calling up to me that breakfast was ready. Our four-year-old, who had the nocturnal habit of climbing under the covers with me, bringing the dog along with her—something neither I nor the dog considered quite dignified—would no doubt soon shake me awake to announce I was her prisoner, yet once more tied to the bed with toilet paper.

It was a nightmare, surely. But it was real enough.

Birdie just stood there with a silly grin on his face, clearly relaxed in the unuttered knowledge that time served us at leisure, time to make decisions, time to explain the ancestry of all the bizarre incidents that had happened, of Willy Dunkle's disappearance and Shirley Weaver's derisive laughter and Mabel Reitz's inscrutable glances, of Jim Strong's and the other printers' occasional looks of amusement and Van Jellinek's attitude and that fat little, funny little adenoidal actor, Harvey Kressnach . . . time now to solidify the amorphous nature of the ghosts that permeated the half light between Birdie Johnson and myself.

"Why, Birdie?" I heard myself asking. I cleared my throat, which was as scratchy as an old washcloth, and tried to lower my tone a bit. "What—what's going on?"

Birdie whimpered then, half snickering, half something else as little needles of fear pricked at my throat. My words seemed weak and hollow in contrast to that strained whimper of his that hung between a laugh and a cry.

The chief still stared silently at me without looking back at Birdie, giving me time to place events and incidents in order. His face was grave in contrast to Birdie's whimsical expression. They made an odd combination, abiding one another without communication in a limbo of peaceful coexistence, like a lumbering grizzly bear and a sinewy mountain lion. I felt like a hunk of fresh meat between them.

"It—it was all some sort of trick, wasn't it?" I finally asked.

The chief suddenly turned toward Birdie and said in a businesslike manner, "I just had my men check out the *Dispatch*. All those nosynewsies have gone over to Kelly's place. The dispatcher's also contacting Doc up at Boynton's. He's bringing the others over now."

"Good," Birdie replied matter-of-factly. "Let's go upstairs and have a drink while we're waiting."

Up until then, the atmosphere had been as gothic as one of those corny Vincent Price mystery midnight thrillers, but the anticlimax of Birdie's return to reality and the chief's chummy manner in following him up the stairs, leaving me standing in the cellar with those ridiculous theater props of phony spindle and shears in my hands, was a dénouement that left me no choice but to follow suit. Part of my mind was relieved, yet another part strangely aware of disappointment, like that of a boy in a cinema who thinks he has come to see a melodrama only to realize he is watching the kind of drama that makes, at best, weak soap opera.

So I went upstairs, too. Showing easy familiarity with his surroundings, Birdie took some brandy out of a sideboard in the dining room and poured it into some expensive crystal. He gave the chief a glass, then offered me one.

"None for me, thanks," I said as Birdie offered me a glass. "I've had enough for one day."

Birdie shrugged, smacked his lips as he tasted the amber liquid, and studied the crystal apprehensively. Then he smiled abruptly at me over the edge of his glass.

"The 'others' that the chief is talking about," he said, sitting in an expensive Roman chair by the dining-room table, "are the staff members of the paper—all but Willy Dunkle, that is."

I waited, still marveling at the fact Birdie was alive and sitting there, talking. He took another sip of his drink, slumped in the chair, and chuckled.

"Okay, Steve, relax. It's all right—you can count on that. Yes. It *was* a trick—in part, a long-drawn-out, dirty trick on you, I admit. But a trick well worth it to you and the rest of us in the long run, believe me. We're all going to the top, pal—all of us."

He looked at the chief, who swallowed his brandy with a certain distinction and poured himself another one.

"Here," Birdie said, "take a gander at this while we're waiting."

He pushed a folder across the smooth top of the mahogany dining-room table. It contained a file of letters to Birdie from Irwin Caxton, as well as carbons of Birdie's answers. I was amazed to see one as recent as two weeks before I had come to town. As I browsed through them, I sensed something of what would be Marksburg's reaction to them. That is, I understood, I think for the first time, just how much hatred Marksburg's citizens could really feel for a man like Caxton.

The letters were patronizing—overtly snobbish. I had not quite pictured Caxton as that obtuse. I saw him with more polish—certainly better grammar—than these letters revealed. But, in any case, he clearly bore no love for Marksburg. Writing from the West Coast, he made it clear he was planning to return and that he wanted Birdie's help in doing so. He may have been scared off after someone had taken a shot at him (and Willy Dunkle, he implied, was his chief suspect), but he had too much invested in the future of the *Dispatch* simply to run like a whipped dog. He still considered the paper his, even if Terrill had bought it back, and he had solid plans for the future. As I read the letters, I pictured in my mind again the new equipment I had discovered in the upstairs area of the paper's offices.

"Those letters started everything," Birdie explained, settling down comfortably. "You see, Steve, the reason Caxton took off like a cat with turpentine on his backside was because of Willy Dunkle. Willy's a hell of a good man on the streets, but he hated Caxton, as did most people. The guy paid you in peanuts, for one thing. And he looked down his nose at everyone. A real dood. At first I thought, when I joined the *Dispatch*, that the ad revenue and fairly substantial income of the little sheet was being pumped East to Terrill. But Caxton had other ideas—big ones. He was buying equipment as though Hearst was his backer. Any money his family would give him—and that was a considerable pile—plus his ill-gotten gains over the years, he also pumped into material. Terrill wasn't getting anything.

"You've probably seen all that offset equipment, haven't you—that new gang-run press and other stuff upstairs? Well, Steve, you can see as well as anyone that Caxton had, and no doubt still has, big plans. I know personally that he was outlining ideas for a leading daily in the Northwest, plus a Sunday-supplement magazine with national distribution—the lot—as well as a journalism review of a new type, a raft of community printing . . . the works."

"Yeah," I said, putting down the file, "I was wondering about all that stuff."

"Well," Birdie continued, "he wasn't—and isn't—about to kiss it all goodbye, just like that, scared as he may be. Those letters show that he wants to come back one way or another. He was becoming a big name in politics, as you know, and he had other big projects in land and wheat and who knows what. The thing is—this town won't take him anymore. I know that, and so does everybody else in Marksburg. He has million-dollar ideas, but he just doesn't fit in here. He'd never make it work. Pass the brandy.

"Anyway, Willy Dunkle was fed up, doing most of the ad work, starving on a pauper's salary while fronting for Caxton in a lot of phony deals. Furthermore, he was in deep with Caxton in a crazy wheat scam that went sour when Willy got emotionally involved with that Koenig girl. I know Mabel has told you a bit about that, right? And, as I say, that Willy's trigger-happy. I suppose you know he's got a record."

"I found that X-2 file of yours," I said, "in the front office."

Birdie's eyes shifted slightly. He frowned, letting me know that in spite of his recent high jinks, he was still in charge and didn't like anyone snooping around his private papers unless he approved of such actions.

"Not much in that file," he said, with a shrug. "But you did see, then, that Willy could be—well, obstreperous. He believed in short answers to long problems: the more physical the better. He was a good hunter. Trouble is, he decided after too many drinks one night to stalk Caxton. Took a potshot through the curtains in the study and missed. But Caxton was right to suspect him."

"I know," I replied, looking again at the folder of papers on the table. "So there was a real attempt, huh? But if Willy Dunkle was such a good hunter, how did he miss?"

"Some say he was too drunk. Some say he only wanted to scare Caxton off. You could tell by the holes in the drapes, though, that he came close."

I was just going to ask why I only found one bullet hole in the bookshelves when Birdie, anxious to get to a larger point, elaborated: "But do you get the picture? I *had* to figure some way to beat Caxton at his own game, Steve. Caxton would never be able to make a go of his dream here, but that didn't make the dream impossible. He fooled Terrill once and he thought he could do it again—with my help, as those letters show. We were all afraid Terrill might fall for some pitch from Caxton and relent, allowing him to come back. But Terrill isn't Marksburg—ain't ever been here, not even once. And I tell you, Steve, Willy may have missed Caxton, but this town is full of snipers who would make sure they were on target next time. I just had to figure some way of stopping Caxton from returning.

"I thought everything was hunky-dory when Caxton pulled out of here after Willy made his move. But then these letters started to arrive, and that's when I got a brainstorm. . . ."

&. XLV

Birdie's discourse, which left countless questions still unanswered, was suddenly interrupted by a commotion at the front-hall door. One by one, the staff of the *Dispatch* walked in. Mabel, looking a bit smug, I thought, sauntered in, throwing me a flirtatious, sidelong glance, and collapsed in a chair. Jellinek, looking at me nervously, also sat down. Harvey Kressnach simply waddled up to the sideboard and opened a bottle, giggling. Jim Strong nodded at me silently. He and Shirley Weaver passed around the drinks Kressnach was pouring, obviously used to such meetings in this dining room. Ermann maneuvered past me on his crutches, swearing as he banged the plaster cast on his leg against the table. The three apprentices were with him. Even Jim Brownlee, the attorney, was there, accompanied—to my surprise—by Mabel's father, the banker. The doc brought up the rear.

Suddenly it hit me. Now I knew why Mabel's father had seemed so familiar. He was a sort of refined version of Chief Laken. I looked at the chief, who sat opposite me at the table. He had put on a pair of glasses to scan the file of letters that Birdie had shown me, and there was a definite family resemblance.

"I don't quite . . . ." I started.

"Hold the phone," Birdie said, lifting up his hand. Everyone turned to him and fell silent, responding to his air of authority with mute obeisance that said more than words could just how much this show was really his. "Now listen, Steve, we've all taken a big gamble on you and I want to assure you before we start some long series of explanations that there's a real profit in what we're doing—that is, if you don't let us down."

"Me? Let *you* down? I don't get it. What do you mean?"

"Well, in a way," Birdie said, seeming to be off the point, "this is Mabel's idea."

Everyone chuckled. I looked at Mabel and she smiled.

"You see," Birdie continued, "after Caxton took off, the chief here wanted to lock up Willy for assault—or, well, who knows what?"

"Yeah—and I still think I should have," the chief grumbled. "Look how he's ratted on us."

"I'll come to that," Birdie snapped at the chief. I was surprised the way Laken accepted the implied rebuke. In spite of his general gruff manner, the chief turned suddenly lamblike whenever Birdie spoke. Looking thoughtfully at me, Birdie added, "I guess I'd better fill you in a bit, Steve."

"I guess you had."

"Well—I knew that if I didn't do something when I started receiving Caxton's letters, he'd come bouncing back from the Coast with some surefire scheme or other. He was shrewd enough not to write Terrill or anyone in town but me. In a sense, he still had Terrill in his pocket, but I was his angle and he was looking for a comeback. You can see that those letters show that. I'll say this for Caxton—he's tenacious."

"What'd you do?"

"I called a general meeting of the staff. The whole bunch begged me not to let Caxton back here."

The others all nodded enthusiastically, looking at one another with knowing expressions.

"We all have our homes here," Birdie went on. "We all have invested in Marksburg's future. You know yourself how much the printers alone have put into the paper. And the town had a lot to lose, too. Main Street can't stand Caxton."

Mabel's father grunted. "You can say that again."

"I talked over the situation with everyone, and we were a pretty glum crowd, right, Shirley?"

Shirley Weaver laughed. "Go on," she prompted. "Tell him about Harvey."

Birdie also laughed as everyone helped themselves to the bottle being passed around. Kressnach giggled.

"I'm coming to that," Birdie said. "You see, I wrote to Caxton—you can see the carbons of my letters in that file—stalling him. I talked about the importance of timing, of letting things cool down—after all, there was Willy to contend with. Meanwhile, we all agreed that if we had some sensational news and if we could build up the paper rapidly—well, Terrill just might come around to our way of thinking and ignore Caxton's persuasive powers. It was a gamble, but we had Mabel's dad, and, of course, Chief Laken—and Brownlee, too—in fact all of Marksburg on our side.

"But I'm afraid," he added, smacking his lips, "that Terrill didn't have much faith in me, Steve. He knew the advertising linage was soaring and he believed in me as an adman—even as a publisher. I think in fact that he was impressed with the way I'd cleared up a lot of back bills and was slowly picking up on the financial end. But—well, I'm no editorial man, as you know. The editor I had working for me was hopeless. I had to fire him. He was the type who just couldn't think big. Oh yeah—incidentally, he didn't run off with Leon's wife. He couldn't. Ermann's a bachelor."

Everybody laughed then when Leon Ermann shuffled in his chair nervously and actually blushed.

"So I needed a man on the editorial side," Birdie continued. "These people"—he waved around the room—"didn't need any convincing that we would have to have an experienced editor to carry out my plan, especially since that plan depended on hot news."

"Hot news?"

"Right. If Terrill ever caught on to Caxton's dream about a

mammoth printing plant to serve a lot more than Montana, he'd be furious about Caxton's tying up the profits in it and keeping the money from going East. But it's my guess that the idea would ultimately appeal to him. Yet he'd never have faith in our carrying out the dream without Caxton, unless, of course, we could prove to him that it could be done. Terrill would see the business reasons for pursuing the project. Caxton had gone too far—buying that Goss press, for example—for Terrill to cut his losses and run. So we saw the danger of his going for Caxton's return to Marksburg, unless we could convince him in time that we were the right crowd. Hot news was the answer. We had to come alive . . . or die."

"I see."

"So—as I say," Birdie added, "Mabel's rather melodramatic mind concocted the thing. At first, we all thought of it as ludicrous. But when she said she knew a man in the theatrical world who could, so to speak, direct the show—and when I thought over some of the finer points involved . . . well, I ask you, what did we have to lose?"

"You mean," I offered, "that you cooked up a scheme involving your own death *as a news story?*"

"Uh—and coming to life again, don't forget," Kressnach added.

"That wouldn't have been enough, though, would it, Birdie?" Mabel asked. She had gone over to the sideboard and her eyes glowed as Birdie unfolded the story. In fact, everybody was enjoying it immensely. I decided I needed a brandy, after all, and gave Mabel the high sign.

"Exactly," Birdie replied, studying my reaction as Mabel passed a drink my way. "We had to make it look like someone was trying to kill the staff—and the *Dispatch* itself."

"We were counting," Jellinek chipped in, "on your exploitation of Birdie's murder and the subsequent phony events to make page 1 news that would hit the wire services and especially the papers in the East that Terrill would see." He had been silent up to then, and I had forgotten about him in the midst of all the chatter; but even though I realized that he hadn't really walked out on me that day, after all, I still felt a sort of silly resentment. But he didn't even wince.

"Actually," he was saying, "I was supposed to suggest to you once in a while that we put stories on the wire, phoning Helena and all that. But I didn't have to, since you usually brought up the subject yourself first. Have to hand it to you, Birdie," he added as Birdie grinned. "You had Hadleyman tapped."

Birdie's mood changed abruptly. It startled me how he had been grinning one moment and then, like Hitler addressing his generals, became downright solemn.

"I don't know about *that,*" he said seriously, "but I do know you were the newspaperman I needed, Steve—and still need. I have to admit I was gratified to see you plunge into things the next morning after discovering me dead. The way you rolled in with our plan was great."

They all agreed to that, nodding and smiling at me as I studied their faces, still finding it hard to accept that I had been so completely taken in from the beginning. Yet important parts of the puzzle were beginning to fit.

"Then you just kept things going like that the next day, huh?" I asked. "I mean, about the poisoned milk and the cat and all that."

"That was my idea," said Kressnach. "While you were downstairs, I slipped a Mickey into Porno's milk."

"A Mickey?"

"Yeah. You couldn't kill that cat if you tried," Leon Ermann added with a chuckle. Anyway, it wasn't strychnine. Just a heavy tonic the doc gave us that knocked Porno for a loop. He's over at Shirley's place now, living the life—or should I say lives?—of Reilly."

"Well, I'll be . . ."

"The cat was the best actor in the crowd," Kressnach said dryly.

"And then," Birdie added, "it wasn't hard to set up a phony

fight in the pressroom—a sort of red herring to make you suspicious of the boys downstairs, too."

"But the karate punch?" I asked, looking at Strong.

"Karate, hell," Strong replied. "I wouldn't know karate from Indian wrestling. The only person hurt in that fight," he added apologetically, "was you. Didn't intend that."

"But if the fight in the pressroom was a setup," I asked, "then what about the bomb in there—you know, after I was through identifying Birdie's—uh, body?"

"All a gag," Birdie said.

"All except my broken leg," Ermann added thickly. "That was real."

"Yeah," Strong added with a nod. I remembered seeing Strong's anxious expression when the incident occurred and wondering why he was so concerned about a man who was reputedly his enemy. Now it was clear enough. Strong and Ermann were good friends, not enemies, with Ermann playing the heavy, and when the roll of paper had fallen on Ermann and broken his leg, obviously that was not part of the act.

"I'll be a son of a gun," I said, shaking my head. "Then you two guys—and the apprentices—you weren't really scared off?"

Strong laughed.

"It was a joke," Ermann said.

"And the identification of Birdie in the funeral home, and you, Doc—and—and the funeral itself . . . and the remarks from the crowd at the grave . . . *everything?*"

"All set up," Birdie answered.

"But why that cellar bit at Caxton's Folly and Mabel's jacket and scarf and—"

"Good copy," Birdie added cryptically.

"Better drama," Kressnach chirped.

"And the best kind of economics," said Mabel's father, the banker.

ॐ XLVI

The various expressions on the faces all around me explained many of the curious and seemingly eccentric actions of the past few days, and in spite of my first shocked reaction to what I was hearing and thinking, I could not help admiring the ingenuity, the cooperative undertaking involved in this new and dramatic dimension. I could picture Birdie arranging the cellar like some melodramatic soap-opera setting. I could imagine him discussing with, say, Brownlee—yes, Brownlee would be the one—which books to put out on the shelves in the study in order to create just the right ghastly atmosphere. When I asked him if he had started the record-player going with the Rachmaninoff prelude blasting away, he startled me with a brief account of past days at the Pennant.

"It was a joke with all the boys in the Pennant," he said as politely as he could, "just how often you would go on about your uncle's concerts—and that piece in particular. It didn't take much remembering to come up with Rachmaninoff."

I could also picture Birdie and Mabel setting up that grave in the cellar with her jacket and scarf, and his waiting in the cellar until the proper hour to lure me down there with strange sounds, and then dashing away in the night.

No—I couldn't help admiring them all. But I was still incredulous, still irked.

"But you can't do things like that," I protested. "The day of the hoax is dead."

Kressnach snorted. "Oh, is it?" he asked in his squeaky little voice. "This is child's play compared with what goes on in any Hollywood public-relations firm these days. And," he added, looking at Chief Laken, "nobody's really been hurt. No serious crime has been committed. It worked, didn't it?"

"Right," said Birdie, looking gratefully at Kressnach. "When I was in California, I first ran into Mabel. That's how I cottoned on to the ad job on the *Dispatch* in the first place. I knew in those days that, in spite of her attempts to get into films, Mabel had gotten around pretty well. So when she told us all about Kressnach's ability at stagecraft and whatnot—well, I knew she had contacts. It was worth a try, and, as Kressnach said, it's how it came out that matters."

The others laughed—even Ermann, apparently the only real casualty in the entire affair.

"I still don't get it all," I said, and Kressnach moaned. "I mean, why didn't you just fold up, Birdie, and go somewhere else? Why go to all that elaborate trouble?"

I must have hit a special nerve, because Birdie's face once again became deadly serious. His eyes took on a hot, wild look that clearly affected the others in the room. It reminded me of the expression I once saw on the face of a man I was interviewing in Great Falls as he stood on the edge of a railroad bridge, threatening to jump into the Missouri River. I had got to the scene before the cops and firemen, and the man and I had a chance to talk for a few minutes. I convinced him not to jump, actually. He explained later that he had been depressed over his wife's infidelity. He also said that he realized it was stupid to be like that or to think that commiting suicide would be the answer. So he thanked me. Then he went home and shot his wife instead. Anyway, his eyes had the same glint in them that I could see in Birdie's.

". . . wasn't all that easy," Birdie was saying. "As I told you before, the people in this room have built their lives in Marksburg. We *have* to make a go of it here. If Caxton came back, everything would be ruined. And I'm talking about a big operation, man. I'm talking about a first-class offset operation serving

the coming thing: community printing on a large scale. No—
regional printing, with all kinds of possibilities. Do you know
that a huge think-tank recreation area is being built in the Little Rockies, just like the one on Lake Constance in
Switzerland? And in ten years, Steve, a lot of the industrial
headquarters will have switched from the crowded East to the
West."

Birdie shook his head vehemently. He wasn't talking to me
anymore, or to anybody else in the room. His eyes were slightly
glazed, quite disconcerting to me, but apparently emotionally
gripping to the rest of the group. He stared above me, out the
window.

"No! No—I'm not turning my back on all that, either. Not
after all these years. No sir! A large commercial plant, maybe a
women's mag or national kiddies' insert, a journalism review
that'll curl Seldes' hair and make Columbia's and Missouri's syc-
ophantic critics face some facts about the news game . . . our
own future syndicate for the West Coast . . . Picture it, Steve.
Caxton knew what he was doing, okay. He would have gotten
the town and Terrill hooked. Once I took over, there was no
turning back. But we've got to prove to Terrill that we can
do it."

I looked over at Mabel, whose eyes glowed like Czarina Al-
exandra's in a conversation with Rasputin. Van Jellinek's
mouth was open. Birdie was a persuasive talker. I was still marveling at the force of his personality when he added, "I had to
convince Terrill, and I think I—that is, *we*—have done just
that. The paper is now a viable product—thanks to you, Steve.
We had to keep publishing, not fold up."

I laughed. "And all this time," I replied, shaking my head, "I
was under the impression someone was trying to kill the paper.
It was just the opposite."

"Now you've got it," Kressnach said sarcastically.

"But how could you people be so sure that I wouldn't just
pack it in and go back to Great Falls? I mean—right from the
start Chief Laken was implying that I should hightail it out of

here—and you even advised me to do so, Brownlee. And it was quite a shock, seeing you sitting at the desk with shears through your throat, Birdie."

"Frankly," Brownlee said, breaking a long silence on his part, although he had been carefully studying Birdie and me for several minutes, "that's what I was wondering all along. From the beginning, Birdie stressed that we should all try negative psychology. The chief was to tell you first off to get out of town. If you remember, the more we tried to discourage you, the more you seemed to get your back up, old boy. But even after I met you and heard your stubborn answers myself, I was worried that we might overdo it and you would suddenly depart, especially after we pared down the staff to the printers—and then they deserted the ship."

Birdie smiled, looking at his hands. "The difference between me and the rest of them here," he said softly, "is that they didn't know you in the days of the *Independent*. I figured, remembering when we used to talk at the Pennant, that you'd get the old taste back in your mouth and, what with your being so broke and needing a job and all that, the more Marksburg put the pressure on you to quit, the more you'd sink your teeth into the *Dispatch*."

Some of them chuckled over that.

"But did you also figure," I said, "that I'd keep publishing once *everybody* left? Especially Jim? To tell you the truth, I wasn't sure what I'd do myself. I just got mad and kept on going."

This time Strong laughed. "Actually," he said, "I won ten bucks on that one."

"That's right," Birdie added. "I guess that's the only time I really overestimated you, Steve. Strong came to me and said he thought we had pushed you too far. But I bet him ten bucks you'd get the paper out anyway."

"Well, I did."

"Yeah," Birdie continued. "But I bet Strong you'd roll with a four-pager. You came out with a one-page sheet."

"You expected a four-pager? In as many hours?"

"Yeah," he replied, "I thought you'd try it. I was *sure* you would."

I shook my head in amazement. "How could I?" I protested. "I couldn't operate that run-down rotary press and the folder if I tried."

"The truth is," Strong put in, "that the press is okay, really. Old, yes, but doing fine. And Birdie thought you'd get the news kids to fold the paper with combs."

"But you said—"

"I know. But Birdie thought you'd be mad enough to try to run the rotary and everything else. We were all kinda pleasantly surprised when you got that old Babcock going and even used that terrible ink in the old vat. It made a great yarn."

Birdie changed the subject as everybody started laughing and drinking up. "The best stroke was putting out this last issue with all of the media involved. Wow! I tell you, Steve, that was a brainstorm none of us had counted on! That was a hum-dinger. We just didn't figure on that extra bonus. And that proves that I had the right idea in bringing you down. I imagine Terrill's delighted."

"I see," I said. Oh, how I saw!

"I've been keeping in touch twice a day with Terrill," Mabel's dad commented in a businesslike tone. "He doesn't know about Birdie yet, of course, but all good things in their own time."

"It almost fell through," Jellinek commented, rubbing his stomach and grinning widely, "when Willy overdid things. I was worried when he made your head bleed that first night."

"That was Willy Dunkle?"

"Yeah," the chief grunted, interrupting. "We should have used one of my men. But no. That hot-rock bastard had to get in on the whole thing. He's a violent character, anyway. I *knew* he'd overdo it—you have to admit I warned you, Birdie."

Birdie nodded as if to say that he would be the first to admit that there were snags in his master plan. That, I could see, was in fact one of Birdie's most persuasive qualities. He was never a know-it-all, yet he was always fully in charge.

The chief turned to me. "That's why I was so doggoned mad when you came to," he said. "The plan was for you to be lured out the front doors after you had discovered Birdie's body, and then, seeing a dark form running away (that would be Willy), to chase after it to the bus depot. We figgered you'd call us from there."

"But what if I'd decided to inspect your—uh, body, right at the start, Birdie? What if I hadn't been fooled?"

"Easy," Birdie replied. "I'd have just given you a big smile, apologized for the morbid gag, and tried another approach. We were desperate, Steve. We thought we'd try for a big story right off. What was there to lose?"

"Trouble is," the chief went on, "Willy always had to try something rough. I was really mad about the whole thing when you came to. I'm afraid I ain't much of an actor."

"You did all right," Kressnach said.

"I dunno," the chief said. "I'm still worried about Willy Dunkle. He could bring the whole thing down on us."

"Nonsense," Birdie said confidently. "No need to worry on that score, Chief. We'll have this all wrapped up and rolling before Willy can spoil anything. And as for exposing the hoax, in a few days we can do that ourselves."

"I still think we'd be safer if he was in the jug where he belongs," the chief protested.

There was a long silence in the room. Then Shirley spoke up. "I agree," she said. "He can be nasty."

⪦ XLVII

I waited for a moment in the ensuing silence of that sumptuous dining room as everyone pondered Shirley's words.

Finally I said, "What *is* the score on Willy? To tell you the truth, I think he's taken off for good."

The chief swore.

"The way it was," Birdie said, "is that Willy got greedy. You can see that we had to work as a team. Kressnach made that clear from the start. Willy, though, is a loner. At first I convinced him to go along with us, when I pointed out after you arrived that you would keep publishing. The fact that you were more determined to get the *Dispatch* out following each crisis impressed him. But as he began to realize the *Dispatch* would catch national attention and as the advertising potential became obvious, I think Willy saw for the first time that Caxton's dream of a giant operation just might turn into a reality. That hit him right in the pocketbook."

"How so?"

"He came to me and threatened to expose the entire hoax—my so-called death, and all that—wrecking everything, unless I promised him a good share of the whole thing."

"The nerve of that guy," Mabel said.

Birdie sipped his drink thoughtfully. His jaw was set and his mouth kept working between compressed lips. I could see that he was very angry, as were the others in the room.

The chief grunted again.

"What did you do?" I asked.

"The only thing we could," Birdie replied. "We had already all agreed to a plan. Variety was the ticket. That is, I was to be killed when you arrived; Shirley was to vacillate so that you'd never know if you could count on her; Kressnach was to be scared off; Mabel was to be apparently in some kind of trouble in Caxton's Folly here, and then ultimately pulled off the paper by her dad; Jellinek was to take off abruptly; and Strong—the last straw—was to go for union reasons."

"I played the stereotyped alky doc," Doc said.

Everybody looked at him. He had spoken so mildly, eager to join the conversation for the first time, that his meek voice sort of shocked us all.

"That wasn't hard," Kressnach quipped, and everyone—even the doc—laughed.

"But Willy was supposed to hang in there close to the end, since we really did need the adman, right? I called a meeting," Birdie said, "and we took a vote. The chief was for arresting Willy pronto. I made another pitch and we voted right here in this room. The group went for my proposal."

"Which was?"

"We'd give him a choice. Willy could have the paper's station wagon and a month's salary in advance—and that was all—plus a chance to hightail it to Canada. Or he could shout all he liked to the world about the hoax, but it wouldn't do him any good. He might spoil our plan, but the chief would still throw him in the jug for attempted murder. Not only did the shooting at Caxton hang over Willy, but the chief was mad enough to file an assault charge against him for slugging you. Furthermore, spoiling our plan would mean that Caxton would be back, and, as I told you, he had his own vendetta with Willy. No—we have too much of a hold on Willy for him to give us any trouble—right, Chief? He took our offer for Canada mighty quickly, once he saw that we were sticking together. He won't be back."

"But tell me something," I interrupted. "Where does Willy's Chemfact Company fit in?"

"Willy's what?" Birdie asked quickly.

"Chemfact Company."

"What's that?" Brownlee asked in surprise.

"Never heard of it," said Mabel.

"Isn't that the firm you mentioned to me at the funeral?" asked Mabel's father.

Everyone looked at me suspiciously. I told them that I'd seen a letterhead of that name with Willy's initials on a receipt.

Mabel laughed. "I'm not surprised," she said matter-of-factly. "He and Caxton were always cooking up companies and schemes. Probably just one more get-rich-quick plan."

"Anyway," the chief added, "I can't help wishin' I'd booked him. He was trouble from the start. I think he'd have called our bluff about the Canada offer if he didn't have such a lousy record in the first place."

"Right," Birdie said thoughtfully. His face had turned very pale and he was suddenly moody again, his fingers tightly gripping his glass. "That guy almost blew it."

"I've been wondering all along," I said, turning to the chief, "about you, Chief Laken. I mean—if you don't mind my asking—why did you go along with all this? Isn't this—uh, hoax—well, stretching the law? Fraud or something? Isn't it?"

The chief shifted uneasily in his chair. He wasn't used to being questioned or having his authority challenged, except maybe by Birdie, and my suggestion of fraud made him turn beet-red.

The others looked slightly amused, however, as though I were stepping tippy-toe over a point they had mauled to pieces. They were sitting around the table like one happy family— except for Jellinek, of course, who never sat still anywhere. At the moment, he was standing under what looked like a Currier & Ives original, spilling liquor on the carpet as he tried to pour a drink and watch the chief's reaction to my question at the same time.

Frankly, I didn't think the chief was going to answer me. He just sat there uncomfortably, picking up the phony shears and playing with them.

"Might as well tell him, Lucas," Mr. Reitz, the banker, said. I was surprised to hear Mabel's dad speak, let alone call Chief Laken by his Christian name. Hard to believe, that: Lucas Laken. Not bad, I thought. "Hadleyman should know, after all," the banker said, his voice surprisingly gentle and personal.

"Well," the chief drawled. "I had my reasons."

"Yes," Mabel said suddenly, getting up from beside her father and walking over to the chief's chair, "and you're too shy to tell Steve that I'm one of them."

"You?" I asked.

"Yes," Mabel replied. "Me. Irwin Caxton tried to—well, he—"

Mabel looked at Shirley, then back at me. "Well—he attacked me. He may have looked suave and debonair and all that, but when he was alone with a woman . . . Anyway, he was a mess from the start. When I returned from California and Caxton took over the paper, I suggested an astrology column. Oh, I know—it's terrible. But it's popular in Marksburg and furthermore it attracted Daddy's bank with an ad and with general support, and all. Caxton went along with it, so I wasn't suspicious of anything when he said he had a lot of books on the subject that would interest me. That was true enough, and like a jerk one night I accepted his invitation to see them. They're in the study there. And—well, there's just no trusting him. Another time in the plant—"

"It's true," Shirley put in. "There was Willy's fiancée, Rena—and others. He was like that with all the girls."

She suddenly flushed, realizing what we were thinking, and added, "He . . . I know . . ."

"And then," Mabel started up again, "after I told Daddy, Uncle Luke—"

"*Uncle* Luke?"

"Yes. Thought you'd know that by now. Chief Laken is sort of my uncle. Daddy's half brother."

I recalled the looks that had passed between the chief and Mabel in the office, not to mention the paternal—or should I say avuncular?—manner in which Laken had kept his men at bay around Mabel. I had, I am afraid, placed the wrong kind of emphasis upon the relationship.

". . . and when Irwin Caxton left town suddenly," Mabel was saying, "we were all pretty happy. But when he threatened Birdie that he would be returning—well, Daddy here talked to Uncle Luke and they decided it would be better to go along with Birdie's plan or somebody just might commit a *real* crime. Besides, my idea of using a California pro like Harvey here had a lot of fun in it, and—"

"Plus," Jellinek added with a touch of irony in his voice, "the Marksburg Central Bank has a big stake in the *Dispatch* and its future, right?"

"I've gotcha," I said, looking at the chief with a feeling that I was seeing him for the first time, really. He stared at the floor, oddly awkward and apparently even embarrassed at showing the slightest hint of tenderness and protectiveness toward his beautiful niece.

"Well, I'll tell you this," he said in a low tone, looking up slowly. "I've told Birdie and I've told Mabel. One reason I didn't push any harder for the prosecution of Willy Dunkle for taking a crack at Caxton is that I could have done it myself. It wasn't just Mabel—although that was enough right there. You'd be surprised what's on the books about Caxton's shenanigans, the stuff that he tried at one time or another with half the people in this town.

"An' when Birdie told me Caxton might try to come back to this town—*huh!* Birdie's plan was peanuts next to what I felt like doin'. The more I thought over the plan, though, the more it seemed to solve a lot of problems and to help Marksburg at the same time, just like Mabel's dad said. I mean, hell—no one was hurt. No serious law was broken, really. We may have bent a few rules and looked the other way, but since Brownlee's the local magistrate, anyway, between the two of us, I didn't see how anythin' could go wrong—"

"You also knew no one would dare prosecute," Jellinek again interpolated.

The chief continued, "And since Mabel's dad here is also the mayor, as well as head of the bank—well, we had the whole town behind us, right? At least the part of the town that counts—and all my men were briefed about the whole thing, except for that new guy, Jerry Hannibal, and *he* took off."

"Jerry? The rookie?" I asked. "Oh, I know. And now I know, too, what he meant when he said he thought something peculiar was going on down at the station."

The chief nodded. "He caught on to the fact that the doc an' me kept comin' over to Caxton's Folly at odd hours. Well," he said defensively as he looked at the others, "we had to coordinate things, didn't we? And somebody had to keep bringing Birdie food and stuff like that, and I think that damn rookie saw some of our black-and-whites goin' over here, too. He was pretty nosy, that guy. Since he was gettin' chummy with you, Hadleyman, I thought he'd spill things too soon. So I told him to take off."

"I liked him," I said coolly.

"All the same," Brownlee added, "the chief was right. That kind of guy doesn't fit in here in Marksburg. We don't like strangers nosing around in this town, Steve. Birdie had a tough time convincing us about bringing you in. But it's worked out okay."

"You mean it *might* be okay," Mabel's dad said.

"That's right," Kressnach added, "if . . ."

"If what?" I asked.

"What they all mean," Birdie said, "is that things can work out perfectly for our plan, Steve, including a good deal for you, if you're agreeable."

"Agreeable to what?" I asked, but I think I already knew the answer.

❧ XLVIII

That may have been the strangest conversation among some of the most bizarre characters ever to collect around a dining-room table since *The Man Who Came to Dinner*, but I'll say this for Birdie. He never hedged his bets. When he went for something, he went all out—as I concluded when he laid out the final phase of his big plan.

The idea was this: I was to go back to all the news people, right away, with an exciting announcement to be made from atop a pool table at Kelly's Southside Bar & Laundromat, since that was where practically the whole town had assembled for libations and general riot in an extension of what I had facetiously called earlier "an old-fashioned press party." The announcement was to be that I had talked to the staff of the paper and all had agreed, except Willy Dunkle, to come back to work. They had all rallied, I would say, after seeing the Friday special.

On Monday, I was to reveal my suspicion about the staff and Birdie's so-called murder, indicating that strange things were happening in Caxton's Folly. The newsmen could nose around, and it would only be a matter of time before they would discover the shallow pit in the cellar, where Birdie would have replanted the phony shears and spindle. No doubt the newsmen would do the rest.

"We won't make it too easy for them," Birdie said, indicating that the story of the hoax should break gradually. Chief Laken and his men, Brownlee and the Merchants Association, and Mabel's dad and the bank must never be involved, Birdie stressed.

The point was to have the news people discover for themselves first that a hoax was involved in which I was as much duped as the rest of the media people, a hoax fabricated by the entire staff of the *Dispatch*. Then, by means of a calculated and subtle orchestration, the staff could unfold the story of Birdie's nuclear position in the plot in a cooperative effort to save the paper. Naturally, Birdie would make a dramatic, midweek appearance, but only after the stories had been leaked one by one to milk the plan for all national publicity possible. Meanwhile, Mabel's dad would be filling in Terrill on each step, softening his wrath when Birdie was finally resuscitated, pointing out all business advantages in the long run.

I would be in the clear, Birdie argued—the idealist who came out on top, a rare phenomenon in the news game. No doubt the various media representatives still in Marksburg would be pretty sore about being duped, but they wouldn't blame the struggling Steve Hadleyman, who, after all, had been sucked into the nexus. And if they were mad at Birdie—well, he said, so be it. What were they going to do, prosecute? The worst that could happen would be for them to ignore everything.

"Who cares if they get a bit cynical and sarcastic in their postmortem prose?" Birdie commented. "As long as they spell the names right, we get the publicity."

It was true I was beginning to see my portrait on the cover of *Time*. And if Birdie appeared to be pulling the strings of the hoax, as indeed he was, he was acting in the time-honored tradition of the star publishers of the nineties and throughout American newsdom. In any case, no one was really hurt. The newsmen would have a story involving a mystery that they could be led to believe they themselves had solved. Books could follow, then diaries—films! And it all concerned the printed word, the great electronics revolution from hot metal to video terminal.

"Think of the possibilities!" Birdie exclaimed. "The *Dispatch*—the desperate, struggling *newspaper* in a small American town—would be saved by the knights-errant of the Fourth Estate, a triple play—okay, triple ploy—that would make Marksburg and its voice the American feature story of the year!"

I argued a bit about those newsmen who were currently sloshed and still celebrating down at Kelly's. I wasn't sure I could face them, in spite of their condition. Those guys were sharp. They knew their way around. The way they had slapped together several columns of news in a few minutes without missing a stroke in filing their own stories was impressive. They may have pitched in on the Friday issue for a lark, but they were dead serious about their own stories.

"And they'll get 'em!" Birdie argued back. "And it will be the truth! Well, some of it." He pointed out that all I had to do that night was make the first announcement. It would be an easy start. Timing, from then on, would be everything.

It was clear that the involvement of anyone outside the paper would be a mistake. And when I again expressed fears over some kind of litigious reaction, Brownlee pointed out that no one was really being libelled.

It was a good story. It did seem as though no one was really getting hurt. I could picture all those media people and newsmen with good features to their credit, and laughing over it afterward. And it certainly seemed that Birdie had thought of all the angles. No one would get to Willy Dunkle—he wasn't about to involve himself, with a murder-attempt charge hanging over him. The others were all willing to go along with the gag. Even as I uttered more protestations, I remember weakening. Yet, at the same time, that weakening sensation was opposed to my growing confusion over things I simply could not at the moment concentrate on.

"You're always telling me that it's important to get the small details of a story straightened out," Maura had said to me one time, and now that remark came to me, but it was only fuzzily in my thoughts. I felt dizzy. I couldn't get the next thought straight, even though I could imagine her level gaze—a gaze that said she was not easily fooled about people.

I wanted to straighten that out. Maura wouldn't have been satisfied at that point with all the explanations going on. I wished I could talk to her right then.

"Uh—I'll—I'll have to go up to Great Falls next week," I stammered. "I promised Maura."

"Fair enough," Birdie replied.

"All the better," Kressnach added. "Family tie-in is good."

"And," I added, almost whispering, "uh—what's the ulti-mate—uh—role that I'll play?"

Birdie paused, smiling at me as only an adman can smile, then said crisply, "Editor-in-chief of the whole operation."

Now I paused. Birdie raised his glass. There was a strange look in his eyes that seemed to be meant just for me. It spoke of the past and of our path-crossed careers.

"Well," he said finally, "what about it, Steve?"

I knew I should have said then to forget the whole thing. I should have gotten up immediately and told them all, right then and there, to take their marbles home and let me play another game. I should have walked right out the door.

But I didn't. Marksburg had done its work well.

All I could see in my mind's eye at that moment was that brand-new Goss double-decker offset press in full swing, and my new office on the second floor of a rearranged editorial section with a shiny plaque on the door, EDITOR-IN-CHIEF, and the growling staff down below busily manning the largest and most diversified up-to-date printing operation north of Denver and west of Minneapolis.

I looked back at all of them then, my gaze finally setting on Birdie. He stared at me, a thin smile on his lips and small gold flecks glinting in the pupils of his eyes. I felt hypnotized. At the back of my forehead, little facts kept flashing and going out like sparks before I could comprehend them. Somewhere, Maura's voice kept echoing, "No—no—check the facts," but things were terribly mixed up. The heat of the room oppressed me. The apparently innumerable pressures I had faced that day seemed to collect at once with a sort of invisible weight, borne down upon me by the gleam in Birdie's eyes.

I knew my thoughts weren't collected and that, in fact, my real intent had yet to be summoned up. I must have sounded as though I were in a trance: "And all you want me to do is make an announcement?"

"Right," Birdie said quickly. "That's all."

"Well," I said, "there doesn't seem to be anything wrong with that. . . . Okay."

There was a sort of corporate sigh throughout the room. Someone said, "Great!" Brownlee raised an eyebrow. But Birdie said nothing. He just straightened up, giving me a long, thoughtful look, then glanced around the room, his chest expanding as he took a deep breath and tucked in his shirt. He sipped his drink then, and the others followed suit.

I also lifted my glass. But it was empty.

❧ XLIX

I have often wondered since those long, emotion-ridden days, which left me feeling like a battle-shocked newsman just back from an Ernie Pyle briefing, exactly what might have happened if I had gone through with the plan Birdie and the staff of the *Dispatch* so persuasively proposed. Anyone on top of the news is now well aware that the *Dispatch* has not published since that memorable cooperative Friday edition. Its future remains in question, but no one has any doubts about its past. I was responsible for its folding up, I suppose, since I did not go to Kelly's Southside Bar & Laundromat that night and tell everyone the staff and I would be back on the job on Monday.

Although I left Caxton's Folly without any clear notion of Birdie's plan or my part in it, the truth—the hard truth—is, I was more confused than ever about the Chemfact Company, whatever that was, and those bullet holes. I can remember thinking it would be good to get away from Marksburg, to see Maura, especially, and tell her all about everything, just to try to make clear what connection there was between the unexplained details. I can remember still feeling scared, too.

I'd like to say that I still felt as though I had the honest outlook I had been reputed to possess before coming to Marksburg, and that I was simply bluffing when I told Birdie Johnson and all the others in the dining room that I would go along with them. I'd like to say I had remained uncorrupted, but it would not be quite true. It just wasn't that clear-cut. Whether I had meant it or not, I had more or less shaken on it with Birdie and the rest of them, and the staff all went home to hide out until Monday. I started out from Caxton's Folly toward Kelly's, and Birdie once more went into hiding in the mansion. I can remember actually beginning to compose a speech for the media people as I proceeded down the street.

But anyone who has ever said, "I wish I'd said that," will know what happened to me. I'm one of those people who, say, at a party, never thinks of a quick riposte when someone makes a smart remark. I always mumble or give a nervous laugh or just sit there mute and desperate for thought. Then, maybe on my way home from the party, or the next day or something, I think of a very clever answer. I come up with the perfect rejoinder, but it is too late, and I always think, I wish I'd said *that.*

Well, it was only after I was halfway down Main, when the pressure of the staff around me and the influential tone of Birdie's rationale had abated, that I remembered I had not asked anyone clearly and definitely about two things that had simply been smothered in all the discussion.

The first was, how come there were *two* bullet holes in the drapes but only *one* in the shelf? That ballistics question remained unanswered, and I wondered how Chief Laken might explain it.

The second question was one that had been answered in a way, but hardly satisfactorily. It was like the old Sherlock Holmes question about the dog that didn't bark in the night. *No one* in the room seemed to know anything about Willy Dunkle's creation of the Chemfact Company. Yet I had evidence of its existence, at least on paper—a piece of paper I'd found in the X-2 file, which, of course, Birdie had seen. I felt that the staff had been telling the truth. The ring of it was there in their puzzled reactions. But Birdie had literally paled at the mention of that company; his eyes had darkened and he grew withdrawn. I knew him well enough to recognize the meaning of that response. He had to be lying. I should have pushed that point more strongly, I thought.

The effect of those two questions clouding my mind, not to mention the tension, all the hectic action, the heavy drinking, and that strange meeting in the house, was just too much. I needed a break from all the stress, a moment to myself, just to think. It had been quite a day—and the night wasn't exactly just one more quiet evening in small-town America.

Oh, I walked down to Kelly's, all right. Everybody who was nobody in Marksburg seemed to be there, mingling with the media people in what sounded like a bacchanalian rite. The thought of all those revelers—perhaps more than the thought, since the drunken, scatological version of "Mademoiselle from Armentières" they were rendering was enough to drown out traffic on Times Square—prompted me to turn on my heel and head back toward Main.

I thought of the Nugget Lounge, but no doubt whatever vestiges of inebriates who had not darkened Kelly's door were there playing Country Western boom-chang and knocking down ditches. My only sanctuary was the usual one: the bus depot.

It wasn't exactly a fork in a Frostian path, but it was a divergence that made all the difference. The waitress, who had the radio blaring when I came in, turned it down and smiled faintly at me. She was the same one who had waited on me during my first minutes in Marksburg. She seemed to be in the very same spot, serving the same lousy coffee. We were alone. Everyone else was celebrating.

"Gee, Mr. Hollowburn," she said in that fetching, lackluster way of hers, "I thought you'd be over at Kelly's like everyone else."

"Naw. I need a breather. How about some of that great coffee of yours, sweetheart?"

"'Kay. Anything for a superstar. Seems like everyone's talkin' 'bout you. Must be swell bein' a celebrity."

"Yeah. Swell."

"Never saw this town so excited," she added, pouring me a cup of mudlike coffee. "I can get all kinds of stations on that radio. Everyone's talkin' 'bout the *Dispatch.*"

She shuffled down the counter and brought me back a dirty pitcher of milk. "Sure is too bad 'bout Willy, though, ain't it?"

The coffee was even more bitter than usual. I stared at her. "What about Willy?" I asked.

"Well, not Willy, exactly. Dint you hear? Couple of Chief Laken's men stopped in here on the way to the big party. Everybody's over at Kelly's. I don't ever gitta go anywhere."

"What's that about Willy?"

She looked at me as if to say, "Hold your horses," and leaned on the counter, blinking. Then she said, "Laken's men found the *Dispatch* station wagon 'bout five miles outa town. All smashed up in a cavern and burned and everything. No sign of Willy, but they said there was some blood in the front seat."

"Blood?"

"Well, what kinda newspaper reporter are you, anyway? That's what I said. Blood."

I stared at myself in the mirror opposite the counter. Once again, I could hear Maura's words echoing at the back of my mind. What kind of newspaper reporter was I? The kind that would maneuver the news—even other newsmen? What about the kind that *gets* instead of *creates* stories? I stared at my face and barely recognized the image. It was not the kind of face I wanted to take back home with me. I took another sip of coffee and burned my mouth.

"Phew!" I exclaimed, reaching for a glass of water. "This tastes like the ink we've been using on the *Dispatch*. What do you put in your coffee? Acid?"

Maybe it was her remark about Willy Dunkle and the station wagon, which set me thinking again about the puzzle of the Chemfact Company and my inability—as a reporter, mind you—*inability* to figure out that story. Or maybe it was that thought on top of my own use of the word "acid." But a fountain of energy surged through me at that moment and I jumped up from the stool.

The waitress must have thought I was cracking up as I shouted the word "acid," my mind calling back that combined visual and olfactory image of the old-fashioned vat of ink behind the boiler in the stereotype room. The stool tipped over with a crash.

"*That* does it!" I shouted.

"Does what?" the waitress asked. "The coffee ain't that bad."

But I didn't reply. I was in the process of making a decision. I had already decided in that brief moment not to go along with Birdie's plan and not to go down to Kelly's. But now another decision remained. Would I simply hightail it for Great Falls and pretend Marksburg was a nightmare on the other side of reality, or would I take one more try at figuring out the Chemfact Company puzzle?

"What kind of news reporter am I?" I asked myself at the door of the bus depot. And that was that.

I headed straight for the *Dispatch*. I was determined to get one more glimpse into that desk in the front office of the paper where I had found the X-2 file. There had to be more information on the Chemfact Company than just that little bit I had.

When I reached the office, the doors were locked and it was dark inside. I still had my key. I let myself in and stared at the silent interior, so much like that first night when I had come to Marksburg, except now the ticker was off and there was no light back in the editorial section. Just darkness.

I lit a match and went over to the converted front office that had once been a display window. The blinds were closed. I flicked on the desk lamp and went through the desk. Nothing new. There was a small cabinet near it, and I started combing through it.

The search had so preoccupied me that at first I didn't see Birdie. But when I looked up, I noticed the front doors were swinging and he was standing at the entranceway to the small office. He had a gun in his hand and was pointing it at me.

"What are you looking for, Steve?" he asked.

L

I aged considerably in the moments of silence that followed. Birdie's stance had that loose-jointed, casual quality that always made him seem relaxed, like a lion feigning sleep before its prey. The terrifying calmness of his manner was belied by the burning intensity of his eyes, which remained fixed on mine. The blue-black barrel of the gun in his hand—I think it was one of those midnight specials—gaped at me. Its maw seemed a foot wide.

"I—I—" I stammered, trying to break the horrible silence. "I—was—curious. The Chemfact Company, Birdie. I was curious."

He said nothing, but frowned as he looked at the mess I'd made of his desk. There was a question in his eyes.

More silence.

"Look, Birdie," I said, clearing my throat and straightening up. "Did you—have you been following me?"

Birdie laughed then, that sort of whimpering little laugh he had used in the cellar of Caxton's Folly. It made the atmosphere seem like the interior of a Berlin bunker in the last hours of the Third Reich.

"*Following* you?" he sneered. "You *sent* for me."

"What—whattayamean, *sent?*" I asked.

A lump formed in my throat. The gun moved up toward my face. Birdie's tone was darkly menacing.

"Why did you write this?" he demanded, stepping forward a bit and handing me a note. "What kind of an idiot do you take me for?"

I was dumbfounded at his menacing tone. I didn't take the note until he pushed it forward, shaking it. When I read it, all I could do was blink and stare at the floor. It said:

I'm on to you, Birdie.
Let's make a deal.
Dispatch office. Tonight.

It was signed "Caxton."

Birdie smiled as I read it again.

"I didn't write this," I finally protested, the words catching in my throat. "Honest."

Birdie's smile widened.

"Maybe—maybe Caxton's back," I offered weakly, but I was not very convincing, I know. I personally suspected something entirely different, a suspicion based on the way the pieces of the Chemfact Company puzzle and other factors fell into place in my mind only a few minutes earlier at the bus depot while I was drinking coffee.

Birdie's smile became a doglike grin. "Come off it, Steve. I know you've copped on to the Chemfact business. But this is a cheap shot. It won't work. And I'm afraid it means you're out of the project. For good."

"I said I didn't—"

"It's a pity. Everything was going well. But it has its good points. Your disappearance will make even better copy."

Birdie's face twisted grotesquely and the grin disappeared in an instant, replaced by that hot, intense look I'd seen before. It was an insane look. It would have silenced a crowd.

"Anyhow, that's enough!" he commanded. "It's too late for excuses, Steve. I want to know what you're up to—and I want to know *now*! I saw you leave the house, but what did you do then? Slip back after the staff had gone and push this note through the mail slot? Come on, Steve—what's going on?"

Birdie scowled at the gun in his hand for a second. When he looked up, a shadow crossed his face diagonally, making one side appear to droop wearily, as though two major sectors of his mind had waged some kind of cerebral battle against one another, with one of them collapsing in exhaustion. I felt he had just come to some hideous and final conclusion. My throat was drying up, but I knew I would have to. keep the conversation going, considering the alternative.

"Really, Birdie," I said, trying to keep my voice from cracking, "I had nothing to do with any note. I admit I didn't go to Kelly's to make that announcement—I just couldn't. Look, back there at the house you had a pretty good pitch—I mean, about Caxton trying to get back here and all. And those letters to you from him were pretty convincing. But even if you can fool a whole town, you can't fool anyone for long about a thing like murder. Especially the second time around."

That last phrase made Birdie stiffen a little, but he simply waited for me to go on. The gun, which had moved ever so slightly, seemed to have an intelligence of its own.

"Sooner or later," I added quickly, "somebody was bound to check up on the *two* bullet holes in Caxton's study. The second bullet had been stopped by someone standing in the room— and that bullet was head high. It was fatal, all right, and it isn't hard to conclude that Willy did the shooting. But it was a little harder figuring out those letters, and Willy's disappearance, and the creation of a phony company *after* Caxton's disappearance."

I waited again for Birdie to say something, anything. But he just stood there bemused—almost fascinated, it seemed—by what I was saying.

"All right," I added as calmly as I could. "You want to know what's going on? Here it is, Birdie—here's what I think. First of all, I figure you cooked up some forged letters supposedly from Caxton to you. Secondly, I think you made a deal with Willy Dunkle to help cover up his killing of Caxton and then reneged on the whole thing. Thirdly, I think you reneged because it all tied up with something only you and Willy knew about, and Willy was somehow going to spill it. That *something* is the reason behind the formation of the Chemfact Company, isn't it? And, Birdie, now I'm pretty sure what that something is. That's why I didn't go along with your nutty plan, and that's what's going on. I came back here just now to check the facts."

I immediately regretted using the word "nutty" as Birdie stiffened again. Why didn't he say something? I wondered. I was running out of ideas, and that worried me silly, because I knew he was waiting to have the last word. And I mean last.

"So it may be true," I went on, anxious to keep the silence of the small room from closing in on me. "Maybe everyone believes Willy lit out for Canada, but that belief won't last. The facts are piling up, Birdie. Willy isn't in Canada, is he?"

Birdie moved slightly and we stared at each other. I wondered if he was remembering the days when we had worked together on the *Trib* in Great Falls. Or was he thinking back even further? I thought I saw something of his boyhood in his desperate eyes. Was there a hurt there—some remote, almost hidden injustice planted in the distant past that had been the seed for this horrible trauma?

That thought was still in my mind when I said, almost with a sense of discovery, "You killed Willy."

Birdie surprised me then. He sort of chuckled, deep in his throat.

"You always were a dedicated reporter," he remarked at last, though hardly in a complimentary way. Then he added, "If you've figured out all that, what makes you think I'd fall for a stupid note like this? You want to trap me, is that it? Well—it won't wash, pal. You've overplayed it this time."

"Look—I just came from the bus depot. I—"

He stepped back a pace and held the gun steady again. I felt myself backing into the desk chair. For a moment, I thought he was squeezing the trigger of that gun.

"Listen to me!" I exclaimed, swallowing. "I just wanted to figure out all this business about Willy. It's all too late, Birdie. They've found Willy's station wagon and the bloodstains inside. It's only a matter of time. The staff would have gone for a hoax, but once they find out Willy's dead and that you killed him—and they'll find out, Birdie—nothing else will matter."

Birdie didn't even hear me. "What's the angle with this?" he asked, holding up the note again.

"I *told* you! I don't know anything about that!"

For an instant, Birdie's eyes showed a hint of puzzlement, his head tipping slightly like a beagle questioning a scent. But only for an instant.

"It's too late—for you."

"Wait a minute, Birdie," I said urgently.

He simply shook his head. "This isn't some cheap detective film now, Steve," he said. "No long explanations. No talk. Come on."

"Where?"

"Pressroom. We're too close to the street here. Now move!"

I hated to move forward. The entranceway was narrow, but Birdie was tensely alert in every fiber of his body. He only moved aside a few inches. There was no chance to run, no question of getting the gun away from him. No chance.

I stepped carefully past him. He moved like a cat, now almost a yard behind me, but I could sense his easy, stalking pace. He said nothing as we walked slowly through the shadows toward the editorial section and the pressroom stairs beyond. I could see those stairs and his desk and other office furniture, because a light was on upstairs. I hadn't noticed that before. I was sure, in fact, the whole place had been dark. In retrospect, I realize I should have been very curious, because I knew that Birdie couldn't have turned on the light; he had obviously slipped in the front doors shortly after I had, and there was no switch downstairs to work the upper-floor lights.

But my mind was elsewhere as we walked through the editorial section. My mouth was dry. The air was absolutely electric. A thousand thoughts crowded into my mind, but fear made them skitter out immediately. Perhaps it was because the pulsating sensation of myriad ideas going through my brain bore some similarity to the feeling I had had that first night in the *Dispatch* editorial section, but whatever it was, I had a sudden inspiration. I also had a sudden impulse of will, an almost inexplicable compulsion to carry out that inspired idea no matter what happened, which now chills me to the bone. It was a long shot, but it was certainly better than the short shot I knew awaited me in the pressroom.

Birdie was about a foot behind me as I reached the ticker. I brushed up against it, covering my hand with my body, as though I were turning halfway around to say something to him. He said nothing, but motioned at me to keep going.

"Let's talk," I said as loudly as I could. My words covered the sound of my finger flicking the switch on the ticker. I stepped forward abruptly at the same time. My quick move prompted Birdie to do the same, and, like a third person in the room, that run-down old ticker broke the silent darkness with its usual rinky-tink volume just as Birdie stepped beside it.

The abruptness of that startling sound, its sententious, staccato rattling, caught Birdie by surprise. I didn't look back to see if it had broken his remarkable concentration. I merely hoped it would distract him for a second or two, and apparently my hopes were realized.

In any case, I got that second. I shot forward, about as scared as a person can get, the adrenaline coursing through my system with rapid force. I grabbed the nearest thing at hand, a wire out-basket full of copy, and swung around, flinging the whole thing in Birdie's face. It connected.

He toppled backward, losing his balance. I dived under a nearby desk. He must have regained his composure fast, because there was a shot immediately. The sound of it was more of a roar—deafening, horrifyingly real. Later, I found out it had nicked me in the rear, cut right through my back pocket, singeing the skin. Later, it smarted some, in fact—but right then I felt nothing. I only heard that smashing sound.

I don't know what exactly happened then. I remember waiting a second and then, rather stupidly, peering over the desk, only to see Birdie grinning at me. He was partly crouched in the darkness, raising the gun as he saw my eyes. I ducked down again, but I knew—I *knew*—he was stepping toward me. I would be wide open and trapped beneath that desk. A prayer went through my mind.

Instead of Birdie's coming around to my side of the desk, however—instead of the second shot that I anticipated any moment—there was another sound. It was absolutely out of context.

It was for all the world like my brothers, when we were kids, calling "Allee, allee oxen free!" during an after-dinner game in the street. It was like that—a call from the distance—high-pitched, clear, loud. It was human—a siren call, almost an order.

"Biiirrdie!" it called, echoing from the second floor.

I peered over the desk.

"Biiirrdie!"

I could see Birdie staring up, transfixed. His eyes were shining in the shadows, wide-open, clearly terrified. I think he had completely forgotten about me in that moment. His face was as pale as newsprint. His mouth sagged at one end. The gun drooped in his hand. I can only describe his expression, the entirely obsessed expression—as well as the posture of his whole body—as the epitome of madness. It was a frightening thing to see.

"Birdie!" the voice called a third time, this time more sharply, imperative, commanding.

I followed Birdie's gaze. Standing at the railing of the second floor, off at an angle so that the light fell obscurely upon his figure, was a man in an expensive suit. I knew it was expensive because I recognized it. The suit was one that had been hanging in the closet in the main bedroom of Caxton's Folly. I could make out a white shirtfront and a bow tie, and a wide-brimmed hat that was in the style of certain areas of the South. Its brim obscured the man's face.

"Caxton!" I heard myself exclaim.

≈ LI

For a moment, Birdie stood stock-still, his mouth working strangely. Spittle had formed in the corners of that mouth, which only seconds before had been so full of malice.

Then he shouted, "No! What? . . . How . . . *You?*"

"Yes," the voice called back. "Me!"

Then the figure abruptly disappeared in the shadows. Birdie remained still. He looked over at me, unseeing. His eyes were glazed, like those of an animal in the throes of death. He shuffled slightly back and forth, and then, raising the gun erratically, he gave a long, agonizing groan.

He went wild. He waved his hands in the air and did a sort of *danse macabre.* Even then I realized he was terrified. He made motions with his body, as though he were going forward toward the stairs, but in fact he kept backing away from that light, working his way backward in the direction of the front doors.

wild shot, he would shout that dreadful "No!" once more, a man completely deranged, dominated by fear.

He backed into the arms of three men in plainclothes whom I had never seen before. But the way they grabbed him and held him—all business, every movement fast, certain, and authoritative—I knew they were police of some sort.

Birdie didn't struggle.

He had given up—inside, I mean. He was broken, pitifully broken. All the confidence, all the brash daring, with which I had always associated him was gone. He looked into my eyes, pleading for help. But it was not physical help he wanted, I knew. He was crying.

The man who had been at the top of the stairs came down in the shadows. For one zany moment, I imagined it really was Caxton, but as he came close I recognized him.

"Okay, fellas," he said to the plainclothesmen. "That's it."

Then he turned to me. "You okay?"

"I—think so."

"Sorry you got caught up in this, Steve. We didn't expect you to be here."

I took a deep breath, too relieved to explain right then.

"It's okay," I said. "I'm sure glad you were here."

"That's our job," Jerry, the rookie cop, replied.

ಌ LII

It's hard to say now, as I recollect the final stages of that night, which was more disturbing, my own traumatic state, which ranged from a highly disturbed nervous system to a stinging sore on my posterior, or the sight of Birdie's eyes as he groped madly at invisible cobwebs before him while the three plainclothesmen led him through the *Dispatch*'s swinging doors. But Jerry, the rookie cop, turned out to be a considerate as well as efficient policeman, and he had a genuine soothing effect on my psyche as we sat together after it was all over.

His real name was not Hannibal, but the Jerry was real enough, and he explained that he was anything but a rookie. He was a federal marshal from a western judicial district in the state, assigned to the investigation into Caxton's disappearance before I ever got to Marksburg.

"I really was born in Norris, though," he said, with a smile, as I turned on a few desk lamps and went over to Kressnach's desk where I knew there was a bottle of milk in the bottom drawer. "I'm sorry about all the deception. But we had to make sure about you."

I winced as I sat down. The burning sensation in my rear reminded me all over again of that moment when Birdie had almost ended both our careers.

The milk was soothing, however, and I poured a drink for Jerry in a paper cup as he relaxed. His sangfroid amazed me. It was almost comical seeing him in that chair, no longer a rookie cop with innocent anxiety over the operation of a small-town police force, but a professional, trained man with command over three detectives from the capital. Close up, he looked slightly ridiculous in Caxton's expensive suit. As he removed the hat, he studied my face for a moment and chuckled.

"Quite a rig," I said.

"It was bait," he replied, sipping his drink. "I sent a note to Birdie. I figure Caxton's dead. Willy Dunkle did it."

"I know," I replied. "He shot him while Caxton was in his study back in that crazy mansion."

"Well," Jerry said, "it figures that Willy would do it. I mean, he sure had reason enough. He'd been played for a sucker by Caxton more than once, and yet he couldn't squeal on him without getting himself right back in the pen. And when he soured on the scheme to swindle old Mrs. Koenig and, for once in his life, tried to do something noble, it must have been doubly humiliating for him to look into Caxton's sneering face. Especially after Rena jilted him."

"Yeah," I said, thinking aloud, "humiliation and jealousy, not to mention the frustration of also getting stuck with the blame so often, are pretty potent motives in the mind of a man who sees the gun as a quick answer."

"How did you find out about the shooting in the first place?" Jerry asked.

"I came across a small story in the *Dispatch* first of all," I answered. "But later Birdie told me that Willy took a shot at Caxton. Only, Birdie claimed that Willy missed and simply scared Caxton out of town. I was confused about that for a while, because when I was first in Caxton's Folly, I spotted two bullet holes in the drapes, and when I checked the ballistics on two shots, I found that only one had lodged in the bookshelves."

"Very good," Jerry said. "So did I."

"You? When?"

"I was in the house when you were down in the cellar being trampled over by Birdie as he tried to fool you about that grave containing Mabel Reitz's things."

"Then you weren't on your rounds?"

"Hell, no," he replied. "I was pretty suspicious about Birdie holing up there. Chief Laken didn't like my nosing around, and, of course, he didn't know I was on a case. He really thought I was a rookie. But he was scared I would find out too much—he couldn't afford that."

"Then you know about the whole plan—the hoax."

"Right," Jerry said, nodding his head. "Looks like the whole town's in on it, although nobody knew anything about murder—except Birdie, of course."

"Yeah. That's what I thought," I said. "They all figured Caxton was still on the Coast. Birdie rigged up a lot of phony correspondence and they fell for it."

"So that's how he did it, huh?" Jerry mused. "I don't know what Willy did with the body, but I was certain Birdie was in on it after I learned that Willy's station wagon was found earlier today. That's why I decided we should have a showdown here tonight."

"Why didn't you just arrest Birdie?"

"No evidence," Jerry said, studying his drink. "*Corpus delicti.* We were going to arrest Willy Dunkle on suspicion, but he disappeared. Now that we've found the station wagon, we have more concrete evidence. It's my guess that somehow Birdie managed to kill Willy by himself and get his body back into town. I'd say offhand that the funeral you attended was a real one. Willy's probably in that grave. We'll check it out when the men get back."

I nodded. "You know," I said after a moment, "I think I can help you out about Caxton. I mean, I think I know where you can find him."

Jerry stared at me. "Where?"

"I'll tell you," I said, feeling much more secure now, "if you will tell me how come Chief Laken didn't catch on to those two bullets that Willy fired."

Jerry shrugged. "That's easy. Laken, as you probably know, hated Caxton. He didn't push that investigation at all. That's why I came down here. The state attorney general wasn't going to swallow that disappearance story without checking it out. He called me in on the case and we contacted California. Caxton never left Montana."

"What did you do then?"

"Well, I came down here and managed to get on the force. That wasn't hard with the turnover Laken had to put up with. I realized after a few days that Laken had never even bothered to examine the study. He was conned by Birdie from the start. He looked around the place, I'm sure—but no ballistics work. I think he was just like the rest of the town, happy to see Caxton gone."

"But I can't figure out the relationship between Willy and Birdie, exactly," I commented. "Why did Birdie help cover up for Willy?"

"Just another case of greed, Steve. Don't you see? Birdie realized this was his big chance. With Caxton dead and everyone knowing it, that guy in the East, Terrill, would have closed the paper down—I'm certain of that. But with Caxton simply not around, Birdie had a chance to take over a big operation. Even if Terrill didn't close the paper, once he found out about the new project Caxton had started, he would never have trusted Birdie to run it. The guy's crackers. Round the bend."

Jerry put his feet up on the desk and stared at me. "You're in a crazy business," he said, shaking his head. "But guys like Birdie—they're something else. Look—he agreed with Willy Dunkle to protect him if Willy went in on the plan. They got rid of Caxton somehow. Then Birdie started the takeover."

"Okay—but why did Birdie kill Willy, then?"

"You tell me."

"I just think I can," I said reflectively. "Willy saw a chance, too. He wanted a big piece of the cake. He had been frustrated for a long time, picking up scraps for Caxton, being jilted by Rena, and all that. He probably tried to shake Birdie down. Even with Birdie holding a murder over Willy's head, the way Birdie's mind was working, he probably was afraid, one way or another, Willy would spoil everything. So he killed him."

"Sounds right."

I limped to my desk and found my pipe and tobacco. "Isn't it funny," I asked, "how this whole doggoned town fell for it? I mean, the bank, the attorney, Brownlee—the whole larcenous bunch?"

"In a way," Jerry replied, "the town caused it all." He got up stiffly and added, "As I said, it's the old story of greed."

Greed. I couldn't help thinking again of Caxton's series of promotions, phony deals, and bogus schemes—all of which amounted to abusing the press in Marksburg. It wasn't really land that Caxton was greedy for—or, for that matter, a newspaper. Rather, I told myself, it was power. That was it, power. Skinning a few cattlemen of a few thousand or commiting usury or grabbing land or selling phony bonds—they were all means to an end, part of a larger plan, and at last I saw it. They would, Caxton must have thought, bring him social prominence and status in Montana. And real power! He was looking for something he had lost long ago, back in his Southern comfort: respectability. He would show them! A governorship. Maybe senator from Montana. The black sheep dyed white at last! King Irwin Royal Caxton III!

The Birdies of this world, I thought, were happy enough with monetary delusions of grandeur in the newspaper game. What was it Stephen Crane had once written? Something like a newspaper is a game that scores the loser a victory. But the Caxtons of this world? To them the press was something to be used for personal gain. A way to graft in high places. An elevator to the room at the top.

"Greed," I repeated. "Well, Jerry, instead of saving the *Dispatch*, greed really cooked its goose."

"Yes," he commented dryly, "although you almost saved it for all of them."

That made me mighty pensive. Jerry patiently waited for me to speak, as though he knew what I would say next.

"Well, I've got to tell you," I finally said, feeling sheepish. "You—you know, I actually agreed just a few hours ago with all the *Dispatch* people to go in with Birdie's plan. I mean, I'm no different from the rest of them. Marksburg got to me, too."

Jerry smiled and sort of shook his head. "Don't be so hard on yourself," he said. "I think 'agreed' is too strong a word. You proved you weren't really corrupted long enough—or, for that matter, even scared enough—to become a conspirator, right? After all, you didn't go along with them. You went your own way, in the long run. I'd say you were more confused than anything. And who wouldn't be, in your position? Birdie was a pretty good word-spinner. And I tried to warn you about this town, which has a way of twisting or covering up the facts. Besides," he added wryly, "your conscience would have caught up with you sooner or later. You know, at the risk of blowing my cover, I kept trying to open up to you as much as I could from the first time we met. That's because I always figured you'd be straight."

"How so?"

"You told me one time that those newspaper people back in Great Falls that you worked with on the *Tribune* always called you 'Even Steven,' right?"

"Well—yeah."

"And another time you mentioned that except for the occasional character like Birdie, they were a pretty straight bunch, right?"

"Right."

"Okay," Jerry added. "You figure it out."

I felt pretty subdued at the moment, but as we walked toward the front doors—doors that had opened up to me, less than a week earlier, a nightmare of chaos—I looked around the plant.

Then I said, "All this reminds me of an old printers' saying."

"What's that?" Jerry asked.

"Something like 'The devil opens a newspaper and the sheriff shuts it.'"

Jerry laughed. "Make that a printer's devil," he said, giving me a caustic look.

❧ LIII

One of the three plainclothesmen who had helped apprehend Birdie was just pulling up at the curb behind my battered VW as we stepped out of the *Dispatch*. He leaned out the window.

"Lathrop and Dwyer are taking that character down to Helena in the other car, Jerry. Too many newsmen downtown to deal with him here. Thought I'd drive you back."

"Right," Jerry said. "But we'll have to get back tomorrow, Scotty. Have to straighten out Laken and his bunch, not to mention the rest of the town. Probably be some fraud charges filed in Helena."

"Right," the man called Scotty said. Then he looked Jerry up and down and laughed. "You gonna ride with me in that getup?"

Jerry laughed, too. "It worked," he replied. "Don't knock it." Then he turned to me. "I was gambling that Birdie knew Caxton was dead, of course, and—considering his state of mind—a dramatic appearance at the top of the stairs would shake him up. I was going to scare him into talking, then take him over to the cemetery and dig up Dunkle's body."

"That was quite a gamble, wasn't it?" I asked.

"Was it?" he asked back.

I knew by his tone that this marshal was a professional. There was probably much more to the death of Willy Dunkle that he understood which was still very unclear to me. Besides, he didn't look like a man who gambled on such things as life and death. I was going to ask him about it all, but I felt as if I'd been up for three days straight. I was ready to collapse. It must have shown on my face.

"You oughta get some rest," Jerry said, not unkindly. "We have a motel, if you want to pack it in for the night."

"Not a chance," I replied. "I'm leaving right now for Great Falls. All I want to do is get back to Maura and the kids and a little bit of sanity. If you guys want me, call the *Trib* up there. I'm going there first thing Monday morning to ask for a job— any job."

Jerry chuckled. I went up to the VW, wrestled with the handle of the door for a while, and got in. It took some time, but the car finally started.

Jerry tapped on the window and I rolled it down. "Hey, wait a minute," he said. "You told me you had a theory about Caxton's body. Where do you think it is?"

"Oh, yeah," I answered. "That's what all the Chemfact Company business was about. When Birdie and Willy agreed to dispose of Caxton's body, they printed up a letterhead with the company name and wrote to White Sulphur Springs—the chemical factory there."

"So?"

"Well, do you remember my telling you about that vat of ink with its terrible stench and sludgy substance in the pressroom?"

"Who could forget it?"

"Right. When I put out that sheet on my own, I had to use that stuff, y' know? And when the other newsmen and I put out that special edition today—well, I was out of ink again, so we had to use up most of the rest of it.

"Look, Jerry, I think that ink was more than ink. It was a sludge that had been made of other stuff, including sulfuric acid. Gallons of it. Later, of course, it was neutralized. The chemicals were ordered by Birdie and Willy under cover of a so-called commercial firm using sulfur products."

"But that doesn't mean—"

"Well, acid has nothing to do *directly* with printing, except in very small quantities. Ferrous sulfates are used for ink manufacturing, and that ostensibly was the purpose of the order. It fooled me for a while, because I thought some huge ink-manufacturing project was being hatched. But sulfuric acid is a long way from sulfates, and actually Willy and Birdie had another, more sinister intent for it, as I realized almost by accident when I was drinking coffee that reminded me of acid at the bus depot.

"It's my guess now that that old copper vat in the pressroom was used for a purpose far different from holding ink—it was to dissolve something that would have to be neutralized later and ultimately mixed with printer's ink. That ink would turn to sludge and then eventually be thrown out—that is, unless somebody like me came along to use it."

Jerry rubbed his chin doubtfully.

"Look," I added, "if you get your lab boys to examine it, I think you'll find I'm right. That acid was used to dissolve something—something big."

Jerry's mouth dropped open.

"That's right," I added. "Irwin Royal Caxton the Third."

I reached across the seat of the car and grabbed a copy of the *Dispatch* from a pile of Friday editions that one of the newsboys had put in my VW earlier. "You ever hear of Edgar Allan Poe's purloined letter?" I asked, handing him the paper.

Jerry took the paper and stared at it, nodding. "You mean about the missing letter that was right under the detectives' noses?"

"That's the one. I mean, Birdie's nickname might describe his brains, but in his own madness he was clever enough. That's why he killed Dunkle, too, I think. He was an accessory after the fact. He and Willy threw Caxton's body into that vat." I smacked the front page of the *Dispatch* and added, "You're looking at part of Caxton right there!"

I revved up the VW then and drove off. I was thinking of Jerry's comment about how there really does seem to be printer's ink in a newspaperman's blood, but in this case the saying could be turned around.

I slowed down as I passed Caxton's Folly. The old mansion looked as decrepit as ever, and when I saw the blurred swastika on the front door that someone had tried to rub out, I was tempted to stop. If I were one who went in for graffiti, I would have scribbled on the door a new slogan for the town—a slogan that the old judge who had founded the town should have thought of in the first place. I would have written, "Resist temptation." But I didn't.

I just drove straight on, leaving Marksburg behind me, not looking back. I was tired, but I was mighty anxious to get back to Great Falls and to tell Maura and the kids everything that had happened. And I was hoping the *Tribune* would consider me for something—maybe even copyboy—as long as it wasn't printer's devil.

After all, I told myself, even if I couldn't offer a potential employer any references from Marksburg, I could sure point out that I was experienced. Anyway, as Maura would put it, it probably doesn't pay to be overly ambitious in the newspaper business.

Take Caxton, for instance, I thought. In a way he did exactly what he set out to do. Make headlines. Literally.

–30–